Methodical Deception

Methodical Deception

Rebekah Roth

KTYS media

ISBN 978-0-9827571-6-1

Library of Congress Cataloging-in-Publication Data
Roth, Rebekah
Methodical Deception
Fiction
2015949846
ISBN 978-0-9827571-6-1(soft cover)
Library of Congress Number: 2015949846

To contact Rebekah Roth:
www.rebekahroth.com

KTYS media
www.ktysmedia.com

Printed in the United States of America

Dedicated To:

The Crew of the USS Liberty

Attacked June 8, 1967
A False Flag Event

"In a gentle way, you can shake up the world."
Mahatma Gandhi

FROM THE AUTHOR

Following the release of my first book Methodical Illusion in November of 2014, I was truly overwhelmed by the response. Many people contacted me with experiences they had been a part of on September 11, 2001 that not only confirmed the facts I exposed in the book, but shed light on aspects that required additional and new research. Taking off my author's hat and delving once again into the mountains of documents that expose 9/11, I was fortunate to obtain nearly a terabyte of Freedom of Information Act radar data from that day which demanded further investigation.

In between interviews, responding to reader requests, and hosting my own radio show, I attacked this new information with vigor and determination, often at the expense of sleep. What I found in that data, combined with facts I had not shared in the first book, necessitated that another book be written to expose the extent of corruption and planning that went into pulling off 9/11.

This new book entitled Methodical Deception will reconnect you with your favorite characters from Methodical Illusion. Their adventures reveal the pernicious and evil doings of those responsible for orchestrating and executing, not only the events leading up to that day, but the cover-up and deception that has managed to hide the truth.

"There are two ways to be fooled. One is to believe what isn't true. The other is to refuse to accept what is true."
Soren Kierkegaard

one

*A*n official leave of absence allows one to become quite comfortable with time off, yet somehow it acts like a revolving door, with no clearly defined ending. Such was the current situation Vera Hanson found herself in. She had returned home to find her golden retriever, Kelli, overjoyed to see her after so many weeks of separation. Their reunion brought a sense of stability that they both craved, causing neither to want to leave the other's side.

It felt good to be home in Seattle, and to reacquaint herself with Kelli and their routine of walking along the beach, visiting the local Starbucks, and watching the ships glide in and out of Puget Sound. So much had happened to Vera in such a short period of time that she appreciated a break from the commotion in order to put it all into perspective. She poured herself a large cup of tea and settled into her favorite window seat that looked out across the water toward the Olympic Mountains. It was a bright clear day, unusual for Seattle, and though it was too cool to venture outside, the splendor and magnitude of her view allowed her thoughts to become vividly clear.

Her husband Jeff had been murdered in order to keep him quiet about his discoveries concerning the 9/11 terror attacks. Max Hager had been the first to verbalize that truth, and he too had been silenced, suffering the same fate as her husband. She knew the evil cabal responsible for their deaths still lurked in the darkness and was willing to strike out at anything or anyone that threatened its existence. Vera was outraged that they had killed

Jeff, and angry with herself that she had refused to demand an investigation. At least when they chose to murder Max, they made it impossible for the authorities to write it off as an accident— rocket-propelled grenades left no doubt as to the perpetrator's intentions. After that, Vera had begun to question her own safety. After she and her friend, Jim Bowman, had discovered that the four airplanes on 9/11 had been remotely flown to Westover Air Force base, she'd had no doubt that her life, too, was in danger. But to Vera, what she had done was like striking a blow to the head of a snake, and she was willing to risk everything to assault it again and again.

With the truth now in place, she could begin to properly grieve and allow those who had passed from her life to rest, bringing to her own soul some needed comfort. She reached down, letting her hand drift until it found the top of Kelli's head. She scratched her behind the ears the way Jeff did, which always caused the dog to whimper gently with delight. That familiar sound caused Vera to smile and bolstered her inner resolve to move forward.

She slowly sipped her tea, allowing each mouthful to linger, savoring its flavor. It was a habit she had developed whenever she had something weighing heavily on her mind. The piquancy of the tea seemed to focus her attention. When she finally swallowed, it was as if a signal would shoot to her brain indicating that decision time was at hand. For more than thirty years Vera had enjoyed her career as a flight attendant. She was good at it. In fact, there were few better. She instilled confidence in the crew members and passengers she flew with, and they trusted her to handle any situation that might arise. That kind of respect only came with experience. When, on occasion, she had mentioned her possible retirement to some of her pilot friends, they begged her—and then threatened to bribe her—to remain on duty. Their reactions always made Vera laugh, but deep inside it was validation that she had reached the top of her profession, and that was a very comfortable place to be. Most of all, she loved interacting with the passengers. Of course, they could be sharp, demanding and unruly at times, but her smooth manner mixed with an aura of authority always seemed to mitigate any tense situation that arose. There was nothing she wouldn't do for the flying public. On more than one occasion she had found herself in the aisle of a jet, performing CPR on a passenger. She had developed a legacy which she was proud of and a reputation that was the envy of her peers. Her previous thoughts of retirement had never really been too serious, and the bribes from the pilots had never needed to be more than them paying for dinner in a foreign country.

Daylight was fading and Vera's favorite time began to stretch its glistening glow upon the city. She stood, quietly gazing at the beauty of the scenery only a Seattle skyline could offer. Yet even in the ambiance created by such a pleasingly familiar sight, something inside was beginning to shift. Her thoughts returned to the passengers on her flights, the thousands and thousands of faces whose names were never known or if they were known, were forgotten as quickly as they stepped off the plane. The moment she put on her uniform and reported for duty, her life transformed. No longer was she just a woman from Seattle; she was a trained airline professional, responsible for the safety and welfare of sometimes hundreds of people. She often wondered if a similar transformation took place for police officers and firefighters when they donned their uniforms. This sense of responsibility was one thing she loved about her job, and why she had never seriously contemplated retiring.

Kelli sat quietly at the door, waiting to go outside. Vera was completely lost in her thoughts and hadn't noticed. Finally a bark, almost a chirp, came from across the room. "Oh, you poor thing," Vera said, catching Kelli's eye. The dog jumped to her feet, pressed her nose against the window, and patiently waited for Vera to open the door. Vera's mind was still wrapped tightly around her career, the responsibility she felt towards her passengers and her thoughts of retirement. Usually she would leave the back door open and wait for Kelli to return, but this time Vera closed the door and set the deadbolt lock.

She imagined herself walking down the aisles, looking into the face of each passenger and attempting to convey assurance that she was there for them no matter what circumstance arose. After what she and Jim had discovered about 9/11, the thought of walking down that aisle began to horrify her. Methodically, they had uncovered how the flight termination systems had remotely commandeered those airplanes and rendered the pilots and flight attendants helpless. The military that she had always trusted to respond within minutes was nowhere to be found until it was too late. There was no way now that she could look into the faces of the passengers as she once had. In fact, all of the events of the past year, the death of the First Lady in Las Vegas, the plane explosions in Orlando and the murder of her dear friend Grace, made it impossible for her to even think of putting on her uniform again. No longer could she be the professional she knew she had been for the past thirty years. That reality began to cripple her soul. As she stood in the kitchen trying to come to terms with the painful truth, Kelli's bark broke her train of thought, which came as a welcome relief. Vera was surprised to discover that she had locked the door and quickly opened it to let the dog back inside. "What was your momma thinking, girl?" she said as she bent down and vigorously rubbed Kelli's fur with both hands. Just then the phone rang. It was her neighbor, Jenny.

"Vera, I'm so excited you're finally home. I was beginning to worry about you. Then I saw you on television at the State of the Union. You, girlfriend, have got some serious explaining to do. I'd assumed you were at the beach house all this time enjoying some well-deserved time off. Then out of nowhere, you're sitting in the President of the United States' box at what might be the most important speech ever made by a leader of this country. I want to come over and make you tell me all about what is going on with you. I'll bring the wine."

Vera laughed, not fully realizing what an impact the recent events of her life might have had upon her friends. She knew it would do them both good to get together. Talking with Jenny would definitely add some clarity to her thoughts or at the very least, might dispel the sense of gloom she was starting to feel as she considered retirement. "Jenny, I would love that, get over here as fast as you can and bring two bottles. I think we're going to need them."

"Perfect," said Jenny, laughing. "I already have one bottle open and more questions than a Jeopardy contestant."

Vera had hardly hung up the phone when the doorbell rang. The two friends embraced on the threshold as if they had not seen each other for years. This reunion was just what Vera needed. She welcomed Jenny inside and took the wine from her hands. Kelli immediately gave Jenny the once-over sniff, then settled onto her blanket in the family room and waited for the women to follow.

"I forgot how incredible your view is, Vera," said Jenny as she settled into a comfortable chair. "I could look out your windows for hours and never grow tired of it. Being across the street, I don't get to see this panorama; my views are just snippets of what you have here."

"You would make the perfect window washer then," Vera chimed in. "Are you free tomorrow morning, or might we still be talking and drinking wine?"

"Let's hope so," said Jenny. "It's so good to see you. Now, I'm all ears and can't wait to hear absolutely everything. How in the world did you end up in Washington D.C. as the guest of President Sherman?"

"Oh, Jenny, you won't believe this story even if I spend all night telling you."

"I have more wine back at the house. Take as long as you need to, because I'm not going anywhere until I get the entire story and I'm satisfied that I like it." Jenny held her glass in one hand, rested her elbows on her knees, and fixed her eyes on Vera. It was obvious she was there for the duration.

"Okay, remember me telling you about that Stan the Man guy on Facebook, who seemed to have a very nondescript profile, but a rather charming personality?"

"Yeah."

"I don't even know if I'm allowed to divulge any of this."

"What? Oh, you're going to divulge, even if this Stan the Man character turns out to be a Microsoft millionaire with a mansion and his own airplane."

Vera burst out laughing. She tried to hold it in, but the comparison was just too funny and it made her realize how much wine Jenny was going to need to consume before she believed what she was about to hear.

"Oh, this Stan the Man has a mansion, a jet, a bulletproof limousine, all kinds of bodyguards, and access to anything he wants. Actually, Jenny, he puts Bill Gates to shame."

"He's that rich?"

"Well, I don't actually know if he even has any money. He might have some. He makes a pretty good salary, but nothing too exorbitant. He has a valet named Mike, nicest guy in the world, but I don't really know about his money."

Jenny clutched her wineglass with both hands and took a gulp. She knew a mere sip at this point was not going to get her through Vera's sketchy explanation. "All right, sweetie, make this easy on me and help me out. You're not making any sense and at this rate, we'll never get to the State of the Union."

Vera smiled, leaned back in her chair and blurted out, "Stan the Man is Joel Sherman!"

Jenny was savoring the last little sip of her wine, letting it slowly trickle down the back of her throat when Vera's words exploded in her ears. What started out to be a succulent swallow turned into a choking cough. She managed to gain her composure just in time to save herself from spitting wine onto the carpet. She gasped, "That Facebook wimp you've been talking to is the President of the United States?"

Vera smiled as she nodded a slow affirmative yes.

"Now wait just a minute here! Are you telling me that the president puts on his Stan the Man disguise and trolls the internet looking for hot dates to his speeches, and he just happened to snag you?"

Vera began to laugh so hard that she set her glass down and put both hands on her face. "Not exactly," she said. "As it turns out, my friend Jim Bowman and the president have been friends for years. Jim was on special assignment for the president and asked me to join him. He told the president about me several months after the First Lady perished in that horrible crash in Las Vegas. That's why he approached me on Facebook, but of course he couldn't use President Joel Sherman as a screen name, now could he? That's how Stan the Man was born. I think he's deactivated that account now and Jenny, you must promise to keep all of this a secret, no matter what."

Jenny's eyes were opened as wide as she could get them. She nodded in agreement, with her hands in the air motioning for more details.

"Jim and I uncovered some very earth-shattering information surrounding the 9/11 attacks. The president called us back to Washington, more for our safety than anything else. Evidently he was so impressed with our research that he invited us to spend the week with him prior to the State of the Union. He included us in several security meetings. He kept us close. We even stayed with him in the residence and I have to tell you, I learned to like him a lot. Jim was asked to head up a new investigation into 9/11 and we were invited to sit in his box for the speech. It all seems very surreal now. My head is still spinning and I haven't even begun to deal with any emotions."

Jenny's voice had returned and the first thing out of her mouth caught Vera by surprise. "Now wait just a minute here, kiddo. I've heard bits and pieces about you in the news media regarding what you discovered and I have to admit, I don't know a thing about 9/11, airplanes or investigations. And at the moment I don't really care. What I want to know is, was there a spark?"

"A spark?" asked Vera.

"Yeah, a spark—you know, between you and the president. I mean, he sought you out, invited you to stay at the White House residence, and who knows what else I don't know about yet? I want to know, did you feel a spark between you two? Is this going anywhere or is it just going to be a great story to share with your friends until the day you die?"

"Well, I guess I haven't really thought about it that much," Vera admitted.

"Whoa, whoa, whoa, hold the phone girlfriend, you received long-stemmed roses when you were in Paris. Were they from the president?" Jenny inquired, starting to put some of the pieces of the puzzle together in her mind.

Vera blushed and smiled, but did not answer.

"There you go. No man does that unless he's interested in you, no, make that very interested in you," Jenny said with a huge smile. "Now, what happened to that man in black who was trying to kill you? Obviously he didn't succeed."

"Oh him, he's actually Agent Garcia," Vera replied. "He was sent by President Sherman to protect me, both in Paris and here at home. I met him in the White House. He's a very nice man and as it turns out, he did an exceptional job keeping me out of harm's way. Obviously I'm still alive."

"So, let me see if I have this right. Joel Sherman hears about you from his friend Jim, checks you out, and then makes contact with you on Facebook. You have no idea who he is, but you play coy, go along with his flirtations, and then he sends a bodyguard to protect you. Of course he doesn't stop there; he sends you flowers from an ocean away and then when you find out he is the President of the United States he invites you into his home, seeks your counsel, and puts you on display at the State of the Union for the entire world to see," Jenny confirmed, all the while rolling her eyes.

"You forgot about the part where he called the President of France and had me on a plane home the next morning, just in time for Christmas," Vera said, laughing.

"Oh, honey, this man is smitten. Can't you see that? What else does he need to do, propose to you in the Rose Garden with CNN cameras rolling?"

"I don't know, Jenny. I haven't heard a word from him since I got home. I'm sure he doesn't have time for me now that he has set off this nuclear truth explosion right in the face of the elite."

"Well, what did he say to you when you left the White House? Did he just shake your hand and say, 'Thanks for your service?'" Jenny asked incredulously.

"Not exactly. He gave me a big hug, kissed me on my cheek and gave me a secure cell phone like the one he had given Jim, and told me to call him anytime I wanted," Vera replied in a sheepishly soft voice.

Jenny threw her hands straight in the air. "And of course you haven't called because you don't want to be a bother, right?"

"Something like that."

"Oh, you are seriously out of practice. Here you have the most desirable and eligible man in the entire world giving you complete and total access to him, access that world leaders, corporate titans and government officials don't have, and you don't want to be a bother. He wants you to bother him! Get it?"

"Jenny, I've also been thinking seriously about retiring from the airline, and running through all the complications that decision might bring into my life. I just don't know what to do," Vera said with a heavy sigh.

Jenny reached over and poured what was left in the wine bottle into Vera's glass. "You drink that and you listen to me. Retire; do it tomorrow. You don't need the money, the aggravation or the flight benefits. And after you've done that, get on that phone and call that poor man. Tell him you're free as a bird and ready to soar, or tell him whatever it is that lets him know you're interested in him. Inform him that you want to pursue wherever that interest takes the two of you. Do you realize you could become the First Lady and you're sitting here trying to decide if you want to pass out peanuts to passengers for a paltry paycheck?" With that said, Jenny pulled her knees up underneath her, tilted her head back, and emptied her own wineglass.

Vera sat quietly, thinking about Jenny's well-meaning but direct demands that had managed to plow right over all the doubts she had been cultivating in her mind. When she finally spoke, all she could say was, "You make some very good points, and I'll give some serious thought to what you've said. Clearly, my life is about to change. I'm just not sure how or when."

two

You would have thought that the gates of hell had been opened and every demon available had been unleashed on Joel Sherman following his State of the Union address. The night of the broadcast found the political pundits and paid progressives nearly breathless as they attempted to call down fire and brimstone upon the man who had expected the nation to account for itself, and singled out the news media specifically to tell the truth to the American public. President Sherman was not the least bit surprised by the response, but he was taken aback by the vicious attacks on him personally, which developed as the days and weeks progressed. There was not a single news outlet in the entire world that had not proclaimed the utter destruction of the country if even one of the president's outlined objectives was considered, let alone brought to fruition. The opposing party rallied its troops and was out for blood, using the speech to raise money, to encourage candidates to run for office, and to paint a picture of the country sliding into decline. The president's own party attempted to show placid support for him at first, but as the hours and days continued, they backpedaled into oblivion and left the president and his team alone to defend against the slings and arrows directed at them.

Nevertheless, his speech had begun to stir something within the people. Their voice had yet to be heard, but the State of the Union YouTube video shattered all-time records for views. Traditionally, the views for a speech could be counted in the thousands during the weeks following the event. But Joel

Sherman's first address shot into the millions of views within the first few days. People who had not seen the speech live wanted to know what all the commotion was about. Others who had watched the speech on television wanted to see and hear it again, and in most cases take notes. They shared it with their neighbors, family members, and friends. Google revealed that it was included in email attachments the following day at an all-time record, twenty-seven million times. The mail that started to pour into the White House was overwhelmingly positive. Words like 'I had lost all hope until I heard you speak' were common. Many citizens stated that they had not voted for several years, but that the president's speech had stirred within them an American sense of pride and duty that had been missing. They promised to lead the charge in their precincts or districts come the following election.

Privately, Joel was pleased with what was transpiring within the nation. He was prepared to lead all those who would follow to a renewed sense of freedom. He knew it would be difficult—maybe even impossible—but such was the road he had chosen to travel. He needed as many allies as he could get who were willing to take up their swords, set aside their selfishness, and rally others to the cause.

Most of the president's daily schedule consisted of meetings with specific Cabinet officers and party leadership. The leadership was mostly supportive, but many in Congress felt the sting of the president's scolding and were vindictive, even in the face of political pressure from their constituents, which was starting to build. It was the president's job to focus that pressure where it was needed the most and encourage the people to stay the course and demand effective change. Joel understood that Congress will always act in their own interest, and if there is a vacuum of demands and direction from the people, they will create their own. President Sherman had held the mirror to their faces and like most cowards, they were afraid of what they saw. This actually worked in the president's favor, and his spirits were lifted with each incremental success.

"You seem in exceptionally good spirits this morning, sir. Have you heard from Ms. Hanson by chance?" Mike asked, as he set the tray with the president's morning coffee on the table in the private study. Vera Hanson was not a subject that Mike and the president had any reason to discuss, but Mike knew the president so well that he could feel it was time to ask the hard question. Mike was more than capable of dispelling his natural curiosity, so it was mostly out of his realization that the president needed to talk that he inquired about the lady.

"No, Michael, radio silence from that woman. You don't suppose she went back to France and got tangled up with the local gendarmes again, do you? If that's the case, I'm going to have to spring her again. You know my presidential pardons carry no weight on foreign soil," the president replied.

"Not likely, sir. She seems much too smart to fall for anything those Clouseaus might conjure up to catch her off guard."

"Why do you suppose I haven't heard from her? Do you think all the trappings of this office and the constant commotion of Washington and the presidency might have overwhelmed her?" the president asked, almost not wanting Mike to answer.

"I couldn't rightly say, sir. Perhaps she just needed some time alone to decompress from all the horror she and Mr. Bowman discovered, the death of Max Hager, and the feeling of being overwhelmed that newcomers always seem to experience on meeting you. Or perhaps she is not a Redskins fan," Mike concluded with a chuckle just under his breath, yet loud enough for the president to hear.

"Maybe you're right. It might just be too much for her, and I should try to push her out of my mind, but I have to tell you she's stuck in there pretty tight. She's a rare blend of intelligence, beauty and sensitivity that you don't often find, and it's exactly what I need to take on this burden of leadership. I'm convinced there's no one like that in Washington who hasn't been tainted by the political power this town creates. But with Vera I could be assured she would be behind me helping, but not pushing me in a self-serving direction. I was hoping the Facebook interaction could lead to something more substantial, but I guess it's not to be. Remind me to deactivate that cell phone I gave her. If she's not going to use it we can't afford the security risk it presents."

"I'll take care of that for you, Mr. President. Worry no longer about the phone or the female," Mike said as he poured the president another cup of coffee before he exited the study.

three

Jim Bowman had remained in Washington D.C. after the president's address. He was eager to begin his assignment to assist Congress in opening a new investigation into 9/11, but his early efforts had already proven this job was going to require a great deal of time in the offices of legislative leadership. He'd encouraged his wife, Mari, to settle things up in Seattle and return to D.C. to be with him. He had been away from her far longer than he would have liked, and this new job only meant more of the same.

To say that Congress was not amenable to the idea of starting a new investigation was a laughable understatement. If not for the fact that the president had threatened to veto their budget unless money was appropriated for the investigation, Jim would have made no headway at all. As he began contacting committee chairpersons, it became very apparent that a new investigation was never going to take place. He was always greeted warmly and had no problem getting in front of the leadership, but from his experience in the Air Force, he knew the runaround when it was being dished up. It became obvious to him that with various Congressmen and women, it wasn't just being dished—it was being shoveled.

It didn't seem to matter that Congress was beginning to hear from their constituents back home that a complete investigation was warranted; they were not about to rattle the status quo where things stood following the 9/11 commission report. As far as most of them were concerned, the status quo had been cemented into place. The problem for Jim was that he knew that nineteen Arabs did not commandeer four aircraft and fly them into selected targets. His research and discoveries with Vera proved that fact. So for him, it was only natural to want to get the investigation started and to get to the truth once and for all. He felt he owed it to the flight crews, the passengers and all the others who lost their lives that day. This new investigation instilled so much fear into the hearts of members of Congress that even when their words said 'yes,' their meaning was a firm and resolute 'hell no.' It didn't take long for Jim to determine he was getting nowhere with his assigned task.

He scheduled a meeting with Jerald Reitz, the president's National Security Advisor, to discuss some possible strategies to persuade Congress to comply with the president's wishes. In his current position Jerald did not interface with congressional members on a regular basis, but his experience was broad and he personally knew several of the committee chairmen. In addition, he was completely on board with Jim and Vera's findings, which made him a great resource and someone with whom Jim felt comfortable discussing his challenges.

"Jim, welcome," Jerald said, extending his hand as he pointed to a seating area in the corner of his office.

"I can't thank you enough for taking the time to see me on such short notice, Jerry. It's been a rather fruitless few weeks, making the rounds here on the hill. And I have to say, I'm quite surprised at the duplicitous reception I'm receiving. I thought Congress would be more than willing to want to uncover the deceptions that were used to cover up the events of 9/11."

Jerald looked Jim right in the eye. "That might be your first mistake, my friend; Congress doesn't like to get their hands dirty. If you want them to dig through manure you're going to have to sanitize it first. They see this as a real lose-lose proposition. They will be polite to your face to a point, but I tried to explain to the president that it would be almost impossible to get Congress to open up any kind of investigation. He understood, but wasn't willing to back off his demand. I admire him for that, but I realize you have been saddled with the task of making it happen. So how can I help you?"

Jim opened his hands palms up and said, "You might start by helping me understand why Congress is so reluctant to embrace the truth."

"Oh boy, that's easy. Truth has consequences that hold people to a higher standard or compel them to do something they're not predisposed to naturally do. Congress hates truth. They dance around it, bow to its precepts, and salute it at every opportunity, when in reality it's the monster under the bed and they can't bear to look."

Jim slowly shook his head, signaling that he understood, but he wasn't willing to accept what he was hearing. "So how am I going to get them to look deeper into this century's most altering event?"

"You're going to have to make it out to be in their best interest. Look, Jim, Congress's number one priority is to be elected, then re-elected. Their second priority is so far removed from their first that it never even registers on the scale. Do you get my drift?"

"You mean I have to make this an election issue?" Jim inquired.

"Well, not directly, because that would never fly, but you do have to move it into the forefront of their minds by causing them to think that if they fail to act, it may hamper them from fulfilling their primary objective."

"I understand that, but what I don't understand is why they are so reluctant to do what we all think we elected them to do."

Jerald leaned back into his chair before he spoke. "You know as well as I do that many entities were involved in 9/11. They all played significant and mostly independent roles that day. If you start digging into what really happened and who did what, you'll be pushing on the house of cards, and no one here wants that house to collapse. For Congress, it's all about money and their access to it. That's what drives their primary objective. The truth puts that money in jeopardy. That's why they aren't willing to take the risk and why you have to find a way to separate the money from assuring them re-election."

"So in other words, Jerry, I have to find a way to cause the people to put the appropriate pressure on them to do the right thing, thereby making the money a moot issue."

"Good luck with that, my friend, but that's exactly what must be done. President Sherman has kicked open that door. The people are starting to fall in behind him, but it's servants like you and me that will have to keep them focused and involved, otherwise they'll lose interest and become complacent. Which, by the way, is where Congress likes them: complacent and easily manipulated."

"I can see that I may not be fully prepared to meet the demands that are needed to move the president's agenda forward. I wish Max Hager were still alive. He and his group were onto something really big before he was killed. I suspect it's the kind of information that, if revealed, could persuade members of Congress to act. He didn't say much the night before he left for Chicago, but I knew him well enough that I could tell his team was digging into something important. He reassured me his group's discoveries were so monumental that they had to meet in person to show him what it was they had uncovered. They knew they had found something that could endanger their lives, but they wanted to get the truth out and so did Max."

"Oh say, Jim, that reminds me. I have a letter here from a law office, addressed to you. I was going to come by to give it to you today even before you called. The president asked me to deal with anything that involved Max, simply for security reasons, and that's why it was funneled through me. Do you mind opening it and letting me know what it is?"

Jim was a little surprised. He could not think of anything involving Max that might concern him. They had been friends for a long time, but it was more a casual friendship, and only became intense when it concerned specific security issues.

"I see a little smile on your face, Jim. What is that about?" Jerald asked.

"Oh, I'm just wondering if this is from Max's probate attorney, leaving me his ponytail collection. That would be just like Max, somehow." Jim opened the letter and read. When he was finished, he passed it to Jerald. It read: "You have been chosen to be the executor of Maxwell Jeffrey Hager's estate. Your presence will be required in Minneapolis to establish the extent of his estate and to execute the duties thereof. Please contact me at your earliest convenience."

Jim took the letter back from Jerald's hand. "Why would he appoint me to be his executor? I know his family buried him shortly after the incident. Why wouldn't one of them be chosen to be the executor? I can't imagine he had many assets to distribute, and surely they would all go to family members."

Jerald put his arm on Jim's shoulder. "Perhaps there's something that Max wanted you to have, something that might assist in your investigation and continued research. Maybe you were the only one who could be trusted with his information."

"That could be," replied Jim. "He was funny that way. His security assets were his most important possessions, and perhaps there's something there that'll help me with my task at hand. I'll make arrangements to meet with this attorney, if you will inform the president."

"That I can easily do. I meet with him daily, as you know. I'm sure he'll approve of you taking on this added responsibility."

As the men walked to the door, Jim paused for a moment,

then turned and looked at Jerald and said, "I sure miss that Max. He was a rock you could always count on for stability, and I could use a little of that right now. Thank you again for seeing me and for your help. It gives me a much different perspective that's sorely needed."

"You're welcome, Jim. I'm always happy to help you. Come see me anytime."

four

*J*enny had definitely given Vera a lot to think about, as if she didn't already find her thoughts consumed by the decisions she needed to make. One of the drawbacks of being a widow was making decisions that affected her without a partner's input. When Jeff was alive, it was always so comfortable for either of them to slip into the role of devil's advocate and help the other come to a conclusion about how to move forward. It was something that came to them naturally, and one of Jeff's gifts that she loved the most. There was a genuine respect for each other that had an unspoken message of, how can I be the most help? Never was there any contention or attempt to maneuver ahead of the other person's ego. Theirs was a team effort that managed to make decision-making enjoyable. Vera missed that. Often she would talk to friends or family, but they were more interested in offering their opinions rather than helping her arrive at her own. With the exception of Jim and Mari's advice, Vera usually slogged through the scenarios of her life and hoped her decisions would work out for the best. This time, the burden of deciding to retire and if she should listen to Jenny's advice and make contact with Joel Sherman were overwhelming.

The morning sun of late winter was slow in arriving. Vera had spent a restless night and was still working her bed pillows to find a comfortable position when the first light broke through her bedroom window and caused Kelli to stir. Kelli was always patient for Vera to get out of bed before she began to run through her hunger dance. For some reason this morning was different.

The moment the first ray of sunlight caught the dog's eye, she jumped off the bed and started barking for Vera to join her. Vera rolled over and pretended not to notice, but when Kelli pulled the covers onto the floor, there was no denying that it was time to get up.

Vera fed Kelli and proceeded to dress. There on her dresser was the phone that President Sherman had given her. Her initial response was to send it back to the president with some cute quip that would indicate to him that she was not interested in pursuing any continued conversations, at least not on a regular basis. Of course she did not want to offend him in any way and she couldn't think of anything worthwhile to talk about, so there the phone sat. Jenny's words from the night before came rushing back. "He wants you to bother him." Now that she had had a night in bed, even if rest had escaped her, Jenny's opinion seemed to fall right in line with all the other opinions Vera didn't pay much attention to.

Kelli wanted to go outside and she wanted Vera to come along. It was very early for such a walk, but Vera was happy to comply. It didn't look like it would rain right away, so she grabbed her coat and the two of them headed out the door. Kelli immediately ran to scatter a flock of seagulls, and then waited for Vera to catch up. Puget Sound was unusually quiet this particular morning; the only noise that could be heard was the birds scolding Kelli for interrupting their morning gathering.

The question of retirement, however, wasn't going away and in spite of the morning stillness, the commotion that this dilemma created seemed to be exceptionally loud in Vera's head. As she walked up the beach she tried to play out in her mind what life would be like without a schedule to plan and to keep. What would she do with her time? All of the projects she had been putting off were not calling her any more forcefully than they had been during all the years she'd been ignoring them.

Flying had been her life for so long she couldn't imagine herself doing anything else. Just as she felt herself being drawn back into the routine, the terror of the flight termination system and the capricious nature of its engagement ratcheted up her fear. She needed Jeff or someone like him to help her make a decision, but there was no one. She was very alone at a critical moment in her life. Kelli came running up alongside her.

"Want to go to Starbucks, girl?" Vera asked, reaching into her coat pocket to find the leash.

Kelli yelped as if she knew exactly what Vera had said and then ran to the gate near the road, sat down, and waited for Vera to join her. It was so comfortable to fall into her regular routine. Kelli got her Starbucks cookie and seemed delighted to sit out front watching for other dogs and patiently waiting. Vera settled into her favorite seat by the fireplace and began to sip her extra hot vanilla latte. It had been some time since she had seen the 'man in black' sitting there. Memories began to flood her mind of that horrible day when Kelli was hit by the SUV. Had it not been for Agent Garcia intervening, both of them might have been killed. She rested her feet on the edge of the coffee table and looked out the window to where the events of that day occurred. She could see herself kneeling in the street tending to Kelli. She remembered the quick response of the police officers. Her mind tried to fight off the stark reality that someone tried to kill her.

Her thoughts turned to Agent Garcia and how he had followed her around the world at President Sherman's request, to protect her and to keep her safe. For the first time the question entered her mind: Why? Why would President Sherman feel a need to keep her safe? Why would he assign his favorite and most trusted agent to such an insignificant detail? Why would he do that when he hadn't even met her? What was going on? She took a quick sip of her latte and tried to think. Nothing made sense. Jim could have told the president every single detail about her and none of it should have warranted the kind of response the president had exhibited. To the best of her recollection, the president had taken a personal interest in her from the moment he knew anything about her. Naturally, she was grateful. According to Agent Garcia, he had thwarted several efforts made to harm her, and had deflected who knows how many other attempts simply by being present. "I must matter to the president," she thought. It was a feeling that Vera had not experienced in a very long time. And yet Joel wasn't overly forward. He had never tried to interfere with her life in any way, but he had been very interested in everything that had happened to her over the past few months. His interest and concern for her was almost stealth like, which would have angered her had she realized it sooner, but now, sitting in Starbucks and seriously reflecting on all the events, she realized none of it was an attempt to manipulate or to persuade her in any particular direction. It was exactly what Jeff would have done, but on a much higher level because of Joel's office and the circumstances occurring in her own life. Her perspective had subtly undergone a metamorphosis and she concluded she would indeed bother him, even if only to express her gratitude for all he had done on her behalf.

Vera finished her latte, said goodbye to her favorite barista and brought an extra cookie out to Kelli. She fastened the leash to the dog's collar and began the stroll home. With each step the anticipation intensified, causing her to wonder if she really should call the President of the United States for something as mundane as a thank-you. The question of when to call, preferably at a time when he wasn't busy, made her start to rethink the wisdom of her decision. Surely he was always busy with matters of state. That was why he had screeners, staff and secret service agents protecting him from the demands of the outside world. And yet, he had given her a secure phone that called directly to him and encouraged her to use it whenever she wished. Once again she felt like she mattered, only this time the feeling was more intense.

Kelli was more than happy to return home. The early morning walk had tired her and she curled up in her favorite spot in the family room for her morning nap. Vera, on the other hand, was far less subdued. Her decision to call the president was making her anxious and all she could do was pace the kitchen floor and pause long enough to look out the window, but not focus on anything in the distance. She walked upstairs and took the phone off of her dresser. It was the most unusual phone she had ever seen. Like Jim's, it had just the one button that when pushed, connected her with the president. She tucked it into her jeans pocket and returned to the kitchen to pace. She felt a sense of accomplishment having the phone now in her possession, but she still hadn't summoned sufficient courage to actually make the call. Jenny was right; she didn't want to be a bother, and no matter when she chose to call, she knew she would be interrupting something important.

Vera sat down in her window seat, curled her legs underneath her and reached into her pocket for the phone. She held it in her hand and stared at it for several minutes. Then she put it back in her pocket. She thought about calling Jenny, thinking that a good girl talk would relieve all the anxiety and supply her with the fortitude she would require to do the deed. Just as she was about to get up to call Jenny, the phone in her pocket began to ring. Panic shot through every fiber of her body. Even Kelli woke when she heard the unfamiliar ringtone. The dog sidled over to Vera and nudged at her pocket. Vera took the phone out and stared at it, trying to decide whether to answer it or not. Kelli yelped. Vera put the phone to her ear and said, "Hello."

"Ms. Hanson?" a familiar voice on the other end asked.

"Yes?"

"Mike McFee here, Ms. Hanson."

"Oh, Mike, it's so good to hear your voice again. But why are you calling me on this secure line? And please call me Vera."

"Well, that's just it, Ms. Hanson. I'm calling to tell you that the president instructed me to decommission this phone. And personally, I think that's a horrible idea."

"Why are you calling to tell me this, Mike?"

"The president concluded that you had no intention of ever calling him, so he instructed me to have it turned off. Just between you and me, ma'am, I think that was a decision the man in him made and not the president, so I'm calling to tell you that if you have any intention to ever use this phone, now would be a good time."

"Now as in right this minute now? Because I was sitting here trying to work up the nerve to actually use it when you called."

"Ms. Hanson, the president is in his private study at the moment, and now would be a perfect time for you to call him. I don't like to intrude or overstep my bounds, but I'm acting on instinct and my friendship with the president. I'm telling you that it would be a shame for me to have to decommission your phone. So you decide what is best for you, and we'll leave it at that."

Vera was stunned that Mike had called her. She almost couldn't formulate the words to respond to him. Finally she spoke. "Mike, I thank you. Like I said, I was just sitting here contemplating calling the president when you called. I appreciate your concern and I'll give your suggestion serious consideration." Her voice sounded formal as the words came out of her mouth, but inside she was turning to mush. Once more a confirmation that she mattered struck home and it humbled her.

"Okay, Ms. Hanson. It was good to talk to you again. I hope you won't be a stranger and you can return to Washington for a visit sometime soon."

"Thank you, Mike, I genuinely appreciate your concern. Goodbye." Vera hung up, but continued to stare at the phone in her hand. She wanted to call, but couldn't force her finger to press the button. Finally she took a deep breath, closed her eyes and pressed down hard with her thumb.

"Hello, Vera," said the kind, familiar voice on the other end.

Vera cleared her throat and choked out, "Hello, Mr. President."

"Please, never call me 'Mr. President' unless you're asking for a formal pardon."

"What should I call you then, sir?" Vera shyly asked.

"Well for starters, you can take the 'sir' and put it in the drawer with the 'Mr. President,' and then you can just call me Joel. If that doesn't work, I've been known to answer to 'hey you' and if you are in the opposing party, 'dumb ass' seems to be the most common reference of the day."

Vera started to laugh. It was exactly what she needed to calm the tension that had built up inside. "Well then, Joel, I wanted to call and thank you for all you have done for me. I began to realize just how many times you or your agents have interceded on my behalf and made a dangerous situation safe. So thank you."

"Vera, I was and I am only too happy to be of service to you. After what you and Jim have done for this country and for me personally, regarding your research, it is I who should be calling to thank you. I also wanted to express my gratitude for your courage to stand up and be heard when it really mattered. I'm still hearing from members of my staff inquiring about that woman who stood up in the Oval Office and pointed out the direction this country needs to take. I was very impressed with your actions and apparently I wasn't alone. Vera, I'm sure that wasn't an easy thing to do. You felt like an outsider whose opinion couldn't possibly matter, and yet you overcame your fear and allowed your love of country to seize the moment and to take charge. To be honest, that's a very rare quality, especially here in the center of concession."

"Joel, we never did have much of a chance to talk when I was there. With the run up to your speech and then all the commotion that followed, I just felt it was best to get home to my dog and begin to make some important decisions about my life. But I missed not having an opportunity to chat with you about our Facebook conversations, how they actually came about, and how beautiful those roses were you sent me in Paris. As busy as you must be, I'm afraid that conversation might have to wait until you are the former President Sherman," Vera said, beginning to feel more comfortable talking to the President of the United States.

"You know, I gave you the phone for that very reason—so you could call me anytime you wanted. You and Jim are the only ones in the world with that kind of access. Jim, because of what he is doing—and is going to do—about the new investigation, needs my input. He is hardly a bother. I think he has used the phone twice since I gave it to him and I've called him once. You, on the other hand, I had hoped to hear a lot from and this is the first time you've called." The President stood up from his desk and gently closed his study door.

Jenny's exhortation began to reverberate in Vera's mind. "He wants you to bother him." For the first time that thought was not just background noise. It started to have some clarity, and she liked the picture it was painting. She thought she would see what colors were being used, so she bluntly asked, "I have been thinking about retiring from the airline, but I can't quite make up my mind. What do you think, Joel?"

There was a long pause, and when the answer came, Vera was pleasantly surprised. "Do you need to see any more parts of the world dressed in a flight attendant's uniform?" the president asked. Before Vera could answer, his next question was even more poignant. "I'm not always going to be the president. Who is going to bail you out the next time you get yourself into a jam with the foreign police?"

Vera laughed. "I hope there isn't a next time. That Paris trip about did me in."

"Perhaps you've given all you have to give to the airline industry, my friend, and much more exciting adventures await you, that won't need to be scheduled a month in advance. I know Jim could use your help with his new assignments. And I wouldn't mind seeing more of you here in Washington. The gossip columnists have already had a field day speculating about you. Then you suddenly left and all they had to babble about was how my politics would scare any eligible woman away."

The last of the president's words only slightly registered with her. Vera was struck by his earlier questions—how he didn't give an opinion, but rather presented thoughts and left it to her to formulate the answers. It was a style she was used to and exactly what she wanted to hear.

"I think I'll make a decision one way or the other very soon, sir, I mean Joel. I do have a life yet to be lived and if it's not with the airline then there's no sense delaying it any longer. But I don't know about coming to Washington. I don't really fit in, I wouldn't have anything to do, and I don't know what I would do with Kelli." She had more to say, but her thoughts drifted and prevented the words from fully formulating.

"You do need to make up your mind. I suspect all those issues could be worked out if you had an objective you were trying to accomplish. Keep me informed as to what you decide. I'm going to need to know where to send flowers the next time I get the urge."

"You're funny, you know that? Here all this time I was dreading calling you, and now you make it sound like we've been friends for years. Why, wasn't it only recently you were Stan the Mystery Man?"

"I wasn't really very good in that role. I wanted to tell you who I was, but I didn't think you would believe me and if you did, I thought you would think I was crazy reaching out to a perfect stranger."

That got Vera's mind racing around some unasked questions. "Yeah, why did you reach out to a perfect stranger miles and miles away from you?"

"Jim Bowman said you were an angel and that I hadn't been the same since my last angel went to heaven."

Vera was silent, but she knew exactly what he meant. The wholeness that an angel provides is terribly missed, and not easily replaced. She spoke in almost a whisper. "And you believed him?"

"I trusted him. I believed him when I finally met you and brushed up against your wings."

"Joel, that may be the nicest thing anyone has ever said to me. I'm not sure it's true, but since it comes from you, I'm going to give you some executive privilege and not argue."

"You're a remarkable woman, Vera. I want to know you better. That's why I gave you the phone. Please use it; you'll be amazed how I can free up my time when it rings."

"I have a better idea," Vera said. "You call me. I'm never battling it out with a senator, meeting with heads of state, or flying off on Air Force One to negotiate a trade deal. I'm just a soon-to-be-retired flight attendant with extra time on her hands. I know there's more to dig up about the 9/11 event, and I have several files from Max I need to go over with a fine-tooth comb."

"Deal, Ms. Hanson, but you be there to answer it when I do call. I don't want to have to send Agent Garcia out after you again. Now I'll let you go and not keep you any longer. Thank you, though, for calling. It's made my entire day and it's still morning."

"Thank you for being so kind and easy to talk to. I look forward to more of this and I promise to answer. Kelli isn't as fond of Agent Garcia as I am. Goodbye, Joel, and keep fighting hard for this country."

"Count on it, ma'am."

After the president hung up he walked again to the study door, opened it, and called for Mike.

"Yes, sir, Mr. President," came Mike's instant reply.

"I thought I told you to have that Hanson woman's phone deactivated."

"That is correct, sir. You did indeed."

"And you didn't do it, did you?"

"No, sir,"

"Good man, Michael. You know me so well. Oh, and thanks for calling her. She needed the push."

"My pleasure, sir," Mike replied with a smile he didn't even try to hide.

five

*T*here was something about going back to Minnesota this time of year that caused Jim to balk at the idea. The thought was made worse by the fact that Max would not be there. After his retirement, the only reason Jim ever went to Minnesota was to see Max. Now his only reason for going was because it concerned something that was important to Max. When he returned to Blair House he immediately phoned Mari.

"How's it coming, sweetheart? I sure miss you," was the first thing out of his mouth when his wife answered.

"Oh Jim, I'd love to be there with you, but getting things buttoned up here is more difficult than I imagined. For starters, I've just now finished closing up the mountain house. I have this strange feeling we won't be back there for quite some time. Then there's the Seattle house to get closed up. I'd love to find someone that would housesit or live in it while we're gone, and I don't have any idea how long to tell them we'll be away. Anyway, how are you?" Mari asked.

"Things have been rather frustrating since you left, and seem to be more problematic every day. No one is excited about opening a new 9/11 investigation, to put it mildly, and on top of that I have to go to Minneapolis again."

"Why would you go to Minnesota, of all places? I can't imagine anything to do with 9/11 is going on there."

Jim chuckled. "It concerns our friend Max, and I'm learning to never underestimate him, even in death. Who knows, maybe he left me more about his 9/11 findings. I know he knew a lot more than he shared with Vera and me," Jim tried to explain.

"Well, why are you even going?" Mari asked, somewhat bewildered.

"Oh, I forgot to tell you. I've been made executor of Max's will, so I have to go and meet with his attorney. I can't imagine it'll take much time. Max didn't have much of anything and I'm sure everything he did have will go to his two kids. I don't even think his ex-wife is still alive. But like I said, you never know with Max. Jerry Reitz seems to think I'll find something that's important enough to keep me there, looking around."

"You should take Vera with you," Mari chimed in.

"Why Vera? I'm sure she's busy with her own life and doesn't want be bothered with something as routine as this," Jim responded.

"I know for a fact she is trying to decide if she should retire or not, and I also suspect she has a few feelings for Joel Sherman that she's trying to figure out. You know how valuable she would be if you do find something important. She proved that already, and I think you could be helpful to her with some friendly advice."

"I'll give it some thought. That would mean you would have to take care of Kelli again. Are you up for that?" Jim asked.

"Oh, I'd love to take care of that sweet dog again, but I'll be busy getting the house closed up and running errands. I doubt I could give her the attention she needs. That might rule Vera out as far as joining you. But I think you should talk to her anyway and see what's going on with her."

"I'll do that, perhaps later tonight."

"Say hi to Vera when you talk to her. I hope everything goes well for her. She deserves a break after all she's been through this past year," Mari said.

"Will do. Goodnight, sweetheart."

Jim hung up and started thinking about the value of having Vera along with him should he discover something interesting amongst Max's belongings. She had such an analytical mind, and could take things apart and reconstruct them so naturally. Jim admitted to himself that the two of them worked exceptionally well together. The more he thought about it, the more he liked the idea.

After dinner he settled into a comfortable position on the bed with all the pillows behind his head and punched up Vera's number. "Vera, Jim here. How are you, my dear? It's been a while since we've spoken. What are you up to with all your free time?"

"Oh, Jim, I'm so glad you called. I had the most fascinating conversation with the president and I can't stop thinking about him—I mean it."

Jim laughed. "You mean my matchmaker's efforts are beginning to take root?"

"I wouldn't go that far, but I think I'm starting to understand who he is on more of a personal level, and I like what I see. And to be perfectly honest, I like how it makes me feel. Now is that too much information for you? Something I should've just told Mari?" Vera asked.

"Hell, Vera, Joel and I go so far back you can tell me anything. And, of course, whatever you say can't and won't be used against you. I'm just thrilled that it all seems to be going so well, but that's not why I called. Oh, by the way, Mari says to tell you hi."

Vera had to smile at how uncomfortable her little revelation seemed to make Jim. It was as if her one sentence had lowered his IQ by 40 points. "So why did you call?" she asked, hoping her question would get him back on track.

"I have to fly to Minnesota to speak with Max's attorney and go through his things. Turns out I've been asked to be the executor of his will. I wanted to know if you would come with me." That wasn't quite what Jim wanted to say, but his words came out before his mental acumen had returned to normal.

"You know, I can't imagine why you would want me there.

I'm sure I would be in the way, but I'd love to go and I can't even tell you why. The only problem is what to do with Kelli. Howard's place is going to be closed for a few months while he does some remodeling. Is there any chance Mari could take her again?"

Jim's excitement at hearing Vera would like to join him was quickly dampened by knowing that Mari couldn't take Kelli either. Without even thinking, he just blurted out, "Why don't you call Joel and ask if he could take her for a week or two?"

They both burst out laughing at the preposterous nature of that suggestion.

"I'll see what I can arrange here and get back to you, Jim. I feel I need to find some closure with Max and even though I can't imagine how much help I'd be there, I would like to go," Vera said, feeling confident something would work out. "I'll call you in a few days and see if I can make this happen."

"I'll probably leave in a few days, so hurry. I have a feeling this will be good for both of us. Talk to you soon."

After Jim hung up, Vera thought it would be funny to share with the president the ridiculous suggestion that Kelli come to Washington while she went to the Midwest with Jim. She found her phone and even though it was late, she pushed the button and hoped Joel would be available to answer.

"Well, Vera, what a pleasant and unexpected surprise this time of night. I was just getting ready for bed, but I'm happy you called."

"Oh, Joel, I won't keep you long, I just wanted to share something funny with you that Jim Bowman said to me a few minutes ago, that made me laugh so hard."

"By all means, share away."

"Well, Jim asked me to accompany him to Minnesota to deal with Max's estate issues. I agreed, but wasn't sure what to do with Kelli. He suggested I call you and ask if you would take care of her while I'm gone. I don't think he was firing with all synapses, do you?" Vera asked, still laughing.

Joel didn't say anything. Vera listened hard, but didn't hear him laughing. She wasn't sure what that meant. She hoped he hadn't thought she too was out of her mind for calling so late with such a stupid idea.

Finally Joel spoke. "I think that is a great idea. I'd love to have Kelli here. There are all kinds of people who would enjoy having her, and if necessary we can hire someone just to be Kelli's nanny for a week or so. Not only that, the Secretary of Agriculture is in Seattle right now and comes home tomorrow morning. If you can crate Kelli up, she can be on that plane and be here before nightfall. I like it. What do you say?"

Vera was stunned. "You can't be serious, Mr. President."

"I don't know what the president thinks, but Joel Sherman thinks it's a capital idea and that you should start looking for a crate. Truly, she will be no bother, and the best part is that when you're finished helping Jim, I'll insist that you come and pick her up in person. No flying her back to the Northwest with some other government official."

Vera started to squirm. "Well, I just don't know what to say. I thought you would laugh with us, but I think you're serious."

"I learned a long time ago that it's best to be serious with angels. So is she coming in the morning?"

So many thoughts flooded Vera's head at once she nearly had to gasp for air. She knew it was crazy to send her dog to the White House. Who would do something like that? The president himself was actually pressuring her to do it and deep down she kind of liked the idea, not for Kelli's sake as much as for her own. She knew Kelli would be fine with such an adventure. She was used to having Vera gone and it didn't seem to matter much to her where she was as long as her needs were being taken care of and people were nice to her. Joel was quite persuasive that all would be well, so without thinking it all the way through, she answered, "Yes, Kelli will be on the flight in the morning if you promise me she will be loved and taken care of until I can come to collect her."

"You have my word. In fact, she'll be so well taken care of, she might not want to leave here," replied the president. "I'll have specific instructions and permissions emailed to you as to where to bring her in the morning. Meet up with Jim as soon as you can. I'm sure he'll need you. I'll be counting on you two again."

"You know, Joel, this is all still quite ridiculous, but I'm going to trust you until I bump up against your harp."

The president laughed. "Just don't ask me to play anything."

six

*K*elli didn't seem to mind being put in a crate and taken to the airport. She was such an exceptional animal that she complied with anything Vera wanted her to do, without causing a problem. That made the whole crazy escapade bearable. Vera gave Kelli a big hug goodbye, scratched her behind the ears, and gave her a special treat to chew on during her flight.

Vera called Jim and made arrangements to fly to Minnesota to meet him the next morning. She still wasn't certain how she would fit into whatever it was that Jim had planned, but she was excited to once again be engaged with him on behalf of her country. Their research filled a void she knew would occur if she retired. And deep inside she found it both exciting and thrilling to uncover the heinous actions of those who had perpetrated 9/11. It was as if she was meant to do this kind of work, and it lent clarity to the realization that her airline career had parked at its last gate. The men in her life who mattered the most—Jeff, Jim, and now even Joel—had always been engaged in service to their country. It was something she admired in them, and now that service to country was becoming a driving force for her. All of a sudden, the decision to retire was becoming easier and a sense of calm was beginning to wash over her.

As his formal work day began to come to an end, President Sherman phoned over to the staff at the residence to inquire if Kelli, the golden retriever, had arrived. The response was affirmative, yet there was a sense something was not quite right.

Upon further inquiry the president was informed that Kelli

had indeed arrived, but that she would not come out of her crate. "Where is she exactly?" the president asked.

"She's on the East Lawn, sir," came the reply. "Because of the long flight we felt it would be best to let her out there so she could do her business, but when we opened the crate she just looked at us with her big brown eyes and refused to come out. We tried to coax her with some dog treats, but even that didn't seem to help. Should we have a vet come see what he can do?"

"Oh, that won't be necessary just yet. Give me a few minutes and I'll walk over there and see for myself what seems to be the matter," responded the president. Joel finished giving instructions to his Chief of Staff and then hurried over to where he saw a few house staff members and a couple of Secret Service agents gathered around a crate on the East Lawn. He summarily dismissed them all and knelt down in front of Kelli. "Well, girl," he said. "You've had a long day, haven't you? And you probably miss your momma. I'm going to take care of you until she comes to get you. My name is Joel." He stretched his hand out toward the open crate. Kelli didn't get up, but she scooted forward just far enough to where she could sniff the president's hand. Once she was satisfied with how it smelled, she began to lick his fingers. Joel turned his hand over so the dog could be sure not to miss any places. When she was done, Joel stood up and Kelli walked out of the crate and began licking his other hand.

"Clearly she was waiting for the boss," shouted one the agents from across the lawn.

The president nodded and reached down to pet Kelli on the head. After a moment or two she felt comfortable with her surroundings and wandered off to sniff the grass. When she was finished she returned to Joel's side and followed him wherever he went. When it became apparent that Kelli was not going to let the president out of her sight, a decision needed to be made.

"Where do you plan to house this dog while Vera is away,

sir?" Mike asked.

"I had just assumed that the staff would take care of her down on the ground level, and that she would stay in one of the outbuildings during the night and be cared for during the day," replied the president.

"I think you may have found yourself a companion. Do you mind if she spends time in the residence?" Mike queried.

"She doesn't seem to be much trouble and we've become buddies. Ah, let's allow her to come up and see what happens. Bring that dog bed you bought to the great room and Kelli can sleep there tonight."

"Very well, sir," Mike replied, delighted that Vera's dog had made such an attachment.

Everything seemed to go according to the new plan, except Kelli nudged her way into the president's bedroom and slept at the foot of his bed. No one seemed to mind. Especially Vera, when she called the next morning to find out how things were going. It was clear to her that Kelli had adopted the president and all would be fine in her absence. Knowing that her dog was happy and comfortable made getting ready for her flight so much easier.

Vera landed in Minneapolis thirty minutes before Jim. That gave her time to make her way to the executive boarding lounge where private and government planes arrived. She was delighted to be able to see Jim again and hoped he had a better idea of what his assignment would be while in Minnesota.

They greeted one another with a big hug when Jim came up from the tarmac. "Oh, it's good to see you, Vera. You make any day brighter, and it looks like we'll need both warmth and sunshine today."

"Oh, that's just your typical spring weather here, Jim, winter-like but with longer hours. It's good to see you too. How was your flight?"

"These government Gulfstreams are so nice, they can really spoil you if you're not careful. I had half a notion to ask if I could fly in the right seat, but the overstuffed recliner in the cabin wouldn't hear of it."

They both laughed. "So what is the plan for the rest of the day?" Vera inquired.

"We don't have a meeting scheduled with Max's attorney until early tomorrow morning, so there are no real plans for the rest of today. I'd like to visit Max's grave and pay my final respects. I hear his headstone was set yesterday and I'd like to lay a flower or two just to say a final goodbye. Everything happened so fast that I never felt like I had any kind of closure. So if you don't mind, let's head there first."

"I was kind of hoping you'd say something like that. One of the main reasons I agreed to come with you was to find some kind of finality for me with regards to Max. I know I didn't know him as well as you did, but he was one of the most endearing souls I've ever met. I'm more than good with that. Do you know where he was buried?"

"I have the address of the cemetery, but not the actual grave site. I'm sure we can find the sexton's office and inquire there," Jim replied.

The drive to the cemetery felt longer than either of them had expected. Perhaps it was because the traffic was more congested than usual or the air seemed colder than normal for that time of year. Whatever the cause, both of them arrived at the cemetery with very heavy hearts. They followed the sexton's instructions to an older part of the grounds. Max's grave was in a beautiful location. Several mature evergreens grew on top of a small knoll near where Max had been interred. Patches of snow still covered the ground. They parked the car and begin the short walk up to the gravesite. Underneath a group of trees was a wrought iron bench, and on it sat a human figure bundled in warm clothes with his head buried in his hands. As they approached the newly set headstone, emotion began to well up in both of them. Vera began to cry softly. Jim put his arm around her. They stood quietly for a minute, and then both reached down together and laid the flowers at the base of the stone. Jim held Vera close and they both began to weep. They could sense the presence of someone behind them, and assumed it was the person who had been sitting on the park bench. He must have been a friend of Max's, and when he saw them at the burial site felt inclined to join them, to pay his respects. They all stood there in silence until the man behind them spoke up.

"I hated to lose that boy. The truth movement really suffered a damaging blow when we lost him."

Vera knew those words. Jim knew that voice. They looked at each other with their eyes wide. Then they each felt a hand rest on their shoulder.

"Like I always said, Jimbo, I like to stay one step ahead of them freaks."

seven

President Sherman's first question when he met with Jerald Reitz was when Jim and Vera would meet up with Max. Jerry assured him that it would happen later that afternoon and promised to keep the president fully informed.

"Well, won't they be surprised. I know I was when I found out he was still alive," the president said.

"After they meet up at the cemetery, Max will take them to the safe house and explain everything. They'll have all kinds of questions that only he can effectively answer, and it will set the stage for their continuing assignment. At the very least it looks like you got a good dog out of the deal," Jerry said, looking down at the president's feet where Kelli was resting peacefully.

"It's a very small price to pay, my friend. I just hope she'll have something to do with Vera when she returns. Otherwise we're going to have to schedule peace talks to resolve this issue. It has only been a day and I'm becoming quite fond of this dog. And as you can see, she likes me better than many members of my own party."

Jerry laughed. He could see good things happening for his boss, but he made sure to keep most of his thoughts to himself.

In total unison, Jim and Vera's heads turned to look at Max. There was no question it was him, and they were both speechless. Max drew them both into his broad shoulders and hugged them tightly while silently nodding his head. When he released his embrace and before either of them could say anything, he pointed to the headstone and said, "Picked her out myself. I thought the inscription, 'Max went for it,' added a nice touch. Now you two, pick up those flowers from the grasp of the living, put them over on that grave where the dead people are, and let's get out of here. We got a lot of catching up to do."

Max climbed into the back seat of Jim's rental car and directed him to the safe house where he had been staying ever since his assumed 'demise.' Vera kept saying, "Max, I can't believe you're alive." Jim, on the other hand, was mostly silent, questioning to himself why he had been left in the dark and wondering what it all meant.

"I take it I'm not meeting with your attorney in the morning, am I?" Jim finally asked.

"Oh Jim, you know I hate those silver-tongued charlatans. I try to never have a thing to do with them, but I did hire six of them to be my pallbearers at the funeral. I couldn't resist the irony of having a pack of plea peddlers escort me to my final stop. I was even there watching, in full disguise. I about had to swallow my tongue to keep from laughing my wig off. But, no, you don't have an appointment in the morning. You've been talking to one of Jerry Reitz's NSA boys. I apologize for all this, but it'll all become clear when we talk. We're almost there."

"That'll be good, because I feel like I've been left in the dark and led around by the nose. Don't get me wrong, Max, I'm thrilled as hell you're still alive, but I don't like the feeling of being used and I really don't like being manipulated. So whatever you have to tell us, it better be worth it," Jim said, as he turned his head to look directly at Max in the back seat.

Vera reached back and rested her hand on Max's knee, as if to say, 'Don't pay any attention to him.' "We're just so happy you're alive, and I'm sure whatever you have to tell us is worth the wait and the intrigue." Max smiled at her and touched his finger to his temple. Vera didn't know Max as well as Jim did, but she knew the language he was speaking and it all made sense to her. Max directed Jim to make a few turns into a neighborhood and then to slow down. As they approached a small older yellow house, he reached into his pocket and pressed the button to open the garage door. "Just pull her in there, Jim, next to that shiny new SUV. I sure hated to lose that Range Rover—we'd seen a lot of good miles together—but I guess better it than me."

Max brought them inside and seated them comfortably in the living room. He put the coffeemaker on to brew and grabbed some cups. "I'm going to answer all your questions, but first let me give you some background information. I'm going to go back a few years, like over forty. Jerry Reitz and I go back that far. We met in basic training towards the end of the Viet Nam war and immediately became friends. We both could see the war for what it was, but felt obligated to serve with honor even though the whole thing stank to high heaven. Fortunately we were assigned to the same unit once we deployed, which probably was a mistake on the part of the brass, but they're not known for their brains. One morning we were doing recon out of a Huey, and the captain had just set the bird down to let Jerry and me out. Just as Jerry's feet hit the ground, a shot rang out. I watched as the force of the bullet pushed him face first into the muddy field. I don't know if the pilot even knew what happened, but I instantly heard the engines rev up so he must have heard the sniper fire and wanted to get the hell out of there as fast as he could. I couldn't tell where Jerry had been hit, but I could see blood starting to trickle from his right shoulder area. Without even thinking I held onto the bird with one hand and with everything I had, leaned out, grabbed Jerry by the belt and pulled him back into the chopper as it began to lift off the ground. Turns out he wasn't wounded too badly, just a nick in the shoulder, but if we'd taken off without him he would've been a POW at best and more likely dead. Needless to say, we have been pretty tight ever since."

"What does that have to do with faking your death and

bringing us to Minnesota?" Jim asked, still not quite sure that he liked or fully understood what he was hearing thus far.

"I'm getting to that," Max said, leaning forward to reassure Jim. "As you know, for the last several years I've been involved with seeking out truth, particularly where it involves a corrupt government and/or illegal covert operations. You and I, Jim, have done some good work together in the past, much of which has made a significant difference. I'm tied in with a group of researchers from around the country who are like-minded and dedicated to the principles of truth and freedom. We've done most of our work separately and individually for safety reasons, and to avoid group think. However, from time to time when we come upon critical information, we have to share that with one another in person. Going to Chicago that day was one of those important times. About two days before you came to see me here, Jerry called me. The NSA had intercepted some communications from my enemies, outlining a plot to take us out—all of us. As I mentioned to you before, they follow me with their drones, bug my phones, plant devices on my car and anything else they can think of to intercept my information and to generally harass me. Well, I guess they decided that our group had become more of a threat to them than they could tolerate. Jerry wasn't specific about what their plans were, but we knew it would involve a rocket-propelled grenade. That could only mean one thing; they would use it to take out the Range Rover with the four of us inside."

Vera interjected, "So when you left us at the hotel that night, you knew you were heading to Chicago to be killed."

"It was slightly more complicated than that. I would have loved to have stayed with you longer. I could tell you were on the verge of discovering something important, but I had to get my plan in motion and that's why I left when I did," Max replied.

"I guess that explains why you seemed more paranoid than usual." Jim laughed. "You kept looking out the hotel window like a kid waiting for his parents to come home."

"I was checking to see if my team had arrived. Once we knew the bad guys' intentions, we shifted the plan to meet up in Minneapolis. We immediately went to plan B, which in this case was to collect clothing and any kind of DNA samples from the group. We dressed three dummies in their clothing and I drove to Chicago as originally planned. When I arrived I checked into my hotel, but here is where it gets interesting. We leaked the fact that we would have breakfast together at seven the following morning at a Denny's near the hotel. It's something we had done on other occasions when we knew they were watching us, so it would seem natural to for us to do it again. I dressed the fourth dummy in my clothing, complete with my ponytail de jour and then returned to my hotel room. The Range Rover had a remote-controlled operational unit installed about a year ago. I never had the chance to use it prior to that morning. I sat in my hotel room and drove her out of the underground garage, through the parking lot, and over to Denny's. I could see the whole parking lot from my room. I chose a spot away from all the other cars as was always my custom. Right on schedule, from a tree-filled knoll adjacent to the restaurant came an RPG, blowing that sweet ride to never-never land. According to the NSA and the FBI, who were brought in to assist in the investigation, Max Hager and his three friends perished in the explosion. Their bodies were so badly burned it required extensive DNA testing to confirm their identities."

"Did the president know about this?" Jim asked.

"Rocket-propelled grenades don't go off in this country without the president knowing about it, Jimbo, but it was several days before he or Jerry knew that I was still alive. I kept them in the dark for as long as possible. We couldn't take the chance that a leak would expose that we were all still alive."

"So at the State of the Union he knew you had survived, and

yet he didn't tell us?" Vera inquired.

"I'm sure he knew. You have to understand that for all practical purposes, I was dead. I needed to be dead. And to some extent, I like being dead. The freaks don't bother me anymore, and so I plan on staying dead. That whole operation became immediately classified. I'm sure he would have loved to have told you then, but then wasn't the time. Secrets are a funny business, folks. The fewer people who know them, the longer they keep."

"But why now?" Jim asked.

"I've been following your work. I know what you two discovered the night before I was supposedly blown up," Max said with a chuckle. "We had been heading down that path for a while, but we didn't have your expertise or experience to put it all together. You guys are an awesome team. I have also heard the tape you found, Vera, and concur that you getting it into the hands of President Sherman when you did prevented a major disaster. In a way, my demise helped to make that happen." Max stood up and moved into the kitchen to grab the coffee pot. Jim and Vera followed him. Max poured them each a cup. Rather than return to the living room, they remained standing in the kitchen.

"So how long have you been here in this safe house?" Jim asked, feeling a little more comfortable with where Max's account was taking them.

"Almost immediately after the event, Jerry arranged it all. I guess he thinks we're even now, except I don't have a battle scar to show for it, or a Purple Heart. I watched you on television the night the president gave his speech. I must tell you, Jim, Mari looked lovely as always, and I believe you now when you say that she knows all about Vera. The two of them carried on like sisters from what I could see." Turning to Vera, Max asked, "Now tell me, what's up with you and the president? Jerry claims to know nothing, but you, little lady, looked ravishing that night and you can't tell an old coot like me that it's all just beer and skittles."

Vera shrugged her shoulders and smiled as she looked at Jim for some kind of backup.

"The most serious thing going on there, Max, is that Vera's dog, Kelli, is staying at the White House while she is away," added Jim.

Max laughed. "Yeah, that's more serious than if he were babysitting your kids. Trust me, that kind of action has a plan behind it. Let me know if I'm going to need to dig up my old tux. I haven't worn it since the eighties when Regan invited me to a state dinner for Maggie. Let's return to the living room and I'll finish telling you why I've brought you here."

"I'm more curious than ever," added Vera.

"The researchers and I operate under code. It has served to protect us when the Octopus has found its way into our business. We are compartmentalized and that's a good thing, but there are times when we need to blend our intelligence and compare notes. When we all met in Minneapolis, we knew something was going to go down and they planned to take us out. We activated the yellow code. When the news got out that we'd all been assassinated, code yellow jumped to code red."

"What is code red?" Jim asked.

"We've never used it before, but it means we go dark for six months, deep dark as in dead. No communication, no contact, no nothing. I'm sure the team know I made it out alive, but they don't know where I am and they won't even begin to be curious for another four months or so. And that is not good. What you two brought out about 9/11 was monumental. It's changed the whole face of the truth movement and has breathed new life into what was a dying group of people, convinced that 9/11 was not as the government proclaimed, but incapable of generating enough inertia to discover the details of how it was carried out and by whom. Scan the internet—your new information is seriously driving that movement now. People can feel the new momentum. What you two uncovered was the first piece of real significant information about 9/11 in years. Your airline experience and knowledge of the FAA protocols, as well as your uncanny way of methodically tearing down the official story, has created enthusiasm and has gotten people to wake up."

"That may be true, Max, but it's not getting us anywhere. I'm having a hell of a time trying to get Congress to open a new investigation, and I really should be back in Washington working on that project right now," Jim replied.

"I'm not clear at all why I'm here, Max. My sole objective in life, at the moment, has been my decision to retire," Vera piped up.

"You're here because I need your help, simple as that," Max said.

"Help doing what?" Jim asked.

"Your revelations were just the tip of the iceberg. My team was on to something that dovetails with what you've discovered. We can't wait four more months for them to surface. We need them now, and I need you two to help me find them," Max boldly asserted.

"Not going to happen, Max. I have a presidential assignment to fill and I can't let you divert me from that task."

Max leaned back in his chair and rubbed his hands through what was left of his hair. "Yeah, you kind of mentioned that's not going too well."

"That doesn't mean I'm going to stop trying. Joel is counting on me," Jim replied.

"You need to get the people to move Congress, and though you've begun to wake them up, you haven't shown enough evidence to get them angry. If we can get my friends and their information, combine that with what you two already have, you'll move people, mountains, and even recalcitrant congressmen,"

Max said, looking positively animated for the first time.

"But Max, you said that the truth movement was stirred up and ready to push forward and continue looking into what really happened," said Vera.

"That's not going to happen," Max quickly and forcefully replied.

"Why not?" asked Jim.

"It lacks leadership. For years they've been poked and prodded by self-serving blowhards whose 9/11 research has been porous, pious and pitiful. They write books based on theories that they cook up that are not only implausible, but outright impossible. They are petty, jealous and vindictive if anyone with real knowledge invades their space. As a result, they have managed to suck the life right out of the truth movement and have left it to languish in lies. Now don't misunderstand; the people in the truth movement and some of the researchers are tremendous. They form the backbone of this country, but in order to be of any real help they need to be armed with the truth and they need to be moved in a direction they can trust. If you want to open a new investigation you're going to have to be singlehandedly responsible for dispelling the inane theories— like voice morphing, the planes going to Cleveland, and shooting down airplanes over the Atlantic—and replacing them with real documented information that proves the event was planned and premeditated. Once the American people are armed with that kind of truth they'll come to life like a lion and their roar will sweep the halls of Congress, penetrate the lair of the Octopus, and possibly heal that crack in the Liberty Bell."

Jim and Vera could feel Max's passion. It began to answer some of the questions Jim had had as to why the truth movement had been so ineffective at exposing the truth and the real perpetrators. It also reconfirmed to Vera why she had been so afraid of saying or doing anything that might get the attention of those in the truth movement. These self-appointed experts had been responsible for providing the dubious reputations associated with tinfoil hats, limited hangouts, and conspiracy theories. There had been rumors that such movements had been infiltrated and Max's discourse helped to explain what was going on inside those groups that proclaimed a genuine interest in getting to the bottom of 9/11. Even the alternative media only skirted the real truth on occasion, and it appeared to most people to be controlled opposition. Both Jim and Vera were aware of how their investigation into 9/11—and what happened at Westover AFB—had made an impact on the truth movement, but neither of them realized just what a life-generating force their discovery had become.

"This is why you need to help me find my team and assimilate their information. It's not going to be easy. I don't know where they are and I don't have any way to reach them. But the sooner we can find them and expose what they've found, the sooner you, Jim, will be able to make some serious progress with that do-nothing Congress."

Vera took the last sip of her coffee and gently set her cup down on one of the coasters that seemed to be well-placed throughout the safe house. She looked at Jim in an attempt to get a sense of what he was thinking, but she couldn't get a read from his face and his voice gave no indication. Finally she leaned forward and looked at Max. "I'm not sure what it is that you want us to do, Max. Maybe Jim can help you, but I don't see why you need me or how I can help. After my experience in Paris I know that cloak and dagger is not my forte. I have no idea whom I would be looking for and if I stumbled into them by accident, I wouldn't have a clue as to what to ask them."

"Maybe I've oversimplified this entire situation," Max said, nodding. "I'm assuming we can and will find them. It's what we do from that point that becomes paramount, Vera. I need your intellect and your ability to put the pieces of the puzzle together. You have eyes that see what others can't. And you have access to the president, whether you know it or not. That alone may prove to be one of the most important elements."

"Max is right, Vera. I don't know exactly what he needs or wants us to do, but I sense that it's important enough to help him. Obviously, the president is aware we are here today and that we now know Max is alive, which means Joel wants us to assist him. You're important to him. If you don't believe that, ask Kelli when you see her. So here's what I think. Let the three of us fly back to Washington tonight, meet with Jerry Reitz and establish a plan of attack." Jim turned to Max and continued, "I'm trusting you, buddy, and I'm counting on you to make this happen for us. If your team has uncovered something that could have gotten you all killed, you have uncovered something very damning to the real perpetrators of this crime. They obviously have been watching you and probably reading your research with remote access to your computers. They felt the only way to keep their deception alive was to silence your team."

Max pressed his hands together as if he was about to pray. "I knew I could count on you two. In case you're wondering, I'm packed and ready to go. So say the word and I'll fasten my seat belt," he said, smiling in Vera's direction.

eight

*V*era reached the White House later that evening and was escorted to the Oval Office, where the president was working late. It had been weeks since she had seen Joel, but it was Kelli she wanted to greet first, even though it had only been a couple of days since she'd seen her. She had received reports that the dog had adjusted well to her new surroundings, but she had to see it for herself. The president's secretary met her in the outer office. Joel must have known she was on her way and intercepted them in the hallway. Vera could feel her excitement elevate when he approached, and even more as the two warmly embraced. It was a much different feeling this time, being in the executive offices. They stepped into the Oval Office together. A true sense of reverence replaced the overwhelming feelings she'd had the first time she entered this historic room. Off to the side of the president's desk she could see Kelli resting in a large bed that obviously had not been there before. Kelli slowly got up from her resting position, walked over to Vera and began licking her hand. Though she was glad to see Vera, this was the first time Kelli had not displayed an overenthusiastic response at their reunion. Finishing her welcoming licks to Vera, Kelli slowly returned to sit at the president's feet, expecting a head rub, which she immediately received.

Vera glanced over at Joel with a somewhat puzzled look. "I leave my dog with you for a couple days and you've managed to replace me altogether. I have honestly never seen her do that when I'm in the room, unless Jeff was present."

"I don't know what to tell you, Vera," replied the president. "We hit it off right from the start, and now some of the staff are referring to her as the First Lady because she doesn't like me out of her sight."

"Well, I know this: she is a perfect judge of character. So at the very least you should be flattered. Ordinarily she doesn't like men, but the ones she has liked have all proven to be exceptional people. So congratulations. Now is there any way I'm going to get her back?"

"I'm afraid you're going to have to stay here a few days with us, and we can gradually work on reestablishing your relationship," said the president with a laugh.

"I'm glad you think it's funny. I suppose she's been sleeping at the foot of your bed, too?" Vera asked, not wanting to hear the answer.

"I put her out in the great room the first night, but she didn't stay there long. I felt sorry for her, not having you around, so I let her stay in my room when she came in to visit, but I'm sure she won't have any trouble cuddling in with you tonight."

"Yeah, well, we shall see. If she wanders in to see you when I'm here, you are going to have to hire me as an Air Force One flight attendant. You know I'm now unemployed, effective the end of the month, but I have no more trips scheduled and the paperwork has all been filed."

"Good for you! I know that was a tough decision, but I'm sure it's the right one. And to tell you the truth, you are needed here in more ways than one," responded Joel.

"What do you mean?"

The president didn't respond to her question. He gave Kelli another pat on the head, then leaned up against the corner of his desk. Vera sat quietly, pondering the meaning of the president's comment.

"I understand you and the guys are meeting with Jerry

Reitz in the morning," the president said. "I can't tell you how important that meeting is going to be. It's imperative that we find Max's team; from what I understand, they have dug up some very incriminating evidence. It's so alarming that it almost got them all murdered."

Vera interrupted, "About Max. You knew he was alive?"

"Eventually I did, yes."

"It was quite a shock, but a welcome one. Jim struggled with what he felt was a deception, for a while, but he's on board now. I think he realizes this is the path that we must follow, and he knows that these investigators have indeed uncovered something monumental. Even Max is not certain exactly what they have collectively uncovered, but he knows it's what we need to prove who was behind this so-called terror attack. It looks like the real terrorists might have somehow figured out that this team of researchers has found the documents to prove them guilty."

"I understood Max's team was on to something big, and we badly need that information to push this boulder over the hill. It begins in the morning with Jerry, and I'll keep my fingers crossed. Say, are you hungry?"

Vera nodded. "I'm starved, actually."

"Well, on our way to the residence, let's see whom we can pester to make us something to eat. It's late, but they all knew you were coming, so I'm sure they have something exceptional waiting as always. In fact, I know they do. Follow me. You too, Kelli."

nine

*W*hen Vera awoke the next morning, Kelli was nowhere to be found. She had a pretty good idea her dog was somewhere with Joel, but it wasn't until Mike met her with her morning coffee service that she discovered that Kelli had actually spent the entire night in the president's room, and she had followed him to the gym earlier. They were now together on a morning walk somewhere on the White House grounds.

"Have I lost my dog, Mike?" Vera asked, distressed.

"It certainly looks that way, ma'am. Your dog wants to be with this man 24/7 and it's been that way from the moment she arrived. I also must confess that I haven't seen the president this happy since Mica passed away. Somehow your dog and he have found a kindred spirit connection and don't seem to want to let it go," Mike replied, trying to be as forthright as he thought Vera could bear.

"I don't think I like this one bit. When I agreed to let Kelli come here it was on the assumption that she would be well taken care of by staff, and that Joel wouldn't even know she was around."

"We never got the chance, ma'am. Your dog stayed in her crate until the president invited her out, and she hasn't left his side since. I must admit it's most unusual, but let it play out and see what happens. I'm sure only good can come of it. Oh and by the way, ma'am, your meeting with the national security advisor is in an hour. Would you like me to fix you some breakfast and bring it here to the residence?" Mike asked.

"You know, if you would bring me just a couple slices of toast to go with this coffee, that would be more than sufficient," Vera replied. She hurried off to shower and dress for her meeting. It was still unclear to her exactly why she had been recruited to help find Max's team. She felt like a third wheel. When she arrived at the great room to wait for Mike, she was surprised to find Joel and Kelli there.

"Well, what have you two been up to so bright and early this morning?" she asked.

"National security," Joel said with a laugh. "We walked the perimeter of the White House property looking for spies and dangerous contraband."

"Did you find anything of note?" Vera inquired.

"A rabbit, a feral cat and two garter snakes. I probably would have missed them if it wasn't for Kelli here. Should I put her on the payroll?"

"I think you should remind her that her mother is here and that if it's not too much of a security risk, she should pay some attention to me," Vera replied, with a chuckle.

"You aren't jealous, are you, Vera?" Joel wondered out loud.

"I guess I'm going to have to spend time with you if I want to see my dog," she replied.

"I doubt either of us would mind that. Which reminds me, in ten days there's a state dinner in honor of the President of Finland and his wife, and I would like you to accompany me. May I be your escort to the ball, my dear?"

Vera looked at him, perplexed. Staying in the White House was one thing, but being the president's date to a state dinner was something totally unexpected. That wasn't something she had ever experienced and she had no idea how to respond. She began to stammer a little, but before she could utter anything intelligent the president said, "I hope that is a yes, because I would look pretty stupid standing in the reception line with a dog."

Without thinking, Vera replied, "I would be honored, Stan the Man."

Joel laughed, slapped his knee, reached down to pat Kelli and said, "She's on board, girl, your mother's on board." Then with a total change of demeanor, the president shifted the conversation to Vera's upcoming meeting. "I've mentioned before that this meeting you have this morning is extremely important. I'm counting on Max's team to bring me the evidence necessary to help move this country in a direction that will allow it to begin to rid itself of the corruption and the lies that have yoked it to complicity. Your presence is necessary because you represent me. I know where your heart and soul are, and I insisted they include you. I confess that I have orchestrated you and Kelli being here, but the reasoning is sound. I think we are pressed for time and we need to make this happen as soon as possible. The evil cabal never rests. It takes what it wants, uses it up and moves to the next source of wickedness. There seems to be an endless supply of hate, which presently is focused on me and my administration for daring to challenge them. It's more than a challenge, Vera, it's what we'll do to save our country, and you will play a much larger role than you realize. I knew that the moment you set us all straight in the Oval Office a couple months ago." He walked toward her and lightly embraced her. It was all the communication she needed, to feel a sense of unity and belonging. The challenge to gather the scattered 9/11 information from Max's crew was now her commitment.

Once Jim and Max cleared security, they were directed to a conference room on the second floor of the West Wing. Jerry was waiting with briefing material for all in attendance. Max gave Jerry a big bear hug and they immediately started talking like old friends who had just pulled off the best practical joke in years. Jim tried to be amused, but since a lot of the joke had been on him, his enthusiasm level was nowhere near that of his companions. It was clearly apparent that Max and Jerry had a special relationship, and whatever had actually occurred in Chicago had evened the score between them. Jim's understanding of the event meant that it was now becoming acceptable to him, but he was hoping this meeting would furnish some much-needed focus and direction.

Vera entered the room a moment later and the gentlemen stood to welcome her. She greeted Jerry warmly, shaking his hand with both of hers, then nodded and smiled at both Max and Jim.

"Who else is coming to this meeting, Jerry?" Jim asked.

"Now that Vera is here, we're all present and accounted for. We may add a few more folks as we go along, but for now I want to keep this circle tight to avoid any leaks or confusion," Jerry informed them. He looked at Max and said, "Why don't you begin? You have a lot of the information we want to discuss."

Max straightened himself up in his chair and placed both hands palms down on the table. "It's like this," he began. "About two weeks before you contacted me this winter, Jim, telling me you were coming to see me, one of us received a terabyte of data from a Freedom of Information Act request. He had been working on trying to pull information from the FAA and NORAD for years with very little success. They were not about to give him what he wanted or needed. We always felt there was something suspicious about the flight tracking that was released early in the day on 9/11. There were flight paths showing the planes going all over Hell's half acre before they crashed into their targets. The voice recordings from air traffic control, the flight times and the routes just didn't make any sense to us. We thought the only way to figure it out was to get the official data and try to analyze it ourselves. I wish you two had come to Minnesota a few weeks earlier. Your discovery would have been a big help to what we eventually had to dig into. As it turns out, our gal Ruth Ann began receiving bits and pieces of data from a woman at the National Archives. I don't know if she was tired of her constant requests or if she just felt sorry for her. After years of trying, she managed to get an invitation to come to the archives with a blank external hard drive. So, wasting no time, she shows up, gives her the hard drive and offers to take her out to lunch. Smooth move on her part, because what she had planned to give her suddenly multiplied quite handsomely after lunch. She instructed Ruth Ann to leave the hard drive with her and to return the following day. After lunch the next day, she went home with more information than she could analyze in a decade. Being the genius that she is, she bought two more hard drives and copied what she had. That's when she contacted me and asked if Bob and Gil could assist her. I drove here to Washington, picked up the hard drives from Ruth Ann and hand delivered them to the other two. All were to report to me individually, but the files were so massive and complicated that we decided to talk it over in person once the team found something of value. We had scheduled a meeting in Chicago to go over our findings to date and to coordinate our continued efforts. That's when Jerry comes in, and I'll let him pick it up from there." Max slowly exhaled, then turned to look at his friend.

"Ever since I was selected to be head of the NSA, Max has complained to me that someone or some organization has been pestering him, intercepting his calls, spying on his house, and just being a general nuisance. Now, I know Max is a big boy and more than capable of taking care of himself. I watched him do it in combat in Nam, and I've seen him rise to the top in all of his endeavors no matter what challenges he faced. If there was ever someone you don't need to worry about, it's Max Hager. The fact that he kept whining at me caused me to take his complaints a little more seriously. We looked into who we thought was responsible, but couldn't find any significant statute violations and so we had no basis to take any further action other than to report what we found. That was until late last year. Whatever Max and his crew were digging into, it was clearly upsetting some folks. We began to hear specific chatter in which Max's name was being used in association with a hit using a rocket-propelled grenade. Now that concerned us. I arranged to have Max fly out here to D.C. to discuss the potential threat. Max and Ruth Ann confirmed it was real, and they had a pretty good idea who was monitoring them and how. We concluded that if these bad guys thought that Max and his group had been eliminated, they could continue their 9/11 research in peace. Knowing that we were up against some highly trained assassins, we had to be very convincing and very quiet. That meant being very careful how communications were made, and the only details we let them hear were about the fake plan for breakfast at Denny's in Chicago. Max did a superior job of setting the stage and, I must say, driving his Range Rover via remote control."

At this point Jim had some questions and interjected, "So Max, if you knew this was all going down when it was, why in the world did you agree to meet with Vera and me? I mean, our presence alone could have jeopardized the whole operation."

Jerry started to answer, but Max interrupted. "I got this, Jerry. First of all, you are my friend, and that friendship is important to me. You indicated that what you were doing was important; we just didn't know how important. In retrospect, had you not come to see me, I doubt you and Vera would have discovered all that you did. It was a gut call and I went with the belly," he said, smiling and rubbing both sides of his ever-expanding midsection. "In addition, having you two in Minneapolis made it look like I was conducting business as usual. I'm sure you sensed I was a little overly cautious during the time I was with you. I had no doubt I was being watched. I don't have that feeling now, and it's given me a sense of freedom I haven't enjoyed in years. Anyway, that's why you were allowed to come see me."

Jim seemed satisfied with Max's response, and turned to Jerry as if to encourage him to continue.

"When we received the news that the RPG had been fired, we had to assume the worst both for cover, and for painting the scenario. When you called the president that morning, Jim, he had just been given the news of the attack and wasn't privy to all the details. It wasn't until Max surfaced several days later than I even knew for certain what had actually happened. With Max and his team alive, we rolled with the full cover story, had him buried, and posted an obituary for each of them. The safe house in Chicago was already in place and we moved Max in with plans to keep him there until enough time had passed that we could reconstitute the group in secret. You and the president threw a monkey wrench, so to speak, into that plan. With what you discovered about Westover and the tape recording indicating plans for a future and more expansive 9/11-type attacks, we immediately had to move to counter the intelligence on that tape. Once the president gave his State of the Union speech, it became imperative that Max and his group get back together as soon as possible."

Max spoke up again. "We're onto something, folks. I don't know exactly what it is, but we need to get to the bottom of it now. Your mission, Jim, was to move the president's agenda forward and get a new investigation on the docket, and this information will make that happen."

"But there's a big problem," Jerry said, pointing to the briefing packets. "We don't know where these guys are. We don't know how to find them and we're running out of time. Open the packets, if you will. They contain pictures of Ruth Ann, Bob and Gil along with all the pertinent information we know about them. It gives you background into their personalities, a full analysis of their areas of expertise, and possibilities of where they might be, based on Max's experience with them. But to be honest, it's not much."

Vera had spent the entire meeting listening intently to what had been said. It was only after glancing through the packet that she decided to speak up. "Why us? Why have you selected Jim and me to help you find them? We don't have any kind of covert operations experience. We don't know these people and, speaking for myself, I'm not sure what you expect me to do."

"I'm of the same mind as Vera," Jim added. "I'm just not sure how you expect us to help."

Max signaled to Jerry that he would field their concerns. "Wherever they are, I know what it is they are doing. They are poring over that FOIA data as fast and as furiously as they can. Just because we fired off a code red to them doesn't mean they stopped researching. It's in their blood. What will be frustrating for them is not having contact with me or with each other. Often their best work develops when they can discuss their theories amongst themselves and take advantage of the synergy that comes from their experience and friendship. But to the question of why you two, that's simple. They'll trust you. I know they watched you on television the night of the State of the Union. I doubt any of them have missed that event in the last thirty years. I also know they have followed the news about you, even though it has been negative of late. I'm certain that if either of you were to approach them they would follow your lead."

Jerry added, "If we were to solicit help from the CIA and their agents got close to them, they'd close up shop and disappear in a heartbeat. They know who the enemy is and they know who they can trust. It's not difficult for them; it's how they have lived for years."

Max spoke up. "You see, in reality you two are the only ones who can do this. I doubt they would trust anyone else except me, and I can't be three places at once. This is why you are here and why we need your help."

Jim looked at Vera and shrugged his shoulders. She nodded gently, indicating that she believed enlisting in this proposal was the right thing to do. Jim reached over and rested his hand on top of hers, and then spoke for them both. "Okay, we're in, but we still don't know how to go about this. Since you don't have any idea where they are, we sure can't be expected to just randomly select cities and try to find them. That doesn't seem very productive."

Jerry again assumed the floor. "No, it wouldn't be, and that's not what we are proposing. What we are suggesting is that as soon as we get a lead, we'll send you out to find them. Based on their profiles and Max's experience, we think we can make that happen."

"But how will you ever know where they are?" Vera asked.

"Here's where it gets a little interesting," Max said with a huge smile. "When we instituted our alert system, we build in a mechanism in case we needed to separate and go dark. We have never had to use it and it's not completely foolproof, but here's the gist of how it works. We created a Facebook page entitled 'Just Desserts.' It wallows in obscurity for months at a time, and then when we want to contact each other, we will post a delicious cake or pie and invite people to like it. Naturally they do, but here's where it gets fun. Each of the four of us has a Facebook page made up of all fictitious information pulled straight out of thin air, but with three exceptions: the middle name for all of us is Sidney, and the city that it says we live in is actually our legitimate birth city. That is how we know who's who. Finally, the stated birthplace is the actual city in which each of us is presently located. We never communicate between ourselves online for obvious reasons." Max couldn't help but turn to Jerry and smile. "With this information, we're then able to find one another, and no one on the outside is the wiser. We have never activated this plan, but I check Facebook every morning for what's going down in 'Just Desserts,' and I have no doubt the others do the same. Bottom line, if I activate a photo, within a few days we should know their general whereabouts. Our task then is to find them and bring them inside so we can get everyone's research collected and disseminated."

"Make no mistake, these guys are targets. If the enemy gets wind they're alive there's no question they'll move to take them out. That's why the need for secrecy, and yet another reason why you two can do this job unnoticed and unfettered. I don't want you to think it'll be easy, because it won't be. Even if we know where they are, finding them is still going to be problematic. So my advice to you is to go about your business as usual. Max and I will set the hook on Facebook, and then we wait. If and when we get any contact, we'll let you know. Of course, you'll have all the resources available to allow you to succeed at this mission." When Jerry finished he leaned back in his chair and softly said, "Now, are there any questions?"

"I have one," Vera said. "What if your Facebook plan doesn't work? Then what?"

Before anyone could answer, Jim interjected, "This whole thing sounds like landing an F-15 on a rolling carrier deck at night with the low fuel light on: possible, but risky as hell and quite unlikely."

"Yeah well, it's what we've got and we'll just have to make it work," Max replied. "As to your question, Vera, it will succeed. My team knows their value and it sure isn't hanging out in some dumpy city. They were excited about what they were discovering, which means it's worth getting their information into the proper hands. Trust me; they'll be working just as hard to make it happen as we will."

"I hope you're right, Max, I really hope you're right," Jim said, partially under his breath.

Jerry stood and motioned toward the door. "Let's adjourn this meeting for now. I'll let you know how to proceed as this mission unfolds. Thank you again. I speak for myself and for President Sherman; in the end it will be the country that thanks you once more."

Jim and Vera huddled in the corner talking while Max and Jerry wandered into the hall, speaking in hushed tones.

ten

*F*ollowing the meeting, Jim headed off to a scheduled appointment he had with a senator. Vera sidled up to Max when Jerry broke away to meet with the president's chief of staff. "Max, didn't I hear you say when we were in Minneapolis that you had been to a state dinner back sometime in the eighties?"

"Oh yeah, those were the days all right. Ronnie somehow got me on his guest list and I had a chance to shake hands with the 'Iron Lady' herself. I loved seeing her and Reagan together. It was like they were twin flames, but without the romance. Nancy saw to that. You could almost sense those two thinking the same thoughts and testing the same theories in their minds. It was a thing of beauty and marvelous to behold. Why do you ask?"

"Joel, I mean, President Sherman, has invited me to be his date, if you will, to a state dinner honoring the President of Finland in a week or so, and I don't have a thing to wear. Remember I was led to believe I was just going to Minnesota to pay my respects to you, and though I love you and all, that wasn't going to happen in a beaded evening gown."

Max laughed. "Why the hell not? Why, if I'd thought of it, I would've had a formal funeral, with engraved invitations and everything."

"Since you've actually been to one of these affairs, I was wondering if you could help me pick out a dress for the occasion."

"Little lady, I can barely dress myself without having the fashion cops put me in solitary. I can't see how in the world I could be of any help to you unless you want to go in a 30-year-old moth-eaten tux."

"Oh, Maxwell, I guess what I'm asking is will you accompany me to Neiman Marcus and give me your opinion on the dresses I try on? You won't have to exert much effort, just tell me if anything I choose will work. Oh, and is it possible for you to check out a car from the motor pool? I don't want to drive in this crazy D.C. traffic and I really don't want to go alone."

"If I tell them it's for you, I could probably get Air Force One along with the 'beast' that travels with it. You kind of can get whatever you want around here, missy. The president has seen to that," Max said with a bit of an 'I told you so' wink.

"Why don't you see what you can do and meet me in the portico in fifteen minutes? You said in the meeting to return to our normal activities. I don't have any responsibilities here other than Kelli, and she's practically abandoned me, so I might as well go shopping."

Ten minutes later Max arrived in the portico with a black presidential Cadillac and a chauffeur. "I had them take the flags off the front, but they wouldn't hear of me driving. Guess they heard about the Range Rover. Anyway, get in and we'll let Josh here take us where we need to go; besides, he can't get ticketed in this baby so parking isn't going to be a problem."

Vera blushed with embarrassment, but did as she was instructed. "This isn't quite what I had in mind, Max. I don't want to make a scene."

"I'm thinking you might want to start getting used to it," Max replied.

"What's that supposed to mean?" Vera asked, raising her eyebrows.

"Ask the damn dog," Max replied, smiling from ear to ear.

The limousine driver let them out right in front of the department store and explained to them that he would be close by when they were ready to return to the White House. Max wasn't particularly comfortable being in Neiman Marcus. To be honest he had never been in one before and being a regular Wal-Mart shopper, he was finding it difficult to establish his bearings. He followed Vera up to the second floor and tried to keep his mouth shut. Everything was going relatively smoothly for him until they arrived at the evening gown department, and a woman greeted Vera and asked if Max was her husband. When the laughing subsided the woman suggested that Max sit in the large leather chair next to the mirrors and wait for Vera to model the gowns she had chosen. Max took one look at the tufted chair and eagerly complied with her suggestion. Vera explained to the woman what it was she was looking for, and the event she would be attending. Without any hesitation the woman escorted her to a sitting room where she and another assistant would bring her gowns from which to choose.

As Max was waiting for Vera to model her first dress, a rather robust woman emerged from the dressing room area and stood in front of the mirrors. She posed from several different angles, admiring what she saw. Max was on the receiving end of every pose and began shaking his head from side to side. The woman could see Max's reflection towards the bottom of the mirror, and couldn't help but notice his perpetual disapproval. Without turning to face him she raised her voice so she was certain he could hear and said, "So this doesn't meet with your approval, I see. And just what is it that's not working for you?"

Max hesitated at first, but then blurted out, "Well, ma'am, it kind of pushes the caboose into the headlights."

This time the woman turned around to face him and with pure indignation asked, "What is that supposed to mean?"

"I think the gown is lovely, ma'am. It's the disease that is causing the problem."

She placed her hands on her hips and demanded to know

what Max was talking about. "I'll have you know I'm free of all communicable diseases and haven't been sick a day in my life since I had the mumps back in Junior High."

"Well, ma'am, it's the same sorry disease I suffer from: furniture disease."

Now she was starting to get angry because she thought she was being made fun of. "And just what the hell is furniture disease?" she demanded to know.

"It's when your chest falls into your drawers."

The woman stood silent with her mouth wide open, then suddenly burst out laughing. Max began to laugh too, but with a bit of hesitancy.

"Well, son, there is no cure for that and as you can see I have it bad, but so do you," she said, pointing to Max's midsection while still laughing. "But otherwise you like the gown, right?"

"Oh yeah," Max replied. "The gown is marvelous. Why, you could wear it to a state dinner."

"That's exactly why I'm here and what I plan to do. The senator and I have been invited to the upcoming dinner, and I think I'll attend dressed in this gown. That is, if it meets with your approval, sir."

"That's fine by me, Madame. I, of course, have not been invited, but I'll tell my friends who'll be there to keep a sharp eye out for you. You'll be the one in the gown with the Maxwell Hager seal of approval."

"Maxwell Hager, I like that name, and I think I like you. You tell it just like it is, and that's a hard commodity to come by in this town. Thank you for the delightful chat; you're a rare one, that's for sure." With that, she returned to the dressing room and Max never saw her again.

It wasn't long before Vera had several gowns she wanted to try on. She checked with Max to see how he was doing and to make certain he hadn't fallen asleep. Max just lifted both eyebrows and shot a friendly grin in her direction.

"Now I expect you to be right here when I come out wearing these gowns. Your opinion is going to matter, so make sure you are up to it."

It wasn't long before Vera had gracefully turned several times in front of the mirrors wearing each of the gowns that appealed to her. Max nodded enthusiastically for each of them, leaving Vera to make the decision on her own. Fortunately for her she looked terrific in anything she tried on, so as far as Max was concerned any one of them would be splendid and he would have been correct. Vera needed the opinion of the saleswoman and her assistant before she could commit to any purchase. That required a little more time, and Max could feel his body slipping into slumber as Vera made her decision and was escorted off to acquire the appropriate shoes and accessories. When she returned, Max was sound asleep. She didn't want to wake him, but she had no idea how to find the car and driver. It didn't take much to roust him, just folding her arms across her chest and tapping her foot lightly sprang him into action.

"So have you got yourself all decked out?" he asked, pretending to be wide awake and fully engaged.

Vera started to laugh. Max was at his most amusing when he was caught off guard. It rarely occurred, but when it did it was memorable.

"So which one did you choose?" he asked, trying very hard to sound interested.

"You'll just have to wait and see. It's being altered and will be delivered to the White House when everything is in order. My attendant was rather impressed when I gave her the address. I just hope it is all worth it. This little excursion has set me back more than a month's salary."

"I don't think you can put a price tag on a state dinner accompanied by the president. You know you'll have to stand in the receiving line and shake the hands of all the guests. I hope your Finnish is as impressive as you'll be."

"I don't know a word of Finnish," Vera quickly replied. "I've been there, but the language was impossible. I guess I'll have to work on that in the coming days."

"Yeah, good luck with that. Only Finnish babies learn to speak that language. Just stay close to Joel and smile. And if you shake hands with a senator's wife in a dark blue gown, tell her she looks divine."

"What's that supposed to mean?" Vera asked with a very puzzled look on her face.

"Oh, never mind. Let's just say you weren't the only one here today looking for something to wear to the dinner. Come on, let's get back and see how your dog is doing before Joel starts talking about adoption."

"I'm afraid we're too late for that. Kelli has already done the adopting."

eleven

*T*he meeting Jim had scheduled with the senator was both tedious and boring. Even though he was firmly ensconced in the president's party he had real trouble aligning himself with the ideals the president championed. He had been in the Senate for more than thirty years and it was apparent that he could not be told anything. He had carved out his space in the legislative process and wasn't going to do anything that would risk his status. He didn't even care if his party was in power or not. It was a good old boy network and he thrived on either side of the equation. Jim was growing very tired of meeting with this type of legislator. It was becoming clear to him that extreme pressure needed to be applied to these lawmakers. That would only happen if they could find Max's friends, coalesce their research, and effectively use it as a wedge to force these nonresponsive representatives into action. These were the thoughts running through Jim's head when Max called to inform him that they had had a hit on the Facebook page. Gil Garrison had responded just as Max had hoped he would. Apparently he was around Reno, Nevada somewhere.

"What have you got, Max?" Jim asked, surprised that he was hearing from him so soon.

"We've heard from Gil and I'll fill you in tonight when I return. Your mission, buddy, now that you have decided to accept it, is about to begin."

"Anything has to be better than what I'm doing now. I'll look forward our conversation later. Stay safe; we need you now more than ever," Jim replied.

Before Jim had time to get to Blair House he received a text message from Vera requesting he come to the White House for dinner. She didn't say, but he assumed it would be with both Vera and the president. He was delighted for the invitation. He hadn't seen much of Joel since he launched into his attempt to push reopening a new 9/11 investigation.

When Jim arrived at the White House, he was escorted to the formal dining room where the president and both Vera and Max were already seated.

"What a wonderful surprise, three of my favorite people," Jim said, feeling almost at home.

The president greeted him with a quick embrace and said, "This is not a formal dinner by any means, my friend, even though we are here in the dining room. Vera has been telling Max and me about the gown she is going to wear at the state dinner and Max here tells me he has a lead on one of his men. That's what we want to talk about. So have a seat and we'll dine while we get caught up with one another."

"Well, I was planning on talking to Max later tonight, but I'm sure this will be more enjoyable," added Jim.

"Good," replied the president. "Jim, when you head out in search of Gil I want you to take Agent Garcia with you. You can be assured if the enemy has gotten word that Gil is not really dead, the forces of the Octopus will be called in. Gordon knows theirs tactics. He has had experience with them and I trust him completely. I think he can be a huge asset to you. I've already talked to him and he can be ready to go anytime you are."

"I think that's a great idea, Jim," added Vera. "Lord knows we can't have anything happen to you, and Agent Garcia knows what he's doing. Besides, he is armed, and I've seen him take action when it was needed."

"I'll take any help I can get," Jim said. "My problem is, I have no idea where to begin to look for this man. Reno is a pretty sizeable town and I really don't have anything to go on."

"Hah, that is where I come in, buddy," Max quickly added. "I know this man. I know what he likes to eat. I can guaran-damn-tee you that you won't find him in an Italian restaurant. So you won't want to spend any time looking at the Olive Garden."

Everyone laughed, but at the same time they could feel for Jim because they knew he was basically on a blind search, and luck would play a big role in finding Gil.

"Another thing, Jim, I know how this boy works. He doesn't wake up before noon, ever. He's your classic programmer type. He probably can't remember the last morning he saw. It's stuff like this that only I know, and I can help direct you to where I think you might be able to find him. Keep in mind he now knows we're looking for him, but he won't do anything stupid to expose himself."

President Sherman had been watching Jim's reaction to what Max was saying. He rested his arm on the edge of the table and stroked his chin as he listened. He asked Max, "Do you think this Gil will tell Jim what it is he wants to know? I worry that the clandestine nature of your codes might cause him to divulge less than he knows. We can't afford to have him withhold information, in this tight timeframe we're working under."

"I think that's why you have Jim looking for him, sir. He combines all the intelligence necessary to locate Gil and the inherent trust required to instantly form a bond that will convince Gil to share what he knows. If you were to send Agent Garcia alone, you wouldn't have the kind of success I expect Jim will." Max spoke with confidence.

Jim glanced at Max with a look of appreciation, but his words revealed his uncertainty. "I sure hope you're right."

"Now enough of all this, I want to hear more about Vera's gown and the joys of taking Max shopping. It has to be better than taking a Secret Service detail with you into a changing room," the president said, laughing. "Of course, I'm not allowed to do that kind of shopping and to be honest, I kind of miss it."

"I think the best part of the entire day was when my sales assistant asked if Max was my husband," chimed in Vera. "I can tell you one thing; it didn't give me a lot of confidence in her ability to make choices." Vera looked over at Max and stuck her tongue out. "That's for dying and not telling us—or, not dying and not telling us."

Max was too busy laughing to even notice. "I figured I was just taking one for the team today," he said, looking in the president's direction. Joel nodded, understanding it all.

twelve

Jim and Agent Garcia boarded the government Gulfstream before dawn and flew directly to Naval Air Station Fallon, just outside of Reno. They wanted to keep their mission and their identities as secret as possible, and using military bases was the best way to insure that privacy. When a base commander receives a phone call from the Joint Chiefs essentially telling him to have a car waiting and to not ask a lot of questions, the message comes across loud and clear. Their jet was taxied into a waiting hanger and a nondescript government vehicle was waiting for them, complete with Nevada license plates and a faded Dump Harry Reid bumper sticker.

They had a few photographs and a basic description of Gil, but had no idea where he was other than someplace in Fernley, which was about a thirty-minute drive from the base. There is not much to Fernley. It sits along Interstate 80 about forty miles east of Reno and serves as the last significant stop southbound along US 50 for several hundred miles. It is big enough to have a Wal-Mart, but if not for the highway traffic, few would even know of its existence.

"How should we proceed, Gordon?" Jim asked. "Stakeouts and manhunts are not areas I've had any experience dealing with."

"We first need to acquaint ourselves with the area. We need to know the roads in and the roads out. That will also allow us to get a feel for if there are any hostiles in the area," Gordon replied sharply.

"Nobody knows we're here except Max, and we aren't even positive if Gil's here. How can there possibly be hostiles in an armpit of a place like this?" Jim asked as they slowly drove through the sleepy town.

"It's what I do, Jim. You always have to plan for the unexpected and assume that anything secret really isn't. I've done this long enough to have developed a sixth sense about people and places and to be honest; I have my doubts that we are alone in our search for Mr. Gil. I hope I'm wrong, but I want to scope it out and plan accordingly."

"I'm willing to follow your lead. You managed to protect Vera in unfamiliar surroundings and you were always one step ahead, so I'll defer to your expertise," Jim said.

They passed a small national hotel not far off the interstate. There was a car in the parking lot, close to the entrance. "What time is it?" Gordon asked.

"It's almost noon. I know it seems later since we left so early this morning, but with the time change and all… why do you ask?"

"See that car parked next to the hotel entrance?"

"Yeah, so what?" Jim replied.

"That's what I call an anomaly. It's past checkout time, and yet the car is still there. Nobody spends more than one night in a hotel in this town, and it's way too early for anyone to be checking in," Gordon said, taking careful mental note of the vehicle. "Remember that car and grab that plate number."

"You're good. Do you think we should be concerned?" Jim asked.

"Only if we see the car in town later, if it follows us, or if I recognize the profiles of its occupants. If it's a mom and dad with three kids I'm not going to be too worried. I know the type that would be looking for Gil and they may think they're clever, but they don't really disguise themselves that well. They are often mocked in intelligence circles; let's just say they don't always get all the details taken care of. Sometimes we have to laugh at their B-movie style, and their lack of complete understanding of us Americans."

They entered the freeway heading east and then exited a mile or so later, making a full loop around the town.

"Take the road to Yerington here at this next intersection. I think that road eventually takes you to Las Vegas and believe it or not, it's the fastest way to get there from Reno," Jim said while looking at the small map on his computer screen.

Gordon turned left at the light and began driving south until they quickly reached the edge of town. "There really isn't much here. If Gil's still in town he should be easy to find."

"So how would you propose to do that? Do we knock on doors? It would be pointless to check hotel registries, since he'd be using an assumed name," Jim said, shaking his head.

"We start by laying out what we know about him. What he likes to eat, what kind of movies he likes to watch, what he drinks when he's at a bar, or if he drinks at all, stuff like that for starters. From there we build on what we know and then solicit the help of those around us to determine if he's even here. Keep in mind, he chose this place for a reason. Obviously no one would look here for him, but there has to be a connection. You don't just choose a random place on a map and go there. The human brain doesn't operate that way; it always seeks what it knows. That's why so many criminals get caught. We just have to be patient. If he is here we'll find him. Now, are you getting hungry?"

"Funny you should ask. I'm starving," Jim answered.

"I saw a little taco restaurant just up the road here. With a last name like Garcia I can never pass up a good taco stand. I seem to recall it had the most unusual name, something like Tacos for Jesus."

They both laughed. "Do you like tacos, Jim?"

"Sure, I guess, but I would never stop at a hole in the wall place like that. You don't know what you're eating."

"Ah, my friend, you're missing out. It's places like that whose names are in Spanish that have the best tacos and salsa. Let's give it a shot. It's my treat today, and I'll ask if they have seen Gil. Who knows, maybe he likes the asada as much as I do. It's worth a try," Gordon said with a huge smile.

They pulled in just past the taco shop and drove down an unpaved alley to park in the back. There were just a few cars in the parking lot.

"Jim, hand me that photo of Gil if you will," Gordon asked.

Jim opened his files and pulled out two different photos. "Hope these are somewhat recent." Jim stepped up to the open window and asked for three beef tacos. The reply coming back was "No comprende." Jim knew just enough Spanish to understand that his English wasn't going to be helpful in ordering lunch. He looked at Gordon and shrugged his shoulders.

"Grab us a table, Jim, and I'll take care of this for us. I'm sure they understood you, but it must be a thing with them that if you don't order in Spanish, no tacos for you."

"Taco Nazis," Jim said with a laugh.

Jim sat down and Gordon, being fluent in Spanish, ordered lunch and started a friendly conversation with the proprietor. Jim couldn't tell what was being said, but there seemed to be a lot of laughing and he was certain some of it was directed at him. After a few minutes, Gordon showed the photos of Gil to both men working behind the order window. He could tell by their affirmative reactions that Gil was someone they recognized. He pivoted around in his seat and looked out into the street. The car that Gordon had pointed to in the hotel parking lot was slowly approaching and Jim recognized it immediately. The two men inside seemed to be looking for someone specific as they checked the faces of all the customers seated in front of the taco shop. When they didn't see the person they were looking for, they increased their speed and returned to the flow of traffic. When Gordon returned with the tacos Jim stated, "Good news/ bad news, isn't it?"

Gordon nodded. "Gil has been here as recently as yesterday evening, but I see you noticed we're not alone in looking for him."

"How did you see that?" Jim asked, quite surprised.

"In my business, Jim, you observe or you die. I kind of like living, so I make it a point to see everything around me. It looked to me like they were so intent on finding Gil they didn't really notice us, but we can't take any chances. You know they'll kill him on sight if they find him. Our job has just become much more difficult. Not only do we have to find Gil first, but we have to protect him, and that won't be easy when he doesn't know who we are."

"So, just who are those guys?" Jim asked.

"It's kind of hard to say exactly. They could be rogue agents that were former Mossad, CIA, or one of the non-governmental mercenary outfits. Their intelligence is usually excellent because they can tap into databases we aren't even completely aware of. They operate around the world with impunity, eliminating risks and any threats to their masters. These guys will often set up patsies to take the blame for many of their operations. Occasionally they simply perform their mission and quietly disappear. Many of us feel that they're essentially the enforcement arm for those who planned and executed 9/11. Clearly they feel threatened by the information that Max and his team were digging into. One thing we do know about this group: they will do whatever is necessary to eliminate anyone that is close to exposing them."

"Can't Jerry Reitz help with this?"

"He can, but he doesn't know to what extent our federal intelligence and law enforcement agencies have been compromised. Like I said, with their software, they can pull intelligence information from almost any computer, and we're just now starting to realize how many government systems have been affected."

"Does this mean they know Max is still alive?"

"It's hard to say. They obviously know that Gil is. As long as Max remains in DC under the protection of the president he'll be safe. The same holds true for Vera, and my job is to protect you. I know you brought me only because the president asked you to, but he knew you would be in far more danger than you realized, and now it looks like we have proven that to be the case. Finish your tacos and we'll figure out what to do next."

thirteen

*W*hen the gown finally arrived at the White House, Vera could hardly wait to call Jenny. She had mentioned something about a state dinner and a new gown on Facebook, but had not gone into any detail. Jenny had been pummeling her with questions ever since and Vera had graciously sidestepped answering, not wanting to make a big deal out of it and not yet having all the details herself.

"Oh Jenny, how are you? I hate to keep you guessing by not answering all your questions. I've been super busy as you might imagine, but I'm all yours now."

"Vera Hanson, you now have to tell me everything that's going on with you. I want to know about the dress, the dinner, the dates, the dog, and the doorman. Tell it all to me, girl. I've been dying over here knowing that you're once again in the White House with that gorgeous man, and all I get are bits and pieces. Am I going to have to start reading the gossip section of the Washington Post to get the rundown on you two?"

"Well fortunately, that hasn't started up yet, but I'm afraid after this state dinner every writer's pen will be a-wagging. Even if they just write about this magnificent dress that was just delivered, they'll have enough material to write articles for weeks. Jenny, it's divine. At first I wasn't all that excited about going, you know being the de facto hostess and all, but now I can't wait. Should I show Joel the dress before the dinner?"

"You owe that to him," replied Jenny. "Obviously he thinks highly enough of you to put you in such an enviable position.

Show him the dress, but make sure you're in it. See if you can turn a politician speechless."

Vera started laughing. "Should I just show up for breakfast wearing it?" she asked.

"You eat breakfast with the president?" Jenny inquired.

"Pretty much every morning, unless he is out of town or has a breakfast meeting scheduled. He's very considerate about keeping me informed. In fact, he has assigned me a social secretary that has begun to keep my schedule and manage my messages. And I kind of like it."

"Exactly how long are you planning on staying there?" Jenny asked. "By the sound of things, it seems to me that you're becoming anchored."

"I'm working with Jim and some others on some important follow-up to the research we did prior to the State of the Union. Kelli has adopted Joel and whines when she can't be near him. I guess if I don't want to lose my dog I'm here for good," Vera said.

"Does that mean what it sounds like, Vera?" Jenny softly asked, but could feel her impatience growing as she anticipated the answer.

"What did it sound like?"

"Well, it sounded like wedding bells from here, and I'm almost three thousand miles away."

"Oh hell no, that's not something we've even talked about," came Vera's reply.

"Ah, but you've thought about it, haven't you?"

Silence. Whatever Vera was thinking, she chose not to share it with Jenny.

"Well, I can see I'm not going to get the good stuff out of you, so tell me more about the dinner and how that all works," Jenny said, trying not to sound too disappointed.

"I've been meeting with a protocol instructor for the past few days. She has been teaching me the right way to do things at a formal presidential gathering. My job, for the most part, will be to keep my mouth shut and not say anything stupid. I can answer questions and respond to compliments, but I'm to follow the president's lead and be charming without drawing attention to myself. Not quite the skill set of a former flight attendant." Vera chuckled nervously.

"Whoa, did I hear you say former flight attendant? Have you finally decided to quit, or does your airline career interfere with being the First Lady?" Jenny said, hoping for answers through the back door.

"Thirty years is enough, Jenny, and to be honest I don't think after what I know now I could ever do that job again with the same attitude and enthusiasm that made it enjoyable for all those years. I turned in all the paperwork before I left Seattle; I'm officially retired at the end of the month. Mike told me that when Joel found out I had decided to retire he clenched his fist, pumped it twice and let out a rather audible 'yes!'. I'm not sure what that all means in guy-talk, but Mike felt inclined to share it with me."

"It means listen to your protocol instructor, kiddo—you're going to be doing a lot more of this type of thing and you'll want to be really good at it," replied Jenny, feeling as if she had all the answers she needed. "Now when you show the gown to the president, make sure you take a picture and email it to me. Don't put it out on Facebook. I want to see it and you want it to be a surprise, got it?"

"Yes, ma'am," Vera shot back.

As evening approached, Vera received word that dinner would be in the formal dining room with just the president. He had requested one of his favorite meals, a pot roast with all the trimmings—his mother's recipe the White House chef had perfected. Tonight Joel wanted to share with Vera what good old-fashioned food from home tasted like, and he wanted it served to them in the dining room.

This gave Vera the idea to come dressed in her new gown. The dress had been tailored to perfection and fit unlike anything she had ever worn. She had her hair and makeup done by the resident experts, and then waited until she knew Joel would be seated in the dining room at the appointed hour.

At precisely seven o'clock, Mike appeared at the entrance to the dining room wearing his tuxedo. The president was seated at the head of the elegant table with a perplexed look on his face and asked, "Vera knows we're dining here this evening, does she not?"

Mike did not respond, but before the president could utter another word Mike took a step back and announced, "Mr. President, Madame Vera Hanson from the great state of Washington."

As if rehearsed to perfection, Vera smoothly glided into the dining room in full view of the president. She hesitated for just a moment, and then with her hands at her sides, offered the slightest of curtseys. The president's immediate response was that he should stand, but he was so stunned by her beauty that he could not seem to move. As he finally managed to stand to greet her, he banged his knee on the table. Vera smiled. Joel was speechless. Vera softly asked, "Does this meet with your approval for the state dinner?"

He wanted to answer, but his eyes were interrupting the connection between his brain and his mouth. All he could do was smile and bob his head slightly as he helped her into her chair.

"Well, you're going to have to do better than that in the receiving line, or people will think you've had a stroke," Vera said calmly.

"If that is how you'll look at the dinner, no one is going to pay any attention to me or anything I have to say. You, my dear, will be the center of attention, and we'll need someone from the State Department to coach you on the answers to all the questions they might have asked me."

"So you like it, the dress I mean?" Vera asked.

"You, in that dress, are the loveliest thing that has graced this house since Mica walked these halls. And since I can't take my eyes off you, I may have to have Mike feed me tonight." That comment cracked Vera up, and even Mike could be heard chuckling from around the corner.

"Well, I'm delighted you like it, and if you'd like, I can quickly go change so you can eat your favorite meal without assistance."

"That won't be necessary," said the president as he returned to his seat, all the time keeping his eyes fixed on Vera's face.

fourteen

"So how would they figure out Gil's here, and that he might frequent 'Tacos for Jesus'?" Jim inquired.

"That's hard to say. My suspicion is that there's a leak somewhere, and they're being fed intel long before you and I receive it," responded Gordon.

"But how's that even possible? This loop is tight: you, me, Max, Vera, the president and Jerry. No way would any of us leak this information."

"Jim, my experience has been that any time you deal with intelligence in any electronic form, it leaks. I'm sure that's why Max's plan called for his team to go dark. He knew the less communication, the better, and the more likely they'd remain safe. It's what we don't know that can hurt us. You've heard about computer viruses, haven't you—Trojans, Suxnet, and the like—installing backdoors into computer systems that can steal information and cause a lot more damaging havoc?"

Jim ran both hands through his hair. "Yeah, I know about that backdoor technology. Max had mentioned that in regard to those two companies, MITRE and Ptech, that were working in the basement of the FAA headquarters before 9/11. He explained how this backdoor technology allowed them to remotely control computer systems. There's some software out there that might have hijacked our entire government. They can doctor up any electronic information that comes over the internet. Changes can be made to any document and you wouldn't even know it, because it all happens after you click the 'send' button."

Gordon slowly nodded. "Not long ago, I met an NSA guy at the gym. We hit the bar after our workout, and he told me that he had discovered some of this type of software that his agency was using to spy on both companies and individuals. Before we could meet up the following week, he had committed suicide in his kitchen, shot twice in the chest. Imagine that?"

"Shot twice in the chest? What kind of guy can pull the trigger on himself more than once?" Jim asked.

"So, in light of all of this, who knows what details might have been communicated out of the Chicago PD after the Range Rover was destroyed? Jerry has a pretty tight grasp on things at the NSA, but all kinds of information flows through there and if someone on the inside is an agent for the Cabal, they'll disseminate it in a heartbeat," Gordon said.

"As far as finding Gil goes, we'll just have to play the hand we're dealt, and today we know we're not alone in our search. Let's hope they're not aware of you and me yet."

"So what's our next move?" Jim wanted to know.

"We don't even know if Gil's still in Fernley. I'm sure if he had become aware that he was being followed, he would have fled. In that case, we'd be back to square one. My gut tells me he is still here, and we'd best hang out for a few more days and try to find him."

Jim and Gordon kept a close eye on both the hotel and the taco stand, where they hoped Gil would soon show up. At eleven-thirty the next morning, Jim and Gordon left the base and drove back to Fernley. They circled around past the small hotel, then cased the taco stand. No sign of Gil. Gordon parked the car, making sure they were in a location that allowed them to keep an eye out for both Gil and the men hunting him. An unfamiliar car pulled into the parking lot behind the taco stand. A man fitting Gil's description exited the car and approached the front of the shop. His demeanor was relaxed, and he didn't exhibit any cautious behavior. He looked straight ahead, reading the menu, while he waited in line behind the other noontime customers. Jim broke out the field binoculars in order to get a closer look at him. He was certain they had found Gil Garrison.

"That's him, it's Gil," Jim said with absolute certainty.

Gordon didn't say a word. He was busy observing the immediate surroundings.

"If that's Gil, then I can assure you that we'll have company soon. How are you with an AK-47, Jim?" Gordon asked.

"Marksman, several years out of practice, but that won't stop me from doing whatever you need me to do."

"In that small suitcase in the backseat is a Secret Service issue AK-47. Assemble it while I drive around to the back of the shop. I'll go inside. After you let me out, pull back around to the curb, but stay out of sight. If the car from the hotel pulls up and stops, wait for the men to get out, then pull up right behind it and park. My guess is they'll attempt to abduct Gil. Ultimately they'll kill him, but not until they know what he knows, which means they'll torture him. They'll flank him on both sides, probably put a gun in his ribs, scare the hell out of him, and throw him into the backseat of their car before he even knows what happened. If that's how this plays out, train the rifle on the head of the man on your right. He'll be the muscle and won't have his gun out. I'll take care of the rest. If this starts to go sideways, shoot him right between the eyes. Got it?"

Jim reached into the backseat and found the suitcase. He opened it and assembled the weapon. "How do you know all this, Gordon? I mean, what makes you think this is how it'll play out?"

"I know how they operate. I know their tactics. They don't deviate much, so they're easy to anticipate. They're usually low-level, no-name operatives on this type of mission. They're good at what they do, but not as good as I am. Keep the gun out of sight until it's time, and you'll know when that is. If you're as good as you say, that one shot will be successful. I'll be in charge of the other guy."

"I'm glad the president insisted you come along. This isn't something I would have wanted to tackle alone," Jim said.

"President Sherman's intelligence-gathering is superb, but his instincts are even better. I'd do anything for him and he knows it," replied Gordon.

"I feel the same way. We've been friends for many years and he's never once let me down."

Jim let Gordon out behind the shop and began to make his way back to the frontage road. Gordon knocked hard on the back door. When it opened, he showed his Secret Service badge and began to explain in Spanish what was about to take place. He cautioned them not to contact the police and to act as naturally as possible. He grabbed an apron and quickly tied it around his waist. Through the window he had a clear view of Gil, who was now just one customer from the front of the line. He could see where Jim had parked and hoped that this would be simple and uneventful. If no one showed up, he would serve Gil his food and then come out and join him to explain the situation. That was the ideal plan. No sooner had the scenario played through in his head, though, than the car from the hotel pulled up alongside the curb. Jim noticed it as well and began to move from his concealed location until he was parked right behind it, just as Gordon had instructed. Jim lowered the passenger-side window and waited. The two men exited their car and approached Gil from behind. Both Jim and Gordon could see a black semi-automatic pistol in the hand of the man on Gil's left. As smooth as machine work, the gun went into Gil's ribs and the man to his right clasped him by the forearm and bicep.

Before either of them could say a word to Gil, Gordon lowered the top window so the distance between his face and the man on Gil's left was no more than two feet, and he pointed the barrel of his 9mm right between the man's eyes.

"Drop that gun on the counter right now, or this round black circle will be the last thing you ever see." Turning to the man on Gil's right, he said, "And you, unhand him or my friend there on the curb will repaint that 'Tacos for Jesus' sign with your blood."

Both men looked shocked and turned to see Jim pointing the AK-47 directly at them. Without any hesitation the man placed the gun on the counter, grip first, then stepped away from Gil. His companion did likewise.

"Now, I want you to walk backwards towards your car, get in and get the hell out of here," Gordon instructed in a crystal-clear voice, with his gun still pointed at the man's head. "Do you understand me?"

Both men nodded and began to slowly walk backwards, keeping their eyes on Gordon and taking turns looking back at Jim. They jumped into the car and quickly sped away into the sparse traffic of Fernley's main highway.

Jim clicked the safety on the rifle, pointed it towards the ground, and slowly approached Gil. Gordon took the gun off the counter, took off his apron, and exited through the back door. Gil stood motionless, completely stunned at what was taking place. He had no idea who these people were; he only knew his life had been in danger. Jim tried to figure out what to say to Gil, but before he could say anything, Gil smiled.

"Hey, I know you. You're Jim Bowman. You were in the president's box at the State of the Union. I've been buried in your findings ever since. You just saved my life. What are you doing here?" At that moment, Gordon appeared and stood silently at Gil's side. Gil looked over at him, turned back to Jim and asked, "Who's this guy? He just pulled off one of the bravest acts I've ever seen, thankfully."

"Gil, this is Agent Gordon Garcia from the president's Secret Service detail. Max sent us to find you. It appears that the word has leaked out that you're still alive."

Gordon shifted the pistol to his left hand and offered his right to Gil. "You handled that just right. I'm very impressed; not many men are that cool under fire."

Gil shook Gordon's hand. "Thank you, sir, I handled it well? Hell, I was too damn scared to move. I don't know how you knew where to be and what to do, but I owe you my life. I owe both of you. My only question is, why did you let them get away?"

"Do you know who those men were?" Gordon asked.

"Well, not exactly, but I assume they're part of the same group that tried to kill us in Chicago, and who Max is either on the lookout for, or on the run from. Correct?"

Gordon nodded. "Generally speaking, that's correct. They're part of an international consortium made up of domestic and foreign agents who are hired to do the dirty work of their masters."

"Who exactly are their masters?" Gil asked, looking rather confused.

"I'll answer that," said Jim. "The masters are those who want to bury, stifle or pervert the truth. They wear faces of cooperation and congeniality in public, but behind closed doors their mission is to subvert the governments of sovereign countries and to control as much of the world's natural resources as possible. They manipulate currencies, start wars, and reign with blood and horror. They eliminate anyone who's a threat to them, and apparently that includes you and the others on Max's team. You guys apparently have gotten your hands on some information about 9/11 that threatens their methodically painted illusion. They're desperate to keep that truth hidden from the public, and I understand they have even threatened a nuclear attack to prevent that truth from being exposed to the American people and the rest of the world. I seem to recall they call that plan the Samson Option."

"That's actually why we're here, Gil; the president needs to know what you guys know. The information your research team has collected could help the president in establishing a new and open investigation into the 9/11 attacks, one that gets to the real truth this time. You heard his State of the Union address, so you know what he wants to accomplish. Trust me, it hasn't been easy so far."

"What about those two thugs?" Gil asked.

"They'll be picked up shortly by some of my colleagues, but they won't stay in custody long. They're probably going to flash some foreign security identification that'll allow them to be immediately released. They're minions, but the money and power behind them makes demanding and executing justice impossible. They're not the problem; they're just evidence of a greater evil—the one the president is fighting and the one you are investigating."

Jim interrupted, "We need to get you back to Washington as soon as possible and get you debriefed. Where are you staying?"

Gil looked down. "I can't go to Washington, at least not yet. I've just learned that Bob is hiding out in Las Vegas. I think he's in trouble and needs my help. I planned to drive down there after lunch. I don't know exactly where he is, but I have to find him. His information is much more critical than anything I have, and now that I know what he might be up against, if I don't get to him before they do our fight for a new investigation will be impossible."

Jim glanced at Gordon, whose expression made it clear this was one for Jim to decide. "Gil, go ahead and reorder your lunch and take some time to fully compose yourself. I'll call Max and see what he knows. If Bob needs to be found, we'll be able to do that with the assets we have. And if he's in the same kind of trouble you were, he's going to need our help."

Gil agreed and motioned for Gordon to join him in line.

"Good idea, Jim," Gordon said. "I need to explain to these

people what just went down here and make sure they didn't call the police. The cops will be of no help at this point, and can only slow us down."

Gil returned to the customer window, hoping his appetite was still somewhere to be found. Gordon went around back to explain to the owner what had just occurred. He wanted to reassure him that everything was all right. Jim retired to the car and called Max.

Max was pleased to hear that Gil was safe. He told Jim that he'd also discovered that Bob was somewhere in or around Las Vegas. Max had a few suggestions as to where Bob might be staying. He told Jim the details of a recent meeting he'd had with Jerry Reitz and the president. Jim could feel the escalating pressure in Max's voice. When he hung up the phone, Jim called the Air Force pilots at Fallon and instructed them to get the jet ready and to make plans to fly to Nellis Air Force Base.

Jim joined Gil and Gordon at the table. "Okay, I've talked with Max and he concurs that Bob needs to be found as soon as possible. How fast can you get ready to leave?"

"I've been staying with my ex-brother-in-law. I have one suitcase, my computers and a few external hard drives. That's pretty much it. If you follow me to his place, I can return his car, collect my things and leave a note. That'll take fifteen minutes tops."

Jim turned to Gordon and asked, "You up for this next phase?'

Gordon just smiled and pointed his finger towards the car.

After a quick stop for Gil's belongings, they headed for the Navy base. The ride back to Fallon was a perfect time to begin to debrief Gil. "Gil, I know this isn't going to be easy for you, but I'm going need you to tell me what you've been working on. Max tells me that collectively your group has compiled enough information to blow the lid off the official 9/11 investigation. So start wherever you think makes sense, and we'll just listen for the most part."

Gil didn't answer immediately. In many ways he was relieved to no longer be on the run. "When we fled Minneapolis, we had no idea when we'd ever meet up again. I knew that the Octopus, as Max likes to call it, was out to silence us and stop our research. I didn't know for sure if Max was able to pull off the plan at Denny's. Of course I'd read his obituary online, but I'd hoped it wasn't true. I watched the State of the Union on television with my ex-brother-in-law, and that's how I recognized you, Jim. For the first time in years, I felt uplifted from hearing a speech. I was filled with hope and encouragement. I finally felt that all of our efforts to get the truth out to the public had been worth the effort.

"I have a friend at the NSA that I sometimes go to for information. I wanted to know more about you and Vera— who you were, why you were at the speech, and mostly, why you were chosen to head up the committee to open a new 9/11 investigation. I called my friend. I probably shouldn't have. That phone call might have led to the leak that allowed those thugs to find me. Anyway, he told me about you and Vera and what you'd discovered. It all made perfect sense to me. We'd been working around the edges of your theory for years, but never had the insight you two did. Your professional airline careers set your findings apart from all the other theories. Personally, I couldn't find a flaw in anything you had found. Your discoveries corresponded with who and what we had uncovered in regards to MITRE and PTech, as well as some of the other corporations. I decided to take up where you two had left off and continued to tear apart their deception."

Jim interrupted, "You know, after we made our theory public, we started getting calls about Westover; several reserves who were based there knew that the base had been evacuated and was put on lockdown. They told us they were locked out for several days following the attacks of 9/11. Vera received a call from a woman who was stationed there; her unit was activated shortly after the second tower was hit. She also reported that Westover was locked up tighter than a prison, and that none of her unit could figure out why they had been locked out. The reserves were all housed in nearby hotels. When she heard about what we had discovered, it all finally made sense to her. She was quite shaken by the realization."

Gil added, "I too was aware of that anomaly, and it adds credence to your theory. Bob had heard rumors of some strange airplane sightings in western Massachusetts and was planning to follow up on them."

"We're approaching the base entrance," interrupted Gordon. "We're going to have to explain Gil. Do you have any ID, Gil?"

Jim responded, "I've already taken care of that, my friend. When I talked to Max I asked him to provide clearance for Gil at both Fallon and Nellis. I'm sure we won't have any problems."

Gordon pulled up to the checkpoint and was saluted, then waved through by the guard on duty. "That Max does good work," he said.

"Not too bad for a dead guy," added Jim.

fifteen

*V*era finished answering her email. All the excitement that surrounded staying in the White House not only made finding time to read her email difficult, but responding to it became impossible. Most of her friends couldn't imagine meeting the President of the United States. She found answering their questions to be very challenging. She wasn't quite sure how much of her experience she could share. Being a guest at the White House presented its own set of unique problems. Her unusual circumstances created moments of melancholy that Vera wasn't used to handling. If she were home in Seattle, she would take a walk along the beach, but here in D.C., she had to make do with the grounds of the White House.

The White House Rose Garden was situated along the West Wing, adjacent to the Oval Office. Many historical events had been held there. Most presidents chose to hold news conferences in the garden because of its intimate setting and private surroundings. Joel Sherman had not been a fan of using the Rose Garden for any particular purpose. The caretakers kept it in magnificent, pristine condition for members of the administration to enjoy. Everyone in Washington was so busy that Vera rarely encountered anyone in or around the garden.

As her day progressed into late afternoon, Vera decided to take a stroll. Joel was still in the Oval Office, with several meetings scheduled. Kelli was curled up in her bed next to his desk. As Vera entered the garden and walked toward her favorite bench, Kelli noticed and stood by the door. Joel opened the door and let her out. Kelli bounded out of the office and ran to be by Vera's side. Vera loved the acknowledgement and knelt down to receive all the enthusiastic doggie kisses Kelli could muster. She scratched her behind the ears and patted her in all the favorite places that only a dog's owner truly understands. When she finished and sat down, Kelli curled up at her feet and provided the companionship that Vera had come to expect but was beginning to miss. Vera sat very still, taking in the garden's beauty. Roses were blooming everywhere, and filled the air with their sweet fragrance. She began to think about the senseless loss of life caused by the terror attacks. She tried to imagine what the real terrorists—the handlers onboard those four flights—had done to kill the passengers and crew members. She and Jim had assumed the fastest method was some type of lethal gas. Were the flight attendants and pilots told by the handlers that their flight was chosen to test the military or the FAA? She wondered if the pilots had been told of the many war games the Pentagon had scheduled that day. What could have possibly gone through the minds of the flight attendants as they realized the gas was not a fake smoke bomb like those so often used in training exercises, but was killing them? Did any of the crew grasp the reality and try to arm and open an exit door? The television anchors, did they know this was some cooked-up charade? Had they known all along what she and Jim had uncovered about the remote-control hijackings of the planes to Westover? How could they sit and lie to the public, and watch as our drones killed innocent families around the world? Tears began to well up in her eyes, and gently one by one slid down her cheeks. Kelli placed her paws across Vera's feet and brushed softly against her legs.

Joel began to wonder where Kelli had gone. It wasn't like her to not hurry back to his side. He began to look for her out the windows of the Oval Office. Kelli was nowhere to be seen. Joel touched the intercom and told his secretary that he was going for a short stroll in the Rose Garden and would be back soon. Kelli heard the door to the office open and raised her head, but quickly returned it to Vera's feet. Joel followed the garden walkway, keeping his head up and his eyes alert for any sign of the dog. At the intersection of two of the pathways, he chose to follow the one which led deeper into the garden. After a few steps, he saw Vera sitting with her head down, surrounded by roses, Kelli at her feet. He hesitated for a moment, not wanting to disturb them, but as he listened, he could hear Vera softly crying.

His first thought was to leave them in peace, but she meant so much to him that any pain Vera experienced, he too felt, even if he didn't understand its source. He walked toward them and sat down quietly on the bench next to Vera. Kelli looked up at him in an approving manner. Vera felt his presence and gently rested her hand on his thigh. Still Joel said nothing. The tears continued to drop into her lap, but the sobs that Joel had seen from the walkway had ceased. After a few moments, he moved closer to her and rested his arm across her shoulders. Vera raised her head and began wiping the tears away with her fingers. They sat together in silence. Finally, Joel spoke. "Vera, what might I do to help you?"

"Just your being here is comforting in so many ways. When Jim and I discovered the details about 9/11, along with the tape recording, it changed my world. I've spent some time since those discoveries digging into FBI documents and sorting through Jeff's files, which have shed light upon who the perpetrators of that horrific event were. These past few days I have been consumed with research that Max has given me. When I'm not buried in documents, I'm fully engaged in pulling every detail from Max that he knows. And I think it has just all overwhelmed me."

Joel pulled Vera a little closer to him and said, "I'm listening."

"Do you know about PNAC, the 'Project for a New American Century'?"

The president nodded his head slowly.

"Those bastards planned to create a New Pearl Harbor—something so horrific, so destructive, and so indelibly imprinted upon the minds of the people, that it would rally the country around a common enemy. There wasn't one, so they created the enemy, devised the plan and then executed it with precision. Sure there were flaws and mistakes, but with the help of the media, its overwhelming magnitude seared into the minds of the people exactly what they wanted ingrained. Joel, they have planned and executed war after war: seven in all. And in the name of patriotism, young men and women, the lifeblood of our country, enlisted to fight those wars. Thousands of them have perished; tens of thousands of them have been maimed and crippled for the rest of their lives. Not to mention the thousands that suffer from PTSD. Pat Tillman, the NFL football player, left a lucrative career to fight and defend this country. When he realized what it was he was really fighting for: drugs, oil, power, and control, he intended to expose the lie. He was killed for daring to let that truth be known to the public. He was just one person. Think of the thousands of innocent people who have been killed, maimed, orphaned, and driven from their homes in the name of freedom, camouflaged by the synagogue of Satan."

Joel softly whispered, "Ah, a Bible verse."

"Yes," replied Vera. "And not found only once, so He must have meant it. Anyway, Joel, I think it's all gotten to me. No one loves their country more than I do, but I'm having a difficult time recognizing my country, and that loss causes me to weep. Do you even know who signed PNAC?"

"I do," Joel said, without hesitation. "Their names are on a list in my desk and to be honest, it's the same people who cause me the most trouble and agitation. It's they who are fighting every effort to reopen a new 9/11 investigation."

"Well, that's not too surprising. That would cause them to

have a lot to answer for, now wouldn't it?" Vera replied, with a touch of anger in her voice that had managed to push away some of her tears. "How in the world did they manage to get away with this for so long? Are people in this country so controlled by fear and political correctness that they'll sit by and watch their own country implode like those towers did? Are our leaders so manipulated that they can no longer speak the truth, if it doesn't point to their chosen enemy? Why is it accepted to falsely accuse Arabs or Muslims and bomb their countries when we can clearly see the involvement of the Israeli Mossad and its fingerprints all over 9/11? For God's sake, they even had a trained assassin onboard Flight 11. That guy was also trained as a hostage rescue specialist. That training means he knew as much about those aircraft as the flight crews did. The real passenger manifests didn't list one of the accused hijackers, yet people just seem to swallow the lie the media pushes without question. Am I the only person that's not blinded by fear of ridicule and political correctness in this country? How can anyone get the truth out to the people when the perpetrators are the gatekeepers that monitor and control every bit of information?"

"I'm working on a plan to beat them at their own game," Joel said. "I can't go into any details just yet, but I've known for years those you can trust to stand up for this country, and who it is that is standing on its throat. And it's time the United States cleared its throat and found its voice."

"That's just the beginning of it, Joel. The voices in the media serve to do all their bidding. Even those who we think share our views are nothing more than controlled voices that will never cross the line into certain truths. Oh, they'll launch mortar fire into liberal thinking, rally the troops around the issue de jour, and raise the standard of moral superiority for all to follow, but do they ever explore the entire truth? Do they want to know what really happened on 9/11, or is their abundant flow of money more important to them? Wasn't it those in the media who began to call anyone who questioned 9/11 'truthers'? Didn't they ridicule everyone who so much as questioned the official story as 'tin foil hat wearers'? They effectively used their power and prominent positions of trust to stifle any inquiries into the facts. Why would they do that if they stand for freedom, truth and justice? Is it because they are controlled by the same people who planned, orchestrated and murdered thousands of people just to satiate their lust for war, power, and money? How many news anchors have been caught embellishing stories, editing videotape or outright lying? All the stations lead with the same stories. No longer is there any degree of investigation into the news of the day. It's served up like pablum for the masses to consume. And if anyone is brave enough to do some investigative work, they are targeted, compromised, and ultimately terminated. Do you see this, Mr. President?"

"Vera, not only do I see it all, I feel it daily as it's choking the life out of the country I love."

Vera pulled away from Joel's grasp so she could look him directly in the eyes. "You might be the last hope, you know. It might all rest on you, to make America what it once was and to instill the determination in its people to overcome the evil that has such a firm grasp on the nation."

Joel took both of Vera's hands in his and spoke softly. "Whatever my role is, history will decide. But I know this: whatever I do, I cannot do it without you."

Upon hearing his words, Vera threw her arms around Joel's neck and hugged him with all the energy she had left. "Joel, you saved me from myself today. I needed that. I needed you to listen to me. You did that, and then you loved me. How can I ever thank you?"

The president was silent. He offered Vera his hand and helped her from the bench. Then he put his arm around her and walked with her back to the Oval Office, Kelli following closely behind.

sixteen

*J*im was hoping to leave immediately for Nellis as soon as they arrived at the hangar. The pilots were just finishing up, and explained to him that there was a slight mechanical problem with the Gulfstream. Since it wasn't an aircraft that was part of the standard Navy fleet stationed at Fallon, it would require a replacement part from another location, which was being flown in and then would require an hour or two for installation. Both Jim and Gordon felt that remaining on base would be the smartest way to protect Gil, but it wasted valuable time which could have been used to find Bob.

Since the extent of the delay was uncertain, the base commander had arranged for a guest house for them to stay in until the repair was completed. This accommodation made it possible for them to rest, shower, and to begin Gil's interrogation. They were invited to dinner at the Officers' Club as guests of the base commander. In spite of all the base hospitality extended to them, Jim could feel a certain amount of tension and frustration building inside him. With the attempt to kidnap or even eliminate Gil, the urgency of his mission took on a new perspective. At the very least he wanted to know what Gil knew, and why a price might have been put on his head.

After dinner, Jim began to fire questions at Gil. Gil didn't like the feeling of being interrogated, and began to be hesitant with his answers. He was still uncertain who these two men were, in spite of them having saved his life earlier in the day. He asked if he too could talk with Max, and Jim agreed.

Jim called Max and handed the phone to Gil. Having known Gil for quite some time, the call didn't come as a surprise to Max. As superb a researcher as Gil was, his tendency to be a loner magnified the sense of general mistrust that naturally accompanied his personality type. After nearly being killed in Chicago, the entire research team would be reluctant to talk with strangers.

"Max, is that really you, and is it safe to talk to these guys?" Gil asked.

"Oh for hell sakes, Gil, you're a nobody civilian sitting in a general's guest house after having eaten in the Officers' Club at the 'Top Gun' fighter pilot training base, and you want to know if it's safe to talk to these guys?" Max asked. "Who do you think managed to arrange all this, the Mafia? Yeah, it's me, and you damn well better tell Jim everything you know, or I personally will fly out there and bring your mother with me." Max let out a loud belly laugh.

That made Gil laugh, and both Jim and Gordon could see him immediately start to relax. Now it was going to be much easier for them to elicit answers to their questions. Gil talked to Max for several more minutes, comparing notes on what they knew about Bob and where he might be. When he was finished talking, he handed the secure phone back to Jim and proclaimed, "Max told me to let her rip, so ask away. The last thing I want is to have my mother here complaining at me." Gil was still laughing at that thought, while Gordon and Jim just let it ride.

Gordon asked, "What do you think it is that you discovered that caused you to become the target of an international hit squad? Those boys and their tactics are not deployed on people who are promoting conspiracy theories on a blog, or writing novels. You must have uncovered something that is potentially very damaging to them. I feel that there could be more than one intelligence agency involved that might fear being exposed."

Gil rubbed his chin rhythmically as he thought. "I've never disclosed to anyone what I was researching. If they were after me for what I knew, they ascertained that information because they have all of my research material, or they have the ability to spy on me through means other than the internet. If they knew what I had and it was a threat to them, then all they had to do was find me, torture me until they discovered exactly what I had uncovered, and then dispose of me. That's how they operate, isn't it?"

"Sadly, that is exactly how they operate. So based on what you've said, they must have some of the same information that you and your team have. You may not have put it all together, but something is hiding in that Freedom of Information Act data that has them scared. They know everything they did on 9/11, as well as all the steps that were taken to cover up the details. They probably fear that a couple of airline professionals and a few good researchers working together will be able to expose them. Chances are they're thinking you or your group has finally figured it out. Just my guess," Gordon said.

Jim glanced down at his watch, then checked for any messages on his cell phone. No word from the mechanics meant they weren't going anywhere any time soon. He had indicated to Max that chances were they'd be departing early in the morning. He was certain their plan was passed on to Jerry, the president and eventually on to Vera. He pulled all his papers into a single stack, then straightened it by bouncing the edges on the table several times, as a signal that he was ready to begin. "So Gil, it looks like we have some time. Share with us what you know."

"Well, I'm not sure where to start; there were lots of people that made millions of dollars off that so-called terror attack. Of the government agencies, several seem to have something to hide, and they're still hiding plenty. Let's begin with the FBI. Nothing I've uncovered indicates that they were involved with the planning and specific execution of anything that transpired that day, although at this point, nothing would surprise me. I mean, you can't point to that agency and say FBI agents piloted planes or activated the remote control devices, or that they planted the explosives in the World Trade Center. What they did do, and did very efficiently, was cover things up. In fact, they were so timely in their execution that there was no question that they had to have had prior knowledge of what was going down: when, where, and how. For example, within minutes of the Pentagon being struck, FBI agents were on the scene confiscating nearly eighty security videotapes from the Pentagon and surrounding businesses. They knew where to look and they knew what they were looking for. Now, those tapes have been in their procession since the incident occurred, and they have never been brought to the forefront of either a defense or a prosecution. They've been buried and, if I recall, they've been sealed from the public for a number of decades. To me, that spells cover-up."

"Did the FBI ever do a chemical analysis on the dust residue from the towers?" Gordon asked.

"Not that I've ever heard of or found in any of my research," answered Jim. Gil continued, "Then there were the phone calls. Within a suspiciously short period of time, agents were at the homes of the people who had received calls from the hijacked planes. They proceeded to confiscate their home phone recorders and contradict what the people were being told. In a sense, they were rewriting the story on the fly, and with the recorded evidence now in their procession, the FBI version could no longer be called into question.

"In the case of 9/11, it appears they knew who was going to receive calls. How did they know? Who provided that kind of information to them? Now, the woman involved that you and Vera discovered—this is where it gets really interesting. You remember the purser down in Florida, the one with the message left on her recorder by a woman with a heavy accent? Why was that woman with the foreign accent not a concern to the FBI? That information was completely buried, never mentioned by the media and never followed up with an investigation. Why? Again, I don't necessarily know or think they were in on the planning, but they sure as hell were, and to this day still are, complicit in the cover-up. Even their own reports for the 9/11 Commission hearings and the Moussaoui trial were inconsistent. Many of the details of the official government story were conflicting."

Jim's mind went back to the story he and Vera had uncovered about the American Airlines purser that had been assigned to fly Flight 11 then at the last minute, replaced. When she got to her home in Miami, a strange message had been left on her home phone recorder. It was the heavily accented voice of a woman and two men, speaking perfect English. The message was, 'If this had anything to do with Israel, there will be a backlash against the Jews.' Jim knew how an airline employee's home phone number and address were protected by the company. He saw a breach of security that indicated to him that the phone lines to and from Crew Scheduling had been tapped. But who could have done that? Tapping an airline's phone system would have had to have been done near the corporate headquarters and by someone that had connections into telephone services inside the United States.

Gil could tell Jim was deep in thought, "What's on your mind there, Jim?"

"Well, I'm still thinking about the Purser and that odd message left on her recorder. From all indications, the corporate phone lines at American's headquarters or somewhere along their system, had to have been tapped. That might also explain the unusually light passenger loads so many have questioned. If their phone lines were tapped so too could their reservation computer lines have been. If they had access to reservations, they could have controlled not only the number of passengers on those planes, but who everyone thought was on them. If those flights had been full, they then would have had nearly eight hundred bodies to dispose of."

Gil blurted out a quick answer without thinking, "The government? But that would indicate they were in on the planning."

Jim was still thinking. "I remember the flight attendant, who called in from Flight 11 on a reservations line. Once the agent knew it was an emergency, the phone call was supposed to be recorded, but they claimed something didn't work right, and only about four minutes was recorded."

Gil added, "I remember reading that United's headquarters near Chicago also lost their phone lines and internet that morning."

"You're right, I remember reading that as well, Gil. "I'd never put two and two together with those phone lines, but it can't be a coincidence that both companies involved had phone problems that morning."

"I understand that the FBI can tap phone lines, but at the time of 9/11, they still needed a warrant and they would have had to have some reason to get one. I doubt that it was the FBI tapping those phone lines." Gil was clicking through some files he had saved on his laptop as he spoke. "Still would be nice of them to release their documents to us."

Gordon interjected. "I've worked inside law enforcement agencies my entire adult life and I can tell you that nobody covers up tighter and more completely than the FBI."

Gil glanced at Gordon knowingly. "We've been trying to get all the Freedom of Information Act documents we could get our hands on, and it's been almost impossible. What we do have probably wasn't fully vetted before it was released. Since you and Vera exposed what you did about Westover Air Force Base, we've seen their door close even tighter. Hopefully one of us is in or around D.C. and is still fighting that battle.

"My cousin was vacationing in the Caribbean several years after 9/11, and met a guy and his wife at the hotel pool. He was a Navy man and his wife had been employed in the Pentagon. She told them her personal survival story. Shortly after she arrived at work that day, about an hour before anything struck in New York, her phone rang and a voice she didn't recognize told her, "Get out of the Pentagon and get out now!" She grabbed her purse and left the building in a hurry. She still doesn't know who made that call, but she's alive today because of it. People knew in advance, and that right there is just one example.

"The sad thing is, ever since that day, people have seen what happens when you speak up against this war machine. Nearly fifty eyewitnesses, or people who had information that could have exposed the real perpetrators, have met an untimely, unexplained, or premature death. I never thought I'd hear myself say this, but I've grown fearful of my government, and it doesn't seem to matter if there is a "D" or an "R" next to their name. Both parties are evil and corrupt, and will do whatever it takes to keep their new world order alive. We're now living under the same type of regime that many of us grew up fearing. People are afraid to speak the truth. What they want you to believe is the illusion they create via the media and their talking heads. A terrorist is defined as anyone they point to: Arabs, Muslims, Iraqis, Afghanis or American patriots. The methodologies used on the world that day were calculated to send the people into a state of shock and awe. In that state of mental trauma, the human mind is most susceptible to programming. Now every time the TV anchors chime in with '9/11 terror attacks' it's a trigger used to pull us all back into a hypnotic trance. Most people were raised to believe they could trust the news. Unfortunately, the CIA has had control over the networks for many years. Remember retired CIA director, William Casey's famous quote, 'We'll know our disinformation program is complete when everything the American public believes is false.' Gentlemen, let those words sink in. They're painful."

Jim's mind was still digesting the depth and meaning of Casey's words. "That's quite the statement for a CIA director to make. Applied to what we think we saw on 9/11, and those trigger words being used constantly over the past decade, it's a miracle anyone can break free from the matrix they've built."

Gil began pacing the room. "It's not just the government agencies involved, either. Let me move on to the MITRE Corporation. Good Lord, they were involved in absolutely everything, but what causes me the most consternation is that they're a nonprofit company and exempt from filing the documents that would reveal where they spend their money. Nevertheless, they are basically a shadow government, involved in absolutely everything. They manage federally funded research and development centers, support the Department of Defense, the Federal Aviation Administration, the Internal Revenue Service, the Department of Veterans Affairs, the Department of Homeland Security, the Administrative Office of the U.S. Courts on behalf of the Federal Judiciary, the Centers for Medicare and Medicaid Services, and the National Institute of Standards and Technology. Now, anyone that has looked closely into the collapse of the World Trade Towers knows all about NIST and how they published the most ridiculous theories about pancake collapse and free-fall acceleration, all mixed in with their nonsensical gobbeldy-goop that even a junior high student knows is against all laws of physics."

Jim's eyes followed Gil around the room. "Max tried to lay out for us what he knew about MITRE and Ptech the night before he left for Chicago. It was evident that he knew a lot more than he shared with us. As I recall, the information was overwhelming, and since then I've discovered that almost all roads of research lead back to them. I'm amazed at how many government officials have spent time working there. It came as no surprise that the new Secretary of Defense following Chuck Hagel's incompetent tenure was someone directly from MITRE's board of directors. I guess they felt a need to have closer supervision and more direct control."

Gil agreed, "It's like a revolving door: politicians, government employees and military officers weave in and out of corporations like MITRE. It's your old-fashioned good old boy network, but these private nonprofit joints allow them to circumvent restrictions they had in the government or military. These people bring their inside knowledge and next thing you know, they are using that knowledge for evil purposes."

"You mentioned Ptech, Jim. I've heard of them, but I don't think that's what they are called today. What do you know about them, Gil?" Gordon queried.

"Oh, plenty! They're the guys, along with MITRE, that made it all happen. With that backdoor installed into their stolen PROMIS software, they became like gods. Both Ptech and MITRE, you'll recall, were working together in the FAA headquarters. Ptech had completely infiltrated all of our national security computer systems, thanks to their inside connections. When the FBI pretended to close them down, they simply changed their name and continued to operate. Certain aspects of the technology world have been penetrated by people who want to control the human domain. I knew when I first read about the PROMIS software's ability to monitor and track any and every activity, that it was only a matter of time before this technology would be turned against the people. This modified software has been installed just about everywhere, and the latest version will be used to create artificial intelligence that will even control our military. This new militarized version is capable of tracking everything every one of us does, how we think, and what our innermost feelings might be on any given subject. It's been integrated into all social media, online reading, even text messages—and particularly private chats and phone calls. They're deliberately pushing out disinformation to us via their controlled media and internet blogs. These new quantum computers of theirs monitor and track each of our reactions. Anything we express about government, guns, religion, or politics is recorded, analyzed and stored. In a sense, we have all volunteered that information by using social media sites, and are encouraged to do so. Why do you think these social media sites are free? Look into the connection between intelligence organizations and one-world funding sources; it will rattle you to your core. Let's say this New World Order being planned decides to limit your freedoms. You're going to wake up and demand your privacy and freedoms back from an overreaching government. By then it will be too late, I'm afraid.

"It's more than frightening; it's the equivalent of every science fiction and horror film you have ever seen rolled into one, and it's now our reality. The equivalent of a cyber-octopus, this new artificial intelligence has the ability to turn us all into slaves. Go online and start talking D-wave and quantum computing, and see how fast you meet the men in black and are silenced.

"After 9/11, we all experienced the government beginning to separate us from our freedoms and protections under the Bill of Rights. A good buddy of mine from the Navy was digging into this new high-tech superfast computing and made a few YouTube videos about what he understood. A few months later, government agents ordered him into silence. He willingly complied. I'm afraid we've given away our rights to privacy, and hell, we can't even express an opposing opinion now.

"Another detail that has stood out in my research centers around the people who were in a position to do something about 9/11 and failed. Most Americans would have lost their jobs for such incompetence. Curiosity got the best of me, and I just had to see what happened to some of those people. As you might suspect, not one of them lost their job. Many of them went into non-governmental security companies, like Blackwater, or one of the military/industrial war machine corporations for a much higher salary.

"Several of the high-ranking military officers that failed to do their jobs that day moved on to private intelligence companies. These companies are connected to the military, but are run privately, which allows them to operate outside the laws and controls that restrict the military. Some of these black operations are running drugs into our country, arms into enemy territories, and even children into prostitution rings.

"It gets worse. The psychopaths that you've seen representing ISIS are homegrown, and are supported or financed by some of our retired admirals, generals and politicians. You heard that right. Many of those ex-military guys, who were sitting where they could have stopped the terror attacks, are now on the boards of directors for black ops mercenary companies. The labyrinth is complicated. People inside corporations like MITRE, Noblis, Booz Allen Hamilton, Los Alamos Labs, the Business Executives for National Security, US Falcon, Anteon, General Dynamics, Bechtel, In-Q-Tel, DynCorp, Rockwell Collins, Lockheed Martin, Boeing, Rand, Iridium, the Council on Foreign Relations, the Trilateral group, and the National Reconnaissance Office, seem to want to take control of all mankind. Most are connected through their past military or government positions.

Jim tilted his head to one side, looked over at Gordon and said, "Well, Gil, I think you've painted a pretty clear and ugly picture of why someone would want to separate you from your tacos."

Gordon agreed, "You probably have tapped into some of those companies that have connections to black op guys who could have easily killed you. You are correct in your findings; they can tap any phone or computer, and as a consequence they can track down anyone they are looking for. I think you understand that now. I'm beat; what do you two say we call it a night and continue this tomorrow?"

seventeen

*J*ust before noon, Jim's phone rang. It was the jet's captain, confirming that the plane had been repaired and that they could be 'wheels up' as soon as Jim arrived at the hangar. He conveyed the message to Gordon and Gil, then finished packing his few personal items. It still wasn't clear what they were planning to do once they landed at Nellis. No new information had been conveyed concerning Bob. If anyone wanted to melt into the masses, Las Vegas was the perfect place to make that happen.

It felt good to be back in the Gulfstream. Gil was particularly impressed, since he had never flown in a private plane, let alone one as sophisticated and well-appointed as a government jet with Air Force pilots. Once he got over the initial excitement and had fully examined every detail of the plane, he settled into one of the plush captain's chairs and reclined it, but not so far as to prevent him from looking out his window.

The flight to Nellis was quick, since they could fly full throttle through restricted airspace not available to commercial jets. They were on final approach just over thirty minutes after leaving Fallon. Jim was on the phone to Max for most of the flight, hoping to glean any more information that would be helpful in finding Bob. They discussed all of the information that Gil had shared the night before, and Max got a real kick out of listening to Jim come to the realization that what they'd discussed in Minnesota was far more encompassing and complex than Max had shared. He could tell that Jim's thoughts were blazing on full wattage, and that made him as proud as it did happy.

Unfortunately, Max did not have any suggestions as to where to find Bob, which meant they would be on their own trying to find him. He did suspect that Bob might be staying in one of the many rent-by-the-week hotels located all around the area. Max made it quite clear that Bob was a tightwad, and Gil confirmed the claim. They ruled out him staying with friends or family, since he never liked being around people, and they knew he could not bear to stay even one night as a guest in someone's house, let alone for days or weeks at a time. The only problem with Max's theory was that there were scores of such hotels throughout Clark County, and finding Bob in one of them would be impossible. Perhaps the only advantage they had was that Gil knew the car Bob drove, and he also knew that wherever Bob was, he would be consumed doing his research day and night. Gil felt if they could find the car, they could find Bob.

The hospitality at Nellis was equally as impressive as it had been at Fallon. They were given a vehicle from the motor pool and escorted to a comfortable guest house, which was far enough away from the flight line that they wouldn't be disturbed.

"In talking with Max, I'm under the impression that Bob has radar data on the 9/11 flights. He seems to think that there are some serious discrepancies between what the FAA has reported, and what NORAD claims were the flight paths of the planes in question. Is that your understanding, Gil?" Jim wondered aloud.

"It is, Jim and you also need to know that Bob is a very interesting character," Gil said. "If you think I was a bit paranoid interacting with you guys, I can tell you that you'll have your work cut out for you trying to convince Bob that he needs to tell you anything. Hell, you guys saved my life, and I still wasn't prepared to tell you what I knew. If you get to the point where you even see Bob face to face, I'm not sure how you'll convince him that he needs to share anything with you. Even in our group meetings, it was clear to most of us that he was always holding something back. And we're the closest thing to family he has. Even Max struggled to get him to tell the whole story on anything. On the bright side, however, he keeps impeccable notes. He documents every aspect of his research, which makes it easy to follow his thinking and his logic. I was fortunate once and got to read through some of his files. I always had the feeling he was testing me. I was impressed with what I saw from reading his notes. It made me wonder who his notes were meant for—I mean, he keeps them hidden on flash drives. But they are current. I'd guess he updates those files at least twice a day. He is obsessive-compulsive about them."

"That may prove to be helpful when the time comes," Jim replied. Then, turning to Gordon, he asked, "How are we going to find this guy? I don't want to hang out at those flea-bag pay-as-you-go hotels looking for him."

"Gil, you mentioned you knew the type of car he drove. Do you have the exact make and model, or even better, the license plate number?" Gordon asked.

"It's an older car—early to mid-eighties model. I think it's an Oldsmobile, but I can't tell you for sure what kind—maybe a Cutlass. It's dark blue and has Indiana plates. I think he actually lives in Illinois, but he registered it in the neighboring state to avoid the higher fees. I'm sure the only reason he never got caught is because he rarely drove the car, so his exposure was minimal. Is that enough to go on?"

Gordon quickly replied, "It's better than nothing, and it'll have to do. I know you don't want to, Jim, but I think we should cruise through the parking lots of some of these hotels where we think Bob might be. It beats sitting here. In the meantime, I'll pull a few strings and get Metro to do a BOLO for a car fitting that description. I know they run through those types of establishments at night checking license plates for stolen vehicles, current registration and anything that looks suspicious. I know one of the division captains here who used to be in the Service. He left a few years ago, when he got married and migrated to the bright lights of Sin City. I'm sure he'll help us. It's still a crap shoot, but it's all we have."

"You're right, Gordon, I don't want to cruise the strip checking out cheap hotels. I'm sure I can find something productive to do if you and Gil would like to have at it."

"Trust me, this is the part of investigative work that isn't fun, but somehow it always pays off. So we do it in spite of the drudgery. One last question to you, Gil—does Bob gamble at all? Based on what you've shared you'd think he was a monk, but I'm trained to ask."

Gil scratched his head, considering. "I do think he likes to play blackjack every now and again. I'm sure he counts cards and does it for the challenge, not the money. I recall he would sometimes hit the Indian casinos when we traveled, but it was never for a long time. He hated losing money."

"I suppose that complicates things, then, doesn't it?" Jim said, looking at Gordon for confirmation.

"It may make him easier to find, but it exposes him, which is a risk to his work. He must know that, and it may be the reason he compulsively backs things up. Except for the wager requirement, blackjack is the same in every casino. So would it be safe to assume that Bob would walk to a casino and find a table that had a one or two dollar minimum?"

"You say that as if you know him. That's exactly what he would do. And he would only stay as long as he was winning, or until they caught him counting cards," Gil said.

"My thinking here is that he found a casino he wanted to play at, then found a cheap hotel nearby. That could make things easier for us. Do you have a photograph of him, Jim?" Gordon asked.

"I do."

"Well, instead of running through parking lots, how about we flash his picture to the pit bosses at some of the casinos we know cater to low limit players?"

Both Jim and Gil smiled. "I think I would like that a little better," Jim answered. "At least it won't be so boring. Let's get started."

For the next several hours Jim drove around the perimeter of Las Vegas, stopping in at any gambling halls that they thought fit the criteria that might appeal to Bob. It was always easy to find the pit bosses; they were the ones standing behind the table games looking at every gambler with suspicion. Unfortunately, their efforts did not prove to be very successful. Either Bob had never darkened the doors of the casinos they checked, or the pit bosses were not of a frame of mind to rat out their customers. People minded their own business, and expected the same courtesy in return should anyone ask about them.

"I had no idea there were so many places to lose money in this town," Jim said as they pulled out of yet another parking lot. "Do you really think this is the best use of our time, Gordon?"

"You obviously are not much of a gambler, are you, Jim," Gordon replied.

"What do you mean? I play a mean hand of baccarat." Jim laughed.

"There are three shifts of pit bosses—sometimes four. What we don't know is when Bob even likes to play cards. Is he a morning, evening or middle of the night kind of player? We'll need to come back to all these establishments at least two, maybe three more times, to hit the pit bosses that might have seen him. And that doesn't even take into account the days they're not here. Can you shed any light on what Bob's habits are, Gil?"

Gil had spent his time looking at the various machines on the floor, which had changed a lot since he had last been in a casino. "I know Bob sleeps late. I doubt he ever begins his day before noon. My guess is that if he hits the tables, it's around midnight. He'd look at it as a reward for having researched all day. And then, keep in mind he wouldn't stay long. He couldn't bear drawing attention to himself. For him, it's not the money, it's the perfecting and the mastering of the process. He knows that if he's on target and wins consistently, they'd tag him. He'd never allow that to happen," Gil responded, with a slight sense of pride at having found a spot to be helpful.

"So what you're saying is that we are probably wasting our time looking for him late in the afternoon, and we might have a lot more success if we come back late tonight?" Jim asked.

Before anyone could respond, Gordon chimed in, "I called my guy at Metro and told him what we're looking for. They'll begin tonight, looking for any vehicle that looks like what you described, Gil. I think that'll be our best chance, but we need to keep doing what we're doing later tonight and hope we get lucky. In the meantime, let's find somewhere to eat. I'm starving."

"We passed a place called 'Flame Kabob' a few miles back. Let's check that out," Jim suggested. "If it's authentic Persian food, we'll have scored big time."

"Not tacos, huh?" asked Gil.

"Think of them as tacos on a stick. You'll be fine," said Gordon.

Their routine continued for several days. No word from Metro, no help from any pit bosses, and no sign of Bob's car. Discouragement was beginning to take hold. Max had not heard anything, and Las Vegas was far too big for them to keep this kind of search up for much longer. Jim had an extended conversation with Max, and the decision was made to fly back to Washington the following day. Gil wasn't sure D.C. was where he wanted to go. His home was in Chicago, and for some reason he felt he would be safer at home. Jim managed to convince him that his explanation of his research was vital to the president's plan. Gil acquiesced to Jim's pleadings, and all of them began making the necessary preparations to arrive at Andrews late the following evening. As darkness began to take hold and the lights of the Strip could be seen from their guest house north of downtown, Gordon received a call from his friend at Metro. A car fitting the description had been reported abandoned at an Extended Stay motel on the Boulder Highway. The police had not yet responded to the call, and wouldn't until Gordon had had a chance to check it out. The east end of Las Vegas was not a section of town they had spent any time canvassing. The three of them jumped in the car with hopes that this new tip would lead them to Bob.

When they arrived at the motel they spoke to the night manager, who didn't know anything about a police report, but he was aware that the car had been parked without moving for several weeks. While Jim and Gordon continued to question anyone associated with the property, Gil looked over the vehicle. He wasn't certain it was Bob's. It was covered in dust, and he could not see anything that he could associate with his friend. The license plate was from Nebraska, which had no connection to Bob as far as Gill knew.

"Well, do you think it's Bob's car?" Jim asked as he approached Gil.

"I can't say for sure. Did the manager have any idea who owned the car?"

"It isn't registered to anyone staying at the motel, nor do they have anyone with Bob's name staying here."

"That figures," said Gil. "He'd never use his real name to check into a place, even if he weren't trying to lay low. Max should've told you that."

Gordon approached them, still trying to size up the situation while taking mental notes of what he saw. "There's an Arizona Charlie's casino just up the block. Why don't you stay here, Gil, and keep looking for clues on this car. I'll see if I can get Metro to run theses plates for any possible connection. Why don't you, Jim, run over to that casino and see what you can find out in the gaming area? This doesn't look all that promising to me, but it's the only possibility we've had the whole time we've been here."

Gil and Jim concurred. While Gordon reached for his phone, Jim started the short walk to the casino. The scenario they had painted when they first arrived definitely fit the current situation; nevertheless Jim still felt the whole exercise was futile. He was starting to wonder if his decision to the help the president was making any difference. It had disrupted his life, and no end could be seen. He walked through the sliding doors of the casino and found himself in yet another gambling hall. By now they all looked alike, and he had no trouble knowing where to go to find the table games. It was as if he had developed a sixth sense which led directly to the roulette wheel where, for whatever reason, pit bosses liked to hang out.

As he approached the man who seemed to be in control, he reached into his shirt pocket and pulled out the photograph of Bob. He held it out in the direction of the pit boss, and before he could even say anything one of the dealers who was standing close by spoke up and said, "Are you looking for that guy?"

"Yeah, I am. Do you know him? Have you seen him?" Jim asked.

"He's in here almost every night for an hour. I haven't seen him in a few days. He only plays blackjack and he always seeks out my table. When I change tables, he often follows, so I've gotten to know him these past few months. He's good player and he's a great tipper. Is he in trouble? Are you a cop?"

Jim didn't answer the questions. Instead, he asked some of his own. "Do you recall his name? Was he always alone? And when exactly was the last time you saw him?"

The pit boss spoke up. "Only a cop would ask those kinds of questions." He then turned to the dealer and said, "Go ahead answer the man."

The dealer responded, "I never knew his name, but even if he had told it to me, no regular in this town uses his real name. You should know that. You must not be a cop. The last time I saw him was two nights ago. He was always alone, but that night he left with two other guys I had never seen before. Does that answer all your questions?"

Jim thought for a moment and then asked, "Had he won much money the last night you saw him?"

"He never won much money, but he almost always won. Every night. Like I said, he was good."

Jim thanked the men and hurried back to the motel parking lot where he had left Gordon and Gil. Gordon was on the phone, and Gil was feeling around behind the rear fender of the car for something. Jim waited for Gordon to finish, and then excitedly shared the information he had learned in the casino. "What have you found out?" he asked, looking at Gordon.

"The car is registered to a June Jefferies in Omaha. It hasn't been reported stolen, but it was given a ticket in Iowa a few months back. The ticket was issued to a Clark Newberg. He never responded to the complaint, and now there is a warrant out for his arrest in Des Moines. Does any of that ring a bell with you, Gil?"

"I've never heard of a Clark Newberg, but I do remember Bob mentioning something about an Aunt June. I don't know where she lives, or even if she's still alive. If the dealer saw him in that casino, then I'm pretty sure this is his car. So now what do we do?"

"We find him," replied Gordon. "Let me go speak with the motel clerk and see what more I can discover. I'll be right back."

Gordon walked over to the small office and waited until he and the desk clerk were the only ones present. He showed him Bob's picture again and asked if he had anyone registered under the name of Clark Newberg. The clerk shook his head no without even looking at the records.

That response didn't sit well with Gordon, and he pulled out his Secret Service badge and made certain the young man could see his gun holstered at his side. "Now I'm going to ask you again, and I'd better like the way you answer this time. No, on second thought, I want the full-time manager. He lives on the property, doesn't he?"

"Yeah, he lives here, but I can't bother him. You'll have to wait until morning when he comes on," responded the clerk.

"You aren't too bright, are you, son," shot back Gordon. "Do you even know what the Secret Service does?" Before the clerk could answer, Gordon explained it to him in the simplest terms. "I work directly for the President of the United States. If you don't call your manager and get his ass down here in five minutes, I'll arrest you for obstruction of justice and see to it you never see a neon light again in your lifetime. Do you understand me?"

The desk clerk's cooperation suddenly improved, and with a compelling sense of urgency he ordered the manager to appear in the office. The hotel manager was in the office in under three minutes, dressed in his bathrobe.

By now Jim and Gil had joined Gordon in the office, convinced that the car outside was Bob's. Gil had found a magnetic box attached to the wheel well. Inside the box were two flash drives. Gil was certain this was Bob's depository for his research. In Chicago, he had seen Bob go out to his car more than once every day, and reach back behind the rear wheel. Gil was never sure what was going on, but he had a pretty good idea. When he found the box, his suspicions were confirmed.

The manger was even more helpful. He told Gordon that a man matching Bob's description and going by the name Elliot Larson had checked into the motel about three weeks ago. He had a Nevada driver's license, but no vehicle, and paid for a month's rent in advance. He had thought that unusual, since most guests paid by the week. He informed them that Elliot was in room 206, and told them he would remain in the office in case they needed any more help.

Within moments all three men were standing in front of the door to room 206. No lights were on, and nothing could be heard emanating from the room. Gordon turned to Jim and asked, "Do you recognize that faint odor?"

"No, should I?"

"I know that smell," piped up Gil. "It's the smell of death."

Gordon shook his head. "Indeed it is. Gil, run down to the manager's office and have him give you a key to this room. If he gives you any static, tell him a drone is overhead awaiting orders to shoot."

Gil looked puzzled, but hurried off to do what he was asked. He returned without any problem. Gordon put the key in the lock, turned the handle and pushed the door open. The stench coming from the two-room apartment was overpowering. All three men covered their noses and mouths, hoping to block the odor. Jim looked at Gordon. The expression on his face signaled he was prepared for the worst. Jim reached in and turned on the light. There, leaning against the coffee table and partially slumped between it and the couch, was Bob's dead and rotting body.

The initial shock was more overpowering than the stench. They stood in the doorway, stunned to have to face their worst fear. Gordon was the first to enter, and he began to examine the body. Gil hung by the door, and Jim began looking through the room for any of Bob's computers and hard drives. The only thing he could find was a portable hard drive on the small table in the kitchenette. It sat on some papers, but there was no sign of any computer or cell phone.

"Do you think it was the guys who were after me?" Gil demanded to know.

"No, Gil, I don't. This was not a professional hit. This was done by thugs, and looks more like a robbery gone very badly."

"How can you say that? You know they had to be looking for him, just like they were looking for me. If my information was worth killing me for, from what I know of Bob's research, they must have sent twice the men and firepower to take care of him," Gil blurted out.

"If that were the case, Gil, they would have taken the hard drive," Jim said, holding it up for him to see. "Whoever killed him had no idea what this was, and so they left it here."

"Look at this." Gordon pointed to couch pillow with a bullet hole in it, and cotton batting around the entry wound on Bob's back. "You remember the gun those guys had in your ribs? It had a silencer on it, didn't it? If it were the same guys or some of their counterparts, they would have shot Bob execution-style with one slug to the back of the head. They would have known exactly what they were looking for, and would never have left without that hard drive."

"So what do you think happened?" Jim asked.

"Bob probably got caught in the middle of some small-time Las Vegas greed. I think those two guys the dealer saw him with realized Bob knew how to win at blackjack. They probably followed him back here and tried to persuade him to place bets for them so they could win big. When he refused to cooperate, they killed him, then stole anything they thought had some value. My guess is that he's been here for two days, and would have been here until the end of the month or until the stench forced someone to take notice."

"What now?" Gil said, still standing in the doorway.

"I hope you're right, Gil, about those flash drives. I say we head back to Nellis and search what is on them. No matter what we find, we fly back to D.C. as planned in the morning," Jim said.

"What about Bob?" Gil asked, beginning to feel the brute

force of his death and its accompanying helplessness.

"I'll call my friend at Metro and report it, but we'll leave it to them to investigate. If Max can give us any kind of next of kin information, we'll relay that, but otherwise we'll stay out of it and let them do their job. It's for the best. There's really nothing we can do, and we don't want to get caught up in the middle of a murder investigation."

The three of them agreed, and went back down to the manager's office to return the key. Gordon called Metro from the office, where the manager could overhear the details. He told them about the car in the parking lot, informed them about the dealer at Arizona Charlie's, and shared his opinion about what he thought might have occurred. The manager was definitely surprised, but it was not the first murder he had experienced on the property. He must have suspected some kind of trouble, because he had gotten dressed and was prepared for the arrival of the police.

On the drive back to Nellis, Jim called Vera. He hadn't spoken to her in a few days, and asked her to break the news of Bob's death to Max in person. Death was an event that hurt no matter the circumstance, the person involved, or the timing, Vera mused. Even though she had experienced more than her share of loss, news of it always deeply affected her. Death stole part of her soul, and she found that to be unbearable.

"Vera, can you share this information with the president when you get the chance?" Jim asked.

"He's sitting right here; you can tell him yourself." She handed the phone to Joel.

Jim explained to the president all that had occurred. They agreed that coming back to Washington would allow the members of the team to begin to compare notes. Not surprisingly, Joel was more concerned with finding Bob's family and helping them endure their loss. Towards the end of their conversation, the president ordered Jim to fly to Seattle to pick up Mari, and then fly back to Washington. He knew they hadn't seen each other for weeks, and they needed to spend time together. He also invited them to the upcoming state dinner, and assured Jim that members of his staff would assist Mari with all her needs so she would feel comfortable at such a prestigious event.

Jim thanked the president for his thoughtfulness. When they arrived back at the guest house, Gil immediately went to work exploring the flash drives. "This is a virtual gold mine."

eighteen

*M*ax met the Gulfstream when it touched down at Andrews. He warmly embraced Gil. "Nice to see you, kid. That taco habit saved your life, I guess. Gordon tells me your Spanish is pretty good. I wish Bob had been a glutton rather than a gambler. He might still be with us."

"It was horrible, Max. He died for absolutely nothing. International hit men were searching for him, and he was murdered by a couple of punks looking to score a few hundred bucks. How insane is that?" Gil replied.

Max put his arm around him. "You know how dirty this whole business is. It's the risk we take trying to nail these bastards. I'm just glad you're okay, and that you were able to help find Bob. They couldn't have done it without you. You're going to need to spend some serious time helping me dig into his work to determine everything that's there. It ain't over—not even close."

Gil nodded in agreement, then stepped back so Max could greet Jim. Max stood there on the tarmac looking at him, his hands on his hips. "You're one of us now, aren't you, buddy?"

"Afraid so," said Jim. "You sort of tried to warn me, but I must have been listening too fast. I'm just happy I was traveling with Gordon and not Vera. She wouldn't have liked this little adventure." Max smiled. "She's busy where she is, and I'm going to need her help finding Ruth Ann. So she ain't going to completely escape this circus."

"She'll be safe, Max, you must promise me that," Jim added.

"Is that Max Hager?" A woman's voice was heard from the

top of the stairs, just inside the jet.

Max looked up. He could see a woman's form, but the sun's glare prevented him from determining who she was. Max glanced at Jim with a grimace and asked, "You haven't recruited another dame, have you?"

"I signed on years ago in spite of old coots like you," the voice said, as the figure descended the stairs. "Maxwell Hager, I'm so glad you're alive—and ornery as ever." Mari rushed to give him a big hug. "When Jim told me you were still alive, it was like the sun came up twice that day. How are you?"

"Not wanting to let go of you, that's how I am." Max held her tight and winked at Jim over her shoulder. "It's good to see you two together for a change. With you here, I won't have to keep Jimbo on the straight and narrow anymore."

Mari laughed. "That's something I've never had to worry about in all the years we've been together, in spite of friends like you." That comment made Max laugh as he put his arms around them both and walked them towards the hangar. When they were safely inside, he turned back to find Gordon, who was following several paces behind. Max stopped and waited for him. He extended his hand and shook Gordon's. "You really are the best, aren't you?"

Gordon didn't respond.

"President Sherman told me why he sent you to keep an eye on Vera, and why he had you go with Jim. I've been briefed. I know what you did. And I can't thank you enough. We would've lost Gil and all of Bob's research had it not been for you. And that little lady there probably would have arrived this morning to greet the casket of her husband, had you not lived up to your reputation."

Gordon could only muster, "You're welcome, sir." And then after a moment, "How is President Sherman?"

"In love, I'm afraid, and I'm not sure even you can protect

him from the effects of that threat."

"Why would I want to? She might be the best thing that ever happened to him—and this country," Gordon softly replied.

"To be honest, I think that's why the president had Mari come out. He's smart enough to know that girls need their friends at a time like this. And it must be getting close."

Again, Gordon didn't say anything.

On the ride back to Blair House, the old friends caught up with all that had passed in their absence. Gil and Gordon both leaned back in the comfortable limousine seats and tried hard to doze off, in between Max's infectious laughs.

nineteen

*L*ater that evening Max called Vera, and asked if she would come to Blair House the following morning. He wanted her to help him to find Ruth Ann, the final member of the group. Of course, Vera was anxious to do whatever she could to help. She missed working hand in hand with Jim. Joel had been filling her in on all the details, and even though there had been an increased element of danger, she still wanted to do her part to help bring her country back to the nation she once knew. The events of the past year had dampened her sense of fear and strengthened her resolve to make the hard choices, and if necessary, to offer the ultimate sacrifice. Her time in the White House, though magical, left a lingering desire in her. She wanted to fight for those whom she had lost and to stand up on behalf of the citizens whose country the White House represented.

"Make it a breakfast meeting and invite Mari, and I'll be there," she said, happy to once again be included.

"All right, kiddo, you got a deal. See you at eight o'clock," Max said.

While Vera and Joel were at dinner that evening, she mentioned the meeting with Max in the morning.

"What is it he wants to involve you in?" the president asked.

"I'm not really certain, but I think it has to do with finding Ruth Ann and getting her information. I'm sure it's just something minor that he and Jim felt I would be good at."

"Surely you're aware of the dangers associated with helping those guys. Bob was killed, and Gil had a very close call in Fernley.

I'm not sure getting too involved with them is the best idea."

"Oh, you can't possibly be serious, can you?" Vera asked. "I've been chased by those guys in the black Suburban, I've had my best girlfriend murdered, my husband killed, my dog nearly run over, and my house broken into. Helping Max with something can't possibly compare to that," she said, almost wanting to laugh.

"It's not that I think you can't handle anything Max throws at you. It's just that I know how unpredictable these types of operations can be, and I prefer that you be safe, that's all."

It was obvious to Vera that Joel was holding something back. It had been a long time since anyone cared enough about her to express this type of concern. She had learned that Joel was someone who allowed others to make their own choice without his influence. He would express what he thought were correct ideas, but allowed others the freedom to choose. Governing, to him, was not a matter of compulsion, but a matter of teaching correct principles. He knew peoples' loyalty was at its most focused when they were trusted to make the right decision. In spite of understanding that about him, Vera could feel his love for her expressed in his desire to keep her safe. Reaching out her hand, she placed it over his. She looked into his eyes and confirmed what she was feeling to be correct.

Joel glanced down to avoid prolonged eye contact with her. His heart was speaking for him, and he could not bear the thought of something happening to her. If ever he wanted to pull rank and make the decision for her, now was the time, but looking away prevented him from making that mistake.

She knew exactly what he meant, and rather than allow it to offend her, she leaned over and kissed him on the cheek. That demonstration of pure understanding calmed the anxiety in him, and he returned his eyes to hers. He could feel a sense of unity begin to weave them together.

The dinner that had been served no longer held much

interest for either of them. Both pretended to return to dining, but it was clearly an exercise of moving food around a plate, as neither wanted to disrupt the magic. The servants were graciously dismissed from the dining room, and the president and Vera were left alone in silence. The head steward had the foresight to dim the lights as he returned to the kitchen, and even Mike knew it was best if he too retired to his quarters.

Vera could feel something stirring inside of her. She recognized emotions that had been neatly folded away for safekeeping, which now were beginning to come to the surface as she felt more secure. Vera was at a loss for words; all she could do was smile. Joel soaked in the smiles and found his own private reservoir into which to store them. It had been empty since his wife died, and though he had felt Vera's tug on his heart, he too had been on guard to keep it safe. After moments of hush interrupted by tender touches, Joel suggested they retire to the residence. They both wanted to talk, but neither was in a hurry to dispel the emotions that had long been missing in their lives. They left the dining room arm in arm, and strolled to the elevator to make their way upstairs to a place that was beginning to feel a lot like home to Vera.

The past several evenings had been spent casually talking and sharing stories from their lives. They had far more in common than either of them had suspected. Hard work had been instilled in them both from an early age, and love of country was as natural as the love they shared for their family members. Events from their lives also had many intersecting aspects which made it easy to establish a common foundation from which to build. Their love of flying and the freedom that they felt in the air fueled their love of travel. Language, culture, and people were also interests that they jointly shared. The most unifying factor in all their conversations was how they were able to share their feelings about the loss of their beloved spouses. Both had been murdered in violent ways by evil, which caused Vera and Joel to have to come to grips with their loss on two distinct levels. Vera had never opened up about how she felt regarding Jeff's death, and Joel's loss was still so fresh that he found Vera's sojourn through sorrow both instructive and comforting. As their talk progressed, the depth of their feelings for one another began to take on a new dimension which neither could deny. Only recently had those feelings been brought to the surface in such a way that both recognized them as love. Tonight's expression was like opening a gift whose content was known, but whose magnificence far surpassed all expectations.

"The night you came up here for the first time, and found out that I was Stan the Man, what went through your head?" Joel asked. He had wanted to know the answer to that question for a long time.

"That whole experience was so dumbfounding that at first I thought, 'well of course he's the President of the United States, and I'm Cinderella, whose job it is to keep the story moving along.' After I got into bed and had time to reflect on all the Facebook conversations we'd had, I remembered what a gentleman you were and how thoughtful of me you had been throughout my ordeals. I think you didn't want me to know you as the president but wanted me to know the Joel in you. You succeeded at that, but when I found out who you really were, my thoughts turned to 'why me?' And to some extent, I still wonder that. Of all the women in the world, it's me you care about, and that's rather humbling. So why me?"

"I wanted your dog."

Vera laughed. "You obviously got what you wanted," she said, looking at Kelli nestled in a ball near Joel's feet. "It wasn't even very hard; she clearly wanted you too."

"At first I was acting only on Jim's suggestion that I reach out to you. Obviously, you came highly recommended. My intentions were pure, and my thought was to be able to report back to Jim that I'd followed his advice. But you changed all that. You were me, in so many ways, and so I felt at home with you. I know myself well enough to realize that that was something I needed. It surprised me. No, it shocked me. I honestly did not think it was possible, especially in my current position. I thought that if anyone was ever going to be a part of my life again, it would occur after I had left this office and retired to the other Washington. I'm more curious about you. Jeff has been gone for some time now. Have you never thought about sharing your life again?"

Vera rarely felt comfortable discussing her plans for the future, even with her closest girlfriends. She never wanted their advice, which was the only reason they were interested in having the conversation with her in the first place. She had become adept at avoiding their questions and circumventing their conversational traps. Joel's question didn't feel like a threat to her, yet she hesitated about answering. Part of her didn't know the answer, and the other part felt content to remain in Jeff's shadow.

"I think I've become a survivor by choice. Survivors tend not to share. I mean, I'm a giving person; it's just that I've not wanted to share me with anyone. Does that make sense?" Vera asked.

"I think that became apparent very early on in our Facebook conversations. I was in a position to help you, and yet everything I did or tried to do for you occurred in secret, not because I didn't want you to know, but rather because I knew you had a desire to be independent. So I helped you and kept silent. Now, was that wrong of me?"

"I have come to realize that most of what has happened to me this last year, I couldn't have survived without you. I chose to help Jim. I chose to voice my opinions in meetings I had no real business being invited to. I chose to retire from the airline. I chose to send Kelli here. I chose to follow her. Do you see the common denominator in all of this? You! I haven't really admitted that to myself until right now, but deep down I know that being around you has been good for me, and so I choose to be here."

Joel leaned forward, knowing what he was about to say was going to take his breath away, and he wanted to preserve it for as long as possible. "When you voiced your opinion in that meeting in the Oval Office, amongst strangers whose job it is to lead this country, and having no idea how your thoughts and feelings would be received, I fell in love with you. If you recall, I started to clap. It wasn't so much for what you said, though I agreed with all of it. I began to clap because you had captured my heart, and I didn't think that was possible. From that moment you have been the dominant focus of my thoughts. In order to conduct the business of this country, I have to quietly usher you from my mind. When the time comes to invite you back in, I'm consumed by you. I wanted you to come here, but I could never have asked you to do that. I doubt you would have agreed to come. I knew if I could get Kelli here you would soon follow. The fact that Kelli and I have hit it off so well was just a bonus. But you being here in this house with me has made my life pleasurable again. And I thank God every morning and every night that I have been able to spend one more day with you."

Vera sat silently for several moments. She was digesting what she had heard, and trying to put it into perspective with how she was feeling. "You're right; I wouldn't have come had you just asked me. I would have seen no purpose in doing so, and would have felt that I was intruding and preventing you from carrying out your responsibilities. So in a sense, you kind of tricked me, didn't you?"

Joel nodded.

Vera moved closer to him so she could touch him, and he could hear her more easily. Her voice softened to a whisper. "You did the right thing. I needed to be with you, and I couldn't have known that unless I spent some time being with you in your world, in your home, and in your heart." She put her arms around his neck and hugged him tightly.

Joel did not want to let go. It felt so good to him to hold the woman he loved. When their embrace began to release he tilted his head slightly and kissed her gently on the lips. Gently was not sufficient for Vera. Her passion focused inward towards his soul, and her lips conveyed the message.

Joel was surprised by Vera's response, but the shock wore off quickly, since the emotions of the moment were everything they both had felt, but had been so reticent in expressing. He questioned what he should do or say next. Eventually he stood up and walked slowly into the study. Vera eyes followed him. He had no business there; he just needed to remove himself from the intensity that had overwhelmed him. He paused for a few moments, then returned to the great room and sat down again beside Vera.

"Is anything wrong?" she asked.

"Absolutely not. It could not be more perfect. My heart is where I have wanted it to be; I'm just not certain what to do next."

"Joel, follow your heart."

"In that case, Vera, I would like to ask you to marry me."

Neither one of them could believe what had just come out of the president's mouth. Joel had always imagined that when this moment arrived, he would be far away from the White House and all of the problems it brought. Vera had never thought such a moment would ever arrive, and her Cinderella feelings were beginning to make a comeback. In spite of the surprise his words had been to them both, neither wanted them withdrawn.

Vera took Joel by both hands and looked into his eyes. "There are a hundred reasons I should say no to you. All of them on good legitimate grounds that make perfect sense and could not be refuted by anyone with a brain, but there is only one simple reason I should say yes."

"And what might that reason be?" Joel asked, feeling slightly insecure.

"I love you, and that means I don't want to be away from you. So yes, I will marry you."

The smile on Joel's face could be felt. He grabbed Vera and hugged her so tightly she was afraid to even attempt to breathe. When he finally released her, she had so many questions running through her head she didn't know where to begin. Before she could even formulate the first one, Joel looked at her and said, "Ask; I know they are in there. Ask and we'll decide together."

He did know her. He knew her thoughts and her feelings. He honored them and respected them, and she loved him for it. "How and when do we tell the world? May I just step out onto the balcony and shout it to all the tourists, and let them disseminate it to the media?" she asked, laughing and feigning a move to the balcony door.

"If it's okay with you, I would like to formally propose to you at the state dinner for Finland. Many of your friends will be there, and of course the media will have a field day with it, if it catches them by surprise."

"Oh, I think that would be so much fun. My new gown is perfect for such a splendid surprise. Now, what shall we do until then? Just let it be our little secret?" she wondered aloud.

"That works for me if it works for you. Are you suggesting we tell no one?" Joel asked.

"Yes, let's keep it our secret and enjoy it while we can. Mike will probably figure it out immediately, but he can be sworn to secrecy, can he not?"

"Mike would be your maid of honor if you asked him. We'll have no problems with him."

"Oh, I am so excited!" Vera exclaimed. "I love secrets, especially really good ones that will surprise the world. Of course, I don't care if we get married in your study under the big red S, but we can make plans as time moves along." Her thoughts seemed to leave her as she jumped into his arms to kiss him again.

twenty

Vera arrived late for the meeting with Max at Blair House the following morning. Mari greeted her as she entered the grand foyer. After a quick embrace, Mari said, "Oh I've been so excited to see you. Ever since President Sherman insisted that Jim bring me back here for the state dinner, I couldn't wait to see your gown and have you help me with mine. This sort of thing is all new to me and I'm not sure where to begin."

Vera's smile was radiant as she replied, "I don't really know what I'm doing either. Fortunately, Joel has given me more help than I could ever ask for. They all know the ropes and protocols for every event and I'm sure they wouldn't mind lending advice and a hand if you need it. In fact, I'll see to that if you'd like."

"That would be much appreciated. You no longer sound like a guest over there. Is there anything I should know?" Mari asked.

Vera's smile shifted from radiant to incriminating, "Oh, we'll talk later. Then you can return the favor and let me lean on you for a while. I'm late for my meeting with the guys so you'll have to excuse me. It's so good to see you, Mari, come over and see me anytime. Just ask for Jan and she'll clear you through security."

Mari knew Vera well enough to know that something definitely was up with her. It didn't take long for her mind to process all she had just seen and heard. Combine that with a dose of feminine intuition and Mari quickly surmised that wedding bells were ringing in the background. But like a good friend her thoughts were muted and her suspicions were safe, even from Jim.

Vera was greeted by both Max and Jim as she entered the conference room on the second floor. She was quickly introduced to Gil and was glad to shake hands with Gordon again. She always smiled inside when she reflected back to her time in Paris when she mistook Gordon for someone who had been assigned to kill her. Now that they were friends, every encounter was fraught with a touch of humor. Being the consummate professional that he always was, Gordon never let his smile show, but inside, Vera had become one of his favorite memories and would no doubt be the subject of many joyful anecdotes when he retired. Of course, had he been as perceptive as Mari, he would have known that such stories were about to take on a whole new arena of significance.

Vera sat down and started looking through the briefing materials. Jim had brought her up to date through the many phone calls he had made. Several new details that tied things together were included in the briefing packet.

"I suppose I could read this information for the rest of the day to get a clearer understanding of what happened in Nevada, but I think it would be more helpful if you just shared with me the salient points and let me ask questions as we go," Vera said.

Max leaned back in his chair and placed his hands behind his head. Part of him wanted to put his feet up on the table, but he resisted the urge. "You've been an instrumental part, my dear, in making all this happen. The purpose of this meeting today is to share with all of you some of what has been discovered. I'm going to say this once; the government of the United States has a lot of explaining to do. They have covered up, altered, buried, white washed, and denied access to critical information about 9/11. Fortunately, we're beginning to get a more clear idea what it is we are looking for. So let me tell you what I have decoded so far from Bob's files."

"To those of us that knew Bob, it comes as no surprise that

he's taken thousands of documents and placed them into files, they seem to be organized until you open them. All the files were identified by codenames that only made sense to Bob. It's going to be time consuming to figure out exactly what he knew."

Max opened his laptop, while everyone in the meeting found a seat. "Seems Bob found some very interesting connections to both people and corporations involved in 9/11. The connections back to the state of Massachusetts are particularly beyond coincidence. For starters, there's a file labeled: MASSMESS. There are some real interesting details surrounding the FAA administrator. Prior to her taking that top position at the FAA, she'd been the director at Boston's Logan International Airport."

"The FAA administrator would have known that Logan International didn't have security cameras installed in the passenger terminal. I'm familiar with the required security plan that must be filed annually with the FAA Administrator. If there were no cameras installed, it would be on that report." Jim added.

"Exactly, Jim, that made Logan the perfect place to begin this deception. Obviously there were no photographs of suspected hijackers or passengers on either of those planes. That adds a real element of mystery doesn't it? With no photographs, they can claim anyone was the hijacker. And with no video, we don't actually know who was on those planes other than the working crew members."

Vera piped up, "I must have flown out of Boston a hundred times and I always assumed there were security cameras because they were in every other airport across the country. If I had known that, I wouldn't have flown out of there."

Max continued reading the file, "I found some information on her husband attached to one of her bios. I was particularly disturbed by the fact that as Sheriff of one of the counties that surrounds Westover, he had total control over of all the information that flowed through the Sheriffs' office. For example, had a report come in about a commercial airliner landing at Westover, he could have buried it. In addition, he was responsible for securing the perimeter around Westover. It seems a little odd to me that a military base that size was unable to protect its own boundaries."

Jim was thinking and spoke out loud. "Even more troubling to me was that the reserve unit based at Westover was locked out that morning. Why would you evacuate a military base, call up a reserve unit, lock them out and then have the local Sheriffs secure the base?"

Max continued. "There's a file called CALLOG, it's full of details I've never read before. On United 175, there were only two phone calls made. Peter Hanson made one of those calls, you remember airline hostess Peter. He told his dad that the hijackers were going to fly the plane to Chicago and into a building. Now, do you really think that Arabic speaking hijackers are going to come to the back row of the plane and in their broken English tell a passenger that? According to the government story, at the time he called his dad, the plane was only seven thousand feet over the Hudson River, which means he could have looked at the window and seen the Statue of Liberty, but Peter thinks he is on his way to Chicago."

Jim interrupted, "We know where those planes were, so who was telling him what to say? Peter couldn't have come up with that story on his own. At that point in history, nobody would have dreamt of deliberately flying a commercial airliner into a skyscraper."

Max looked up from his computer, "Let me tell you something else about this Peter Hanson. He was a vice president of a company called Time Trade in Waltham, Massachusetts. This company is a large government contractor working with Department of Defense, Department of Health and Human Services, Department of Homeland Security, and the Department of Veterans Affairs. And interesting enough, its government contracts have doubled since 2001."

Jim added, "That's exactly like the other caller from Flight 175, the young Navy pilot and MITRE employee that didn't recognize he was over New York, three minutes from impact. In fact, he told his mother he was over Ohio, now how could any pilot make that mistake? What more proof do we need that these two were not on whatever it was that hit the South Tower?"

Max joined in, "Now is that the guy that his friends said he could kill any human being with his bare hands?

Jim nodded.

Max said, "Well then, it gets better. He told his mom that a group of passengers were going to take over the cockpit. Anyone besides me smell something fishy?"

Vera stood up, "Max, you don't suppose these two men were somehow a part of this do you?"

"That's anyone's guess, Vera but you have to question how these two guys, coincidently both employed by companies that work directly with the department of defense and homeland security, knew specific details about the entire day's events.

Vera added, "I find it odd that he was giving the Flight 93 scenario of 'Let's roll' any flight attendant will tell you that's never going to happen especially on a hijacked flight. Flight attendants have protocols to follow and they are not going to allow passenger to interfere. And you have to ask yourself, if these two guys could easily make phone calls, Why didn't any of the other sixty some passengers and crew members make a phone call? That makes no sense at all to me. Max, you are right, this really stinks!"

Jim joined the conversation, "That Navy pilot on Flight 175 was actually an RIO, a radar intercept officer."

Gordon had been quietly listening, "Did you say a radar intercept officer, Jim?"

Jim's own words ricocheted back to him, "Yes, I said radar

intercept officer."

Max added, "Mighty convenient to have someone that was trained in that field when you have this type of charade playing out. Missiles and military drones don't have transponders, somebody would need to make them look like the commercial aircraft on radar screens. The real planes would have disappeared once the flight termination system took over. Someone would be needed to create a different radar picture."

Jim interjected, "Flight 175 also had two professional hockey players onboard." I can't believe they would've just sat there helpless if there really was a hijacker, especially if it was a small, five foot six guy holding a plastic box cutter. I've had hockey teams onboard and any one of them could have easily stopped a hijacker."

Vera nodded in agreement, "Professional hockey players were the worst. They wouldn't take no for an answer and nobody could tell them what to do."

Max continued opening files from the external hard drive. The codenamed WTHFAA caught his attention. He clicked it open. "Hold on folks, you're not going to believe this. That FAA administrator, guess what she's doing now?" Before anyone in the room could answer, Max started reading: "She's now on the Board of Trustees for the MITRE Corporation. She's also on the Board of Directors for United Continental Holdings, the parent company of United Airlines! That's too unreal to even comprehend."

Jim walked over to take a look at Max's computer screen, "That's not funny, are you serious?"

"Dead serious Jim, take a look at these documents."

Jim stood over Max's shoulder reading the screen. "Well, what are we going to find next?"

Max smiled, "It's hard to say Jim, the more files I open, the more appalled I become. And I plan to keep digging."

Vera said, Let me tell you what I found about the passenger that called from Flight 77. She has a very interesting background. After college, she went to work in Hollywood, but for the life of me, I couldn't find out what she did other than work for Stacy Keach at HBO. Ten years in the film industry must have been enough, and she enrolled in law school. Now her wealthy father could have paid for that but he didn't."

Gil asked, "Where did she go to law school?"

"The Benjamin Cardoza Law School at Yeshiva University." Vera replied.

"A Jewish school?" Gil asked. "Was she Jewish?"

"Her maiden name was Jewish, so we might assume that's why she chose that particular law school. Right out of law school, she went to Washington D.C. and landed an incredible job with a prestigious law firm. Then she became an assistant Attorney General. And finally she became a conservative commentator on CNN, which makes no sense coming out of liberal Hollywood, and a Jewish law school. And the icing on the cake, she soon married her husband Ted Olson, Solicitor General of the United States."

Vera continued, "Her husband also has a few rather interesting details in his background. He was the attorney that represented Jonathan Pollard, the Israeli spy in the mid-eighties. He also represented George W. Bush in the Bush vs Gore battle for the 2000 presidential election. And, he will probably go down in history for having the strangest reaction of any spouse ever, after hearing that his wife's plane had crashed. He immediately called CNN and did an interview. Of course the details he gave had to change several times to fit the facts. So in short, what we have with this woman and her husband is a connection to Hollywood, Israeli Mossad, an Israeli spy, the media and the United States government."

Gil added, "Well, if it wasn't for her, we'd never have known the hijackers used box cutters. I think she was the only person to report that detail, wasn't she?"

Max answered, "I do believe she was and since that detail came from a television reporter, it was the story the entire world bought."

Gil was searching through this laptop, "I have an interesting paper here, it's a Chronology from the FAA headquarters. At 8:25 on Flight 11, an intruder entered the cockpit saying, 'Don't move or I'll kill you.'" Gil broke out laughing joined by Max and the others.

Max managed to stop laughing long enough to say, "Oh, I can see I'm not the only one with a visual of some scrawny little guy bursting into the cockpit holding a yellow plastic box cutter and saying that."

Jim was shaking his head, "No kidding, you want to know how fast one of those military trained pilots would have grabbed the crash axe and taught that lunatic a good hard lesson? I discovered some rather interesting details about the heroes on Flight 93. The media built them up to be the 'let's roll' heroes, but their actions don't fit the story. They were all six foot one to six foot four inches tall and over 220 pounds. All of them were very athletic, according to their obituaries and comments made about each of them. The first one was a college rugby player and the team captain. He was six foot two, and a champion black belt in judo. He sat on the phone with his wife for over twenty minutes telling her he loved her and asking her what he should do. His brother-in-law claimed he was a real 'take charge' kind of guy, but that doesn't jive with cowering in his seat talking on the phone. If you look at the FAA radar data, it claims the plane was falling out of the sky at a rapid rate, some six to ten thousand feet per minute, yet oddly, he never mentions that the plane was descending. What he did say is that one of the hijackers was Iranian. How would he know the hijacker was Iranian? Looks like someone wanted to blame Iran for this. There's more here about those athletic passengers who could have easily taken care of those diminutive hijackers, but chose to do nothing. Another one of them was a Physical Education major in college, and he wanted to play professional baseball. His friends said he was a super athlete and extremely competitive. He worked for Oracle and there's an interesting side note here about his boss, the CEO of Oracle, who somehow knew hours before the FBI made public the 'Let's roll' hero story and sent the details out in an email to all Oracle employees."

Jerry Reitz spoke, "That's very telling. How would he have known?"

Max smiled at Jerry as he added, "I remember looking into that one. He had been in Rome for a week and his wife claimed that he was nervous about returning to work, for some reason. He had been in Israel right before the trip to Rome. The story goes, he tried to call his wife from the plane, but couldn't connect, so he dialed the GTE operator and told her he's on a hijacked plane and couldn't connect to his wife's phone. Here's this super competitive athlete who cowered in fear and turned down the operator's offer to connect him to his wife. He's on a plane and about to lose his life, and he chose to pray with a perfect stranger. Why would anyone do that? He claimed that he didn't want to upset his wife, and yet he tried to call her first."

"Maybe he thought his wife knew him well enough to detect the fact he really wasn't onboard a hijacked plane but parked somewhere in a hangar or..." Vera's words slowed.

"Or he wasn't even in the hangar at Westover, but somewhere else following instructions." Jim suggested.

Max smiled, "Anything is possible now that we know the planes were remotely hijacked and there were no Arab hijackers onboard. It looks like there were a few handlers who instructed designated callers as to what to say. Some of whom got a little nervous and blew their lines, forgetting which plane they were supposed to be on. That would explain why the passenger's stories didn't match what the government said the planes were doing. This other passenger, the guy that was so nervous he used both his first and last names as if his own mother couldn't recognize his voice was a super athlete. He was six foot four, over two hundred pounds and he played college rugby. He was still an active player, so he was in great shape. He fought off a mugger with his bare hands, in the Bay Area, that pulled a gun him. Besides these guys, there were several other passengers that could have done something, a weight lifter, a federal law enforcement officer and a paratrooper who was a red belt in martial arts."

Gil stood up to get everyone's attention, "Here in the FAA Chronology, on Flight 11, it says at the 8:44 mark, a passenger was shot. But, only the two flight attendants phoned in, and neither of them reported gunshots. Why in the world did someone at the FAA headquarters come up with that story?"

Vera added, "Those were all big men, I remember in the days, weeks and months following 9/11, nearly every big guy that walked through the boarding door would say to me, 'if anyone gives you any trouble come and get me, I'll straighten them out.' That's human nature, and I'm sure that attitude prevailed onboard all four of those jets. The handlers had to have had guns. Tom Burnett on Flight 93, reported there was a gun onboard. It feels to me like there were a lot of details out of sync."

Max said, "More oddities about Beamer's phone call, the GTE operator he was talking with said that after his historic 'let's roll' announcement, he didn't hang up the phone. She listened for at least fifteen more minutes and never lost the connection. The operator told the FBI that the line just went silent and didn't register the disconnect tone."

Vera asked, "Now how is that possible? How could the call have remained connected after the plane crashed? According to the summary of passenger phone calls presented at the Moussaoui trial, his call lasted 3,925 seconds, that's sixty five minutes, which means that the phone call didn't end until 10:49 a.m. Flight 93 supposedly crashed about five minutes after ten that morning."

Max looked at his watch, "Just one more file and then let's get on with our day. This was coded GUNSMK, and could explain how a gun got onboard. The security at all three airports was handled by an Israeli company called ICTS, and its subsidiary Huntleigh USA. They were hired by both airlines involved to handle their passenger screening and general security. The company was founded by an Israeli who had been convicted of fraud for falsifying documents. Most of the employees were ex-Shin Bet agents, they're Israel's equivalent to our Homeland Security. Many of their top management link back to Israel's Mossad. This same company ran security at Charles De Gaulle in Paris, where the tennis shoe bomber boarded, and at Amsterdam's Schipol airport where the underwear bomber was allowed to board without a passport. So far this company is leaving me unimpressed. But, if anyone could get a gun onboard an airplane, it would be the company in charge of security. They obviously knew there were no cameras in the terminal at Logan and would have had ramp access to the planes. That's one explanation for how the bombs, box cutters, knives, mace, pepper spray, and guns got onboard. They had to have had a gun on each flight to control the passengers and crew after they landed at Westover. There were too many men on those flights that would have fought back. A gun is the only way the handlers could have forced those flight attendants to make those phone calls."

"This was before the TSA and Homeland Security and I remember Huntleigh handled security all over the country." Jim added. "I never realized they were foreign owned, that seems a bit risky to put security in the hands of a foreign government. If these guys behind ICTS were ex-Shin Bet and Mossad agents, then we essentially handed our airport security over to someone who could have…" Jim's words slowed as he continued, "Could have planted guns onboard and hijacked those planes."

Max was still searching the GUNSMK file when he slapped his hand loudly against his knee and shouted, "Well ain't this something, you're not going to believe this detail Bob tagged in here. Guess who now sits on the board of directors of ICTS security?" Without allowing anyone to answer, Max blurted out, "None other than the former Secretary of Transportation at the time of the attacks. Remember he was with Cheney when a young marine came into the bunker and reported: 'the plane is five miles out, does your order still stand?' A few moments later they learned a plane had struck the Pentagon."

The room hushed. Nobody knew what to say. The Secretary of Transportation was now on the Board of Directors with the security company that failed to keep America safe in three major airports. Why would he want to associate himself with a foreign owned company that allowed nearly three thousand people to be murdered?

twenty one

*T*he state dinner with President Jarmo Kekkunen and his wife was rapidly approaching. The Finnish Ambassador to the United States had been in careful planning with the White House for weeks. Invitations had been sent to members of both the House and Senate, a few of the Supreme Court justices, several Cabinet members, and prominent citizens throughout the country, many of whom were of Finnish ancestry or who had business dealings with Finland. The Finnish Embassy was given a number of invitations, and they too were able to select guests from amongst their countrymen and associates. Ordinarily the media was excluded from a state dinner, or at least that had been the policy of the Sherman White House. On this occasion, at the last minute President Sherman had his press office invite a pool reporter from USA Today, along with a cameraman and a videographer. The press secretary tried very diligently to have the president explain the change in protocol, but she was met with both silence and total disregard.

Vera took Mari shopping at Niemen Marcus, where she had developed a wonderful rapport with the women in the formal gown department. All of Washington was abuzz at the length of time Vera had been a guest at the White House. Apparently, it had leaked that she was to be the president's date at the upcoming dinner, and so when she made an appointment to bring Mari to Niemen Marcus, not only were the sales staff curious, but an ample number of paparazzi were also present, which neither of the women had ever experienced before.

"Wait until I tell Max what happens when I come here with you instead of him," Vera whispered into Mari's ear as they skirted past the photographers.

"You probably won't have to tell him, if he reads the papers or watches television," replied Mari. "I take it you didn't get this much attention last time you were here."

"Not exactly. They had no idea who I was, and they only thought it was nice that a working widow from Seattle had been invited to the ball. Guess that's all changed, hasn't it?"

Again, Mari had an opportunity to ask something, but figured now was not the appropriate time. Instead she graciously took a back seat to Vera, and was introduced to the overanxious attendants, who had multiplied in number from the last time Vera was there. Mari selected a beautiful gown, and the seamstress promised her that it would be delivered to Blair House first thing in the morning. On the ride back to the residences, sitting in the far back seat of the limousine, Mari thought it was time to ask the question that had been quietly pushed aside on previous occasions.

"I could be delicate about this, but my curiosity wouldn't be satisfied with just a smile and a nod. Are you and Joel planning on getting married sometime soon?" Mari asked.

"With the reception we received downtown just now, you would think it was happening later tonight," Vera answered.

"Was that a yes?" Mari asked.

"Mari, Joel asked me to be his wife two nights ago. No one knows officially, so you have to be sworn to secrecy."

The squeal that emanated from the back seat fortunately was muffled into silence by the window separating the driver from the women. "Oh, I knew it, I just knew it! You couldn't hide it from me. It was all over your face the next morning when you walked through the door at Blair House. You were a Vera I'd never seen before, radiant from the inside out. If you're trying to keep this a secret you'd best stay indoors, in the dark, and away from people. So when is this going to happen? Tell me everything."

"We haven't planned it all out yet. I promise you, it won't be anything huge and fancy. That is not either of our styles. All I know at this point is that Joel is going to formally propose to me at the state dinner, and then the world will know."

"Oh, how exciting! That must have been why he wanted Jim to come and get me. That is just so romantic," Mari gushed.

"To be honest, I don't think he had even asked me yet when he told Jim to go collect you, but I'm thrilled he did. That is so like him, though. He just knows what I need and makes it happen," Vera said.

"That's what we always loved about him, and why Jim suggested he become acquainted with you. You know it wasn't easy. It's difficult to push very hard on a president. Jim told him he couldn't spend the rest of his time in office being a Mica martyr. I doubt that went over very well with him, but a few days later he called Jim back and asked what would be the best way to get in touch with you. I guess that's when 'Stan the Man' was born." Mari looked over at Vera. "There's that glow again. You really should do something about that, like elope." She laughed.

"Can a president elope?" Vera asked. "I mean, with all that Secret Service protection and responsibility, we could probably only get as far as the East Lawn. But I like the idea anyway. I'll see what Joel thinks."

"The media would go crazy if you pulled that on them. I know they are pretty much good for nothing when it comes to news, but they do their best work at special events, and believe me, having a sitting president get married is a big deal. Besides, the whole country should share in your happiness. I just hope you plan time for a honeymoon, without any media," commented Mari.

The days leading up to the dinner were exciting for Vera. She was asked her opinion on décor and flower arrangements, and even the menu was presented to her for her approval. In many ways she was being treated like a First Lady, and she thought her fiancé just might have had something to do with that. She knew he hadn't told a soul, as was their agreement, but Joel had a way of preparing people for forthcoming events that was unique to his personality. Vera was beginning to recognize it as one of his trademarks, and she liked it.

On the day of the event Vera asked two of her assistants to go to Blair House to help Mari prepare. It was a real treat for her friend to have someone to do her hair and makeup. Vera spent most of the afternoon preparing. As excited as she was for the dinner, her formal engagement to Joel meant far more, and she wanted to look perfect. The staff could sense something different about her aura and did everything they could to accentuate her radiance and beauty. Joel worked a full day before returning to the residence to shower and dress. Of course, as suspected, Mike knew without having to be told what this night meant to his friend. He had taken the opportunity earlier to ask the president if he could help with the procurement of the engagement ring. Joel tried to act surprised, since he had not said a word to Mike about the engagement; nevertheless, such anticipation had become second nature to both of them over the years. The president instructed Mike as to exactly what he wanted and where to obtain the ring to be presented that night.

"Well, how do I look?" the president asked.

"Of all the times I have helped you dress for formal occasions, I must say that tonight you are at your finest. I might add, sir, that I'm very excited for you," Mike replied, almost wanting to salute.

"And the ring, Mike? You have taken care of that, I'm sure."

"Yes sir, it is spectacular," Mike said as he presented the ring box to Joel.

The president opened the box for the very first time. He

gazed at the ring and held it up to the light. He wanted to take it out of the box, but could not bring himself to risk moving it from its perfect position. "Mike, it's extraordinary. I hope she likes it as much as I do."

"Could there be any doubt, sir? The woman is in love with you. She has been dancing around here ever since you proposed, and there hasn't been any music playing. She will adore it, sir."

"Very well, let's go see if the lady's ready," Joel said.

Vera was indeed ready, waiting serenely in the sitting room for her escort, accompanied by several staff. When the president appeared her assistants politely made their exits, which left him and Vera standing alone, gazing at one another. Words should have been spoken, but none were. Both of them were awestruck at the other's radiant appearance. The president offered his arm, and Vera daintily slipped her hand through the crook of his elbow and rested it on his forearm. Staring into one another's eyes, they descended in the elevator and walked towards the North Portico to await the Finnish president's motorcade.

Honor guards and color guards from all the branches of the military surrounded the driveways leading up to the portico, in full dress uniforms. Both American and Finnish flags were positioned along the drive. President Sherman stood at the top of the steps, with Vera standing as close to him as she could. The photographers that had been allowed to attend the welcoming could not stop taking pictures of the president and Vera. Finally the chief of protocol motioned with his hand to indicate that enough was enough, and the clicking distraction began to wane. Presently the motorcade from the Finnish ambassador's residence on Embassy Row entered through the White House gates. When President Kekkonen's limousine arrived in front of the portico, a Marine guard stepped forward and opened the door. President Kekkonen stepped out onto the pavement, and then offered his hand to his wife, Marja-Liisa. They were greeted warmly by the president and Vera, and then all stood at the top of the stairs for a brief photo opportunity.

The president then escorted his guests to the Yellow Oval Room on the residence floor for a brief reception, where dignitaries from both countries had been invited to enjoy hors d'oeuvres, cocktails and champagne. Marja-Liisa Kekkonen had been a student at Stanford shortly after Joel had graduated, so they had a lot to chat about as the reception progressed. Vera shared her experiences in Helsinki with the Finnish president, who was impressed that she was able to pronounce so many of the Finnish names correctly. She didn't bother to mention that she had been there as a flight attendant, and one of her coworkers was a Finn.

As the informal reception came to an end, the presidents and their ladies descended the Grand Staircase to the Entrance Hall where they were met by the United States Marine Band playing 'Hail to the Chief.' This was followed by the national anthems of both countries. In the Entrance Hall a formal receiving line was formed, where the president had the opportunity to introduce each of the invited guests not only to President and Mrs. Kekkonen, but to Vera as well. She immediately became the focal point of the entire reception line and the center of almost all the conversations. People knew of her from the State of the Union address and for what she had exposed about 9/11, but they had never witnessed her in a formal setting where her beauty and elegance was so prominent.

When the last guest had been introduced, President Sherman led the procession down the Cross Hall and into the State Dining Room where he and Vera, along with President Kekkonen and his wife, were seated at the head table. The remaining guests were directed to their assigned seats. The senator's wife didn't seem too thrilled with her location towards the back of the room. Vera couldn't help but wonder if maybe Max had something to do with that. Jim and Mari were sitting up close by the head table, and were obviously thrilled to be in attendance. Unbeknownst to Mari, the president had shared his wedding plans with Jim. He felt Jim should be the first to know, since it was he who had introduced them. As Jim made his way through the reception line, Joel asked him if he would be his best man at the wedding. So both Jim and Mari had secrets they thought the other didn't know, and it made the dinner all that much more enjoyable.

Before the meal was served, both presidents were scheduled to offer some remarks from a lectern at the head table. President Kekkonen was first. He spoke about the long-standing relationship between the two countries, interspersed with nuggets of information such as Finland being the originator of the sauna. He spoke of how Finland had provided a window to the world for the Soviet Union in its day, and how they would continue to help mitigate anything Russia might do to cause a problem for the western world. He thanked President Sherman for his graciousness in offering to have this state dinner, and he closed by complimenting Vera on her beauty, poise, and charm on the world stage. Most intriguing, he invited her to the city of Savonlinna for the opera held on the castle grounds, any summer she could make herself available. His remarks were well received by all present, and then it was President Sherman's turn.

Joel stepped to the microphone and began speaking from his prepared text. His comments were similar in nature to President Kekkonen's, only much shorter in length. When it appeared his speech was about to end, the invited photographer and videographer approached the lectern for much tighter shots, as if they had been instructed to move forward on cue. Instead of sitting down, he remained standing. Those in close proximity could see that he was getting choked up. He turned to Vera and asked her to join him at the podium. She graciously obliged, and once again stood as close to him as she possibly could.

"My friends, for the past several months I have come to know this woman. First, as a true American patriot willing to sacrifice everything for the good of this great nation. Second, as an intellectual peer—no, make that a superior, whose mind acquires and assimilates information better than anyone I know, and whose advice I have come to trust. Third, as a gracious, lovely woman whose beauty knows no equal, and whose soul taught mine to love again. She has been introduced to you as Vera Hanson from Seattle, Washington. At this moment, in front of all of you and before the world who may be watching, I would like to ask her to become Mrs. Joel Sherman, my wife, and First Lady of the United State of America."

He reached into his pocket and grasped the ring box. He opened it slowly under her gaze, and gently placed on her left ring finger the most beautiful Claude Thibaudeau ring anyone could possibly imagine. Vera placed her left hand in her right, moved it closer and stared at the ring. Tears welled up in her eyes and began to softly roll down her cheeks. Joel took his handkerchief from his tuxedo pocket and sweetly wiped each tear. When she had finished examining the ring in all its magnificence, she reached up and kissed Joel passionately, for the entire world to witness. "Yes, Kelli and I will marry you," she said.

That brought laughter to all who knew about the dog who had adopted the president, and then the guests erupted in applause. They stood to show their appreciation and excitement for the newly engaged couple. The applause died down, and since neither President Sherman nor Vera had anything more to say, President Kekkonen asked if he could amend his remarks. Of course permission was granted.

"I would like to be the first to congratulate these beautiful people. Though we didn't know for certain, it wasn't too hard to suspect these two were in love and headed to the altar. I would like to amend my previous invitation to Vera, and extend it to the

Shermans. We would be honored to host the president and the first lady in the land of the midnight sun, where opera knows no twilight."

His comments also received an ovation. The guests were then seated, and the five-course meal, which was a combination of Finnish and American cuisine, was served. It wasn't difficult to imagine the conversation at each table. What was usually a mixture of status, opportunity and politics evolved into the excitement that was sure to engulf all of America as the president and his elegant new first lady were set to be married. The surprise alone made the evening memorable in everyone's mind. No one seemed in a hurry for the evening to end. At the conclusion of the meal, all were escorted into the East Room where renowned concert pianist Neil Rutman performed Beethoven's "Moonlight Sonata" and a Chopin Nocturne that blended into the mood of the evening and enhanced the ambiance of the presidential engagement.

twenty two

*T*he morning following the state dinner, Jim invited Max to breakfast at a small café not far from Blair House. It probably would have been prudent to have had a driver take them, but Jim wanted to walk the few hundred yards. Max was curious about the previous evening's events, so he didn't put up much of a struggle when Jim announced his plans to walk.

It was a brisk morning, but one that did not require anything more than a light jacket. Jim set out, and at first kept to a moderate pace. Max did his best to keep up, but tailed far enough behind that it made conversation impossible. Jim clearly had exercise in mind, whereas Max was more focused on the buttermilk pancakes with the orange marmalade which he knew to be right at the top of the menu at this particular café. That thought is what kept him going. When they arrived they were seated in a corner booth, which limited their view but ensured them all the privacy they desired.

"So, how was the dinner last night? Did your tux fit, or did you to have to skip dessert?" Max facetiously asked.

Jim laughed. "Oh, you know me—I would never miss a good dessert, even if I had to stuff it in my pockets. And I have to admit, the dessert—along with all the other food last night—was incredible. Who would have ever thought the Finns had anything to brag about in the culinary department?"

"That's nice, Jim, but the headline on the front page of the Post this morning was a little hard to miss. Of course, it didn't exactly come as a surprise to anyone who's been paying attention, but I didn't expect the announcement to come at a state dinner."

"Mari tells me he asked her a couple of days ago, and the anticipation of making it all public was more than either of them could bear. It was nice though, real nice. And I'm happy for both of them. They deserve to be with one another, because we both know their lives are not going to be easy as the president pushes forward with his plans. They're going to need one another for comfort and support. If you've watched them together you can see they're both pretty good at that, which leads me to why I wanted to talk to you in the first place. Max, I know you're thinking of using Vera to help you bring in Ruth Ann. In light of last night and their official engagement, I don't think that's a good idea. In fact, I know Joel well enough to know that he wouldn't stand for it, not after what happened to Mica. So just let her be. We'll figure something else out."

Max interlocked his fingers, placed his first knuckle to his lips and let the remaining knuckles press firmly against his nose. He looked down at the table and took a few shallow breaths before sharing his thoughts. "I understand your concerns. Hell, I understand the president's concerns, but I'm not sure any of them are going to matter."

"What do you mean?" Jim asked.

"Vera called me bright and early this morning. Guess she's of the opinion that getting me out of bed to answer the phone is all the exercise I require," Max said, glancing up to check Jim's reaction.

Jim smiled. "And?"

"Let's just say the woman has a mind of her own that the president is going to have to get used to. Keep in mind this was the morning after the engagement heard round the world. She called me at the butt crack of dawn to ask how I'm coming on finding Ruth Ann, and insisted she be involved in helping to make it all happen. Now, do you want me to tell her she's out, or do you want to?"

Jim shook his head. "I know her well enough to know that you telling her won't go over at all well. It's what we love about her. When she gets something in her mind, there's little you can do to persuade her to leave it behind. We wouldn't have found out about those 9/11 planes if it hadn't been for her dogged tenacity and systematic logic. I've already had a few passing conversations with the president about this, nothing real specific, but I know he wants her to back away from what you and I are doing. He feels she's contributed more than enough, and he now wants her to help him in the areas where he's fully focused."

Max chugged his coffee. "Yeah, well, that might make sense to y'all, but you haven't answered my question about who gets to explain it to her."

The waitress arrived with their breakfast orders, giving Jim time to think about how to answer Max. He knew how close Vera felt to the whole operation. In a way, her involvement served to vindicate the deaths of both Jeff and Mica, which to her was necessary in order to give herself permission to marry Joel. He knew that didn't make sense, but it mattered a lot to Vera, and how she felt was always going to be important to him. The two ate in silence, commenting only on how good the food was and how they needed to come there for breakfast more often.

When he was finished, Max pushed his plate away and waited for Jim to finish his coffee. He held his own cup up in the air and motioned to the waitress for a refill. Before she arrived Max said, "I should tell you what I've been working on to find Ruth Ann."

Jim had his arms folded and resting on the table with his head lowered, thinking about how he was going to tell Vera her duties had shifted to West Wing protocols only. He looked up, indicating he was ready to hear what Max had to say. "I have a pretty good idea what Ruth Ann is up to."

Jim tilted his head as if to say, "Go on."

"She's pulling archive documents. I've checked with the National Archives and found someone who claims a woman has been requesting documents that coincide with areas I know Ruth Ann is familiar with, and which align perfectly with her particular interests involving 9/11. I also think she's of the opinion that I screwed up in Chicago, which led to all our assets dispersing. That means, for the time being, she doesn't trust me, and I won't be able to bring her in myself. She never responded to the Facebook page like the others did. I know her well enough to know she'll continue doing what she does best, collecting and analyzing information. If she makes a comeback, it won't be until she has exactly what she's looking for and she can lord it over me. It's her way of saying 'you're forgiven.' I have experienced this with her before. The problem is, I don't know how long that might take."

Jim's face lit up. "I don't see why that'll be a problem. Can't we just run a stakeout and nab her when she shows up to collect her documents?"

"Guess you ain't ever tried to get documents out of the archives, have you?" Max responded.

"Can't say that I have. Why is that a problem?"

"Let's see if I can explain this to you. This woman, who I think is probably Ruth Ann, has been requesting documents. As of yet she has yet to receive anything. Even with her Freedom of Information Act requests, they are stalling and doing anything they can to avoid giving her what she wants. Just typical government behavior, but I've been paying close attention to this one and it seems they're reacting in hyper-denial mode. Which means someone is controlling the information. That's why I wanted to use Vera to set a trap for Ruth Ann, and why I think she could still be helpful with just a little participation on her part."

Jim took a long drink of his coffee and nibbled on the crust of toast still left on his plate. "I don't know, Max; tell me specifically what you're thinking. Try and make it good, because I don't like it to this point."

"Here's what I've been thinking. If we can use Vera as a decoy, perhaps we can lure Ruth Ann to a specific location, thinking she will be given the documents she's asked for along with something extra that Vera leads her to believe will be given to her as a favor. It means we need some time for Vera to develop a relationship with Ruth Ann, and maybe even get some of the documents that have been requested. I'm pretty sure I can get Jerry to procure for us what Ruth Ann wants. Keep in mind we first have to make sure that it is Ruth Ann who has requested all this information, which means we have to lure her out into the open. You and I won't be able to do that, but I'm pretty sure Vera has what it takes to make that happen."

Jim held his hand over his mouth as he pondered what he had just heard. "That doesn't sound too complicated. What are the downside risks?" he asked.

Max's eyes lit up as he replied. "None that I can see. I think worst case is that we find out it might not be Ruth Ann, and then we're back where we started. So what do you think?"

"I still don't like it, but it may be our only play. How long do you think it would take Vera to make contact and establish the trust necessary to lure Ruth Ann out?"

Max was starting to become animated. "If we can do this correctly, it may only take a couple of days. Look, the thing is, Ruth Ann's whole existence is centered on this kind of research. In a way that makes her vulnerable, and she'll respond if she thinks she's about to obtain something that'll move her life forward. I can't really explain her, but trust me. I know what makes her tick."

"Oh, I think I understand. I've known people like that in the service. They're extremely valuable, but so one-dimensional that you almost have to keep them hidden for fear they'll give off the wrong impression."

"That would be our Ruth Ann," Max said with a laugh. "So, is it a go?"

"I'm going to think about it, and I'm going to talk to both Vera and Joel to see what they think. Then I'll let you know. Is that fair enough?"

"I can't complain. It's more than I had when we got here. I have more work than I can do going through all of Bob's information, so you'll know where you can find me day or night."

twenty three

*I*t did not require much thinking for Jim to decide to bring the issue up with Joel rather than to approach Vera with the plan. The president listened to what he had to say and promised to discuss it with Vera. Jim could tell from the brief conversation that Joel was not in favor of involving Vera in any way. Jim was happy the decision now belonged to Vera and Joel, and felt relieved to no longer be in the middle.

Jim waited longer for a response from the president than he thought would be necessary. When the answer came, it was Vera who called him and explained that all the issues had been settled and that she would get in touch with Max to learn her specific assignment. It was obvious to Jim that the discussion between the president and Vera had been long and intense. Knowing them both so well, he could imagine exactly how their conversation must have played out. The fact that Vera had prevailed, and that it was she who conveyed the outcome, told him the president was probably still not on board in principle, but that he had concurred with the decision to be diplomatic. This meant that everything had to run perfectly in order to gain Joel's full support.

The plan was for Vera to establish a relationship with Ruth Ann and to build confidence by providing some of the inconsequential information that Ruth Ann had been waiting to receive. The hope was that Vera could lure Ruth Ann out of hiding with a promise to share with her the more salient parts of the information Ruth Ann had requested. It was uncertain how long this strategy would take to play out, but Max was sure that this approach was the correct one. He explained to Vera that Ruth Ann's personality was ultra-cautious in general, but that trait had been ratcheted up several notches in recent years. A few of her colleagues had died under questionable circumstances, which only served to fuel her paranoia. Ruth Ann was the granddaughter of holocaust Jews that had been liberated from concentration camps when the war ended. Though she never allowed her heritage or its history to affect her research, it was easy to see that she maintained a heightened awareness of her surroundings, which was not going to make Vera's task any easier.

With Jerry Reitz's help, Max was able to credential Vera as a National Archives employee with more than a decade of seniority. Her assumed name was Laura Metcalf. The background and name was important, because he knew Ruth Ann would investigate anyone who was delegated to assist her with documents. It was important to Ruth Ann that whoever was assigned to her had sufficient archival experience, but it was also in her makeup to verify the person's background before she was able to develop any form of trust. Vera spent several days learning the procedures and protocols of the archives. Of course, most everything had to be done off-site, since her face had been plastered all over the media and she would be easily recognized. On the few occasions when Max felt it was necessary to take "Laura" to the archives to familiarize her with the layout of the buildings and the way information flowed through them, he disguised her as only Max could do.

He provided her with a wig that was the complete opposite of her natural hair color. He made sure that it was long enough so that if a pony tail were in order, it could easily come together to form that Maxwell Hager trademark. He also gave Vera contact lenses that dramatically changed her eye color. Those, along with glasses only a librarian would wear, completely transformed Vera into the Laura Metcalf no one knew. Even Mike didn't recognize her the first time he saw her in the disguise, and thought an intruder had breached security and found her way to the residence. Vera was delighted with the change and couldn't wait to show Joel. He was less enthusiastic with the look, but he did like the less formal ponytail possibilities, since that was a style never seen in his White House.

Max's overriding concern was how to determine if their target really was Ruth Ann. Max knew that if it were she, all of the personal information attached to the FOIA request would be bogus except the email address. If, on the other hand, it was a legitimate request from someone else, chances were that most or some of the personal information would check out. Max put Agent Garcia on that task. Gordon utilized all the Secret Service agency's assets normally employed to check out threats to the president, and found that absolutely none of the information provided to the archives was legitimate. Unfortunately, none of it left any leads as to where to search next.

"Gordon, might it be possible to pull the legitimate information we have on Ruth Ann and compare it to what we have from the archives?" Max asked. "Often when people are providing false information, they leave clues that correspond to actual facts. I doubt you'll find anything, but it's worth a shot."

"You must have read my mind; I was thinking the same thing," responded Agent Garcia. "There's a new algorithm we obtained from the CIA that can compare phony information to real facts, and make predictions with a fair degree of accuracy. I was just about to run her information through that program. Let me do it and see what turns up."

"If it comes up zeros, I think it's safe to assume that this is Ruth Ann," Max said.

Gordon nodded in concurrence.

Vera spent her time studying all the possible scenarios that Max had presented. She felt she understood who Ruth Ann was and how she might behave under any circumstances. Vera's flight attendant experience helped her deal with people in changing environments. Max shared with her what he thought Ruth Ann would be requesting. He himself had spent countless hours investigating down the same avenues, so he was familiar with her line of research. This allowed Vera to become conversant with the salient points of what Ruth Ann was investigating. After several days of practicing different scenarios and contingency plans, Vera felt she was ready to set the trap.

Jerry made available to Max two documents that Ruth Ann had requested. They were small in size and had she requested them individually, they would have been sent to her, but because she had included them with her larger request, they had been held up. Vera introduced herself as Laura Metcalf, pledged her assistance to help as much as possible, and included the first small document file in her initial email to Ruth Ann.

"Now we wait," said Max. "If she responds, then in all likelihood we'll be able to work with her and convince her to rejoin our effort. If we don't hear from her, then either it isn't her, or she suspected something was amiss. If that's the case, we may just have to move forward without her."

twenty four

*W*hen Ruth Ann left Minneapolis, her intent was to head to Florida and continue her research. Winter was not her favorite time of year, and she had a friend who planned to be in Europe until late August and had offered a beach house for her to use. It was located along a rough, secluded stretch of beach outside of Pensacola, and was the perfect place to hole up and not be bothered. Ruth Ann had stayed there once before when she was escaping from a boyfriend who had difficulty realizing their relationship was over. She was sure this was the perfect place to hide out until she was ready to rejoin Max.

Money was not a problem for Ruth Ann. Her parents were wealthy and had established a trust fund for her, from which she began drawing when she reached the age of twenty-five. That money allowed her the freedom to do whatever she wanted. For the most part, she was extremely prudent, and anyone who knew her would never suspect she was anything more than a free spirit. Her parents hated her approach to life and never liked the fact that they could go for months without hearing from her. They learned not to complain, and graciously appreciated the time Ruth Ann chose to spend with them. In spite of her Spartan lifestyle, she did have one personality quirk that caused others to take note. She liked all her cars to be yellow. Every few years she would purchase a new car, and they were always the same color. If she could not find the car she wanted in her color, she would have one custom painted. This proved to be her downfall.

After she met with Max and the guys in Minneapolis, she

left at three in the morning for Pensacola, traveling along I-94. She was planning to spend the night in Nashville, and assumed she would arrive close to dusk. As morning dawned, she stopped for breakfast in Rockford, Illinois. She pulled into an IHOP and decided to call a friend who worked in the Chicago Fire Department dispatch. She wanted to know if a call had gone out on a car fire earlier that morning. Her friend reported that a car in a Denny's parking lot had been obliterated, to the point that no one was sure what kind of vehicle it was. That information was all Ruth Ann needed to know; the code red was in play and she was now dark. Max was right; she thought his plan was a colossal screw-up, and even though she liked the idea of being dark on the beach for the rest of the winter, she began to question her loyalty to Max and his research. Being dark meant she could reevaluate her priorities without any interference. She planned to take full advantage of the opportunity it presented.

After breakfast, she headed back out on the road, and wanted to stop in Atlanta for the night. By the time she arrived in Nashville she was tired, and checked into a Holiday Inn Express. When she got ready to leave the next morning, her car was gone. She was certain it hadn't been stolen, since starting it required the key fob to be in close proximity to the car. That meant that the car had been towed. She returned to the hotel lobby and called the police to find out if they had any information as to why her car had been removed from the parking lot. She was told that a detective would be dispatched to the hotel to pick her up and bring her to the station to fill out a report. In the meantime, the police would contact the local tow yards to see if a car matching the description had been impounded.

Within minutes a large black SUV pulled up in front of the hotel. A man in a black suit stepped from the passenger side and walked into the hotel lobby. Ruth Ann was watching him, and could see a gun in his shoulder holster. Naturally, she assumed he was the detective sent to help her. She greeted him and introduced herself as Ruth Ann. He was very cordial and listened to her as she began telling him about her car.

"You know, I think it would be best if we could get you back to the station and take your statement. I think we may have found your car in one of the nearby tow lots. Once we record your statement, we can get this cleared up and go collect your car. Get all of your belongings and check out; I'm sure you won't be back," said the man, ever so pleasantly.

Ruth Ann already had checked out and had a small overnight bag and all of her computer equipment with her. The man grabbed her things and opened the back door to the SUV to allow her to get in, and then placed her belongings in the far back. Sitting next to Ruth Ann in the backseat was a woman who smiled at her as she got in, but didn't say anything.

The SUV pulled out of the hotel parking lot much faster than Ruth Ann thought was necessary. She looked up at the driver, and both he and the man she had spoken with were staring straight ahead. She then looked over at the woman, who was pointing a Glock semiautomatic pistol in her direction.

"Hey, what's this?" Ruth Ann blurted out.

The woman replied in a heavily accented voice, "Shut up and put your arms behind your seat. No more questions. Do it now, or I'll be only too happy to blow you to hell."

Ruth Ann was stunned. She immediately put her arms behind the captain's chair she was sitting in and closed her mouth. The woman then used a set of handcuffs with an extended chain to secure Ruth Ann in place, and reached into a satchel on the floor to get a gag to put in her mouth.

"That won't be necessary just yet," said the man in the front seat. "I have a lot of questions to ask her, and if she cooperates things will go well for her. If not, you can gag her and tighten those cuffs. We have a long drive ahead of us, and I want this to be as painless as possible for us. I don't care about what kind of pain she's in."

Ruth Ann could see that they were heading for I-40, and were probably going to go east. In minutes they were on the freeway, going in the direction she had suspected. Obviously these were not detectives sent from the police station to assist her. It occurred to her that perhaps there were no detectives, and that she had been set up. After riding several minutes in silence, she finally spoke. "Okay, who are you guys and where are you taking me?"

The woman next to her looked at the passenger in the front seat for confirmation before she said anything. He glanced around and nodded to her. Her accent was thick, but it was one Ruth Ann knew all too well. It was the same accent her grandparents had, and so she had no trouble understanding. "Late yesterday afternoon we were heading north on I-94, headed to Chicago, when we saw a bright yellow Lexus coming at us in the opposite direction. Nobody but you would own a car in that horrid color. We were under the impression that you and your cohorts were eliminated yesterday morning. So imagine our surprise when we see your car driving south. We had no choice but to check it out. We followed you to Nashville, and once you parked the car, we verified it was yours. Of course we didn't know if it was you driving it or not, so we had your car towed and waited until morning for you to react. We were less than a block away when we intercepted your cell phone call to the police, so we were able to take care of the situation immediately. Jake here," she said, pointing to the man in the front seat, "knows all about you. He's been following you and your work for months, so it was easy for him to identify you. You are ours now, and you're going to do exactly what we tell you to do."

"I don't understand. Why do you want me? I'm nothing. I'm a low-level researcher working with an obscure group of misfits," replied Ruth Ann.

"We have a pretty good idea what documents you've requested and why you want them. The information that the planes were remotely landed at Westover on 9/11 opens the door to discovering the rest of the truth, and we're not about to let that happen. Bottom line, lady, is we want to know what you know, and we're going to get it if we have to beat it out of you," Jake said from the front seat, without once turning his head to look at her.

The woman spoke up again. "First of all, we want to know who, if anyone, was killed in that parking lot in Chicago. Do you know?"

Ruth Ann flinched. If she told what she knew, it would put everyone's life in more danger than it had been previously. Of course, they now knew she was alive, so she had to find a way to explain that without jeopardizing everything. The woman reached for the gun again.

"No, put that back, Liv. Let's see if Ruthie here wants to be helpful," Jake said. "We won't get to Washington D.C. for nine or ten more hours, so she has plenty of time to see things our way." This time he looked Ruth Ann directly in the eyes, leaving no doubt that he was serious.

It was one thing to be abducted against her will, but mentally Ruth Ann felt trapped as well, and needed to think through how she was going to answer the questions presented to her. Even though she was upset with Max, she knew that if she could persuade them that he was dead and the rest of them were alive, that would give Max the best chance of finding the rest of the team before they suffered the same fate she was experiencing. She ran through some possible stories she thought they might buy, but each of them had a flaw, and so she remained silent. For the time being they didn't seem to mind, but as the miles passed and the scenery changed, the woman became more insistent.

Ruth Ann asked for some water, and indicated she was

hungry and needed to use a restroom. Jake decided that they would stop, get something to eat, let Ruth Ann use the facilities and then move on. "See, we can be amenable to your desires, but in return we want answers. That's not too hard to understand, is it?" he asked.

Liv kept Ruth Ann on an extremely tight leash while they were out of the vehicle. There was no question in Ruth Ann's mind that she was eventually going to tell them what they wanted to know. Once they were back on the highway she said, "Max and I had a falling out when we were in Minneapolis. I basically told him I was done, and no longer wanted to work with the team. That got the other guys to thinking, and both of them voiced their opinions about how things had been going. Neither of them was as adamant as I was about moving on, but I know there were some contentious things said. I honestly do not know what they decided to do, but I do know Max perished in the explosion in Chicago yesterday morning. I called a friend at Chicago Fire. Here, look, you can see the call on my phone. Press it. It will connect you with the fire department."

Jake reached into Ruth Ann's bag and found her phone. "What time did you make the call?" he asked.

"Around eight," she replied.

Jake found the call she was talking about and pressed the 'send' button. It indeed connected to Chicago Fire. He hung up. "So what did you find out?"

"My friend told me that everyone in the vehicle was annihilated beyond recognition, and that it would require DNA testing to determine who was in the car. He said an eyewitness confirmed that someone matching Max's description was driving. There was at least one other passenger in the front seat, but the windows were too dark to tell who, if anyone, was in the backseat. That's all I know. Max, for sure, is dead; the others I assume were with him."

"We'll let our CIA friends check that out for us. In the meantime, tell us what you have been researching. We know your specialty is FOIA and archive documents. And we know somewhere you have a terabyte of information. What exactly are you looking for?" Jake asked.

"Do you have any clue how large a terabyte of information is? I could research that hard drive until they put me in a pine box with a Star of David on it, and still not know everything that's contained in its files," Ruth Ann said.

Liv spoke up. "Hah, a pine box with a Star of David. Haven't you disgraced that honor?"

"Haven't you?" Ruth Ann shot back.

"That'll be enough," snapped Jake. "We've got plenty of time for you to give us what we want, and trust me; you'll give it all up."

The journey continued until late into the evening, when they arrived at a home in Bethesda, Maryland. Ruth Ann was escorted from the SUV and locked in a basement bedroom. The room had twin beds, a bathroom, and bars on the windows—which seemed out of place, since nobody could crawl in or out of the space the window created. Ruth Ann was exhausted, and overjoyed to be out of the handcuffs. She had her bag of clothes with her, but her computers, hard drive and cell phone were of course missing. She stretched out on the bed and instantly fell asleep.

twenty five

*T*he document Laura Metcalf sent to the person she thought was Ruth Ann was opened the following day, and a reply came back thanking her for making the information available. In reality, it was Liv who responded to Laura. Liv did not request anything else, and did not see the email as an opportunity to work together.

Her response left Max and Vera uncertain as to what to do next. They still had the other document, and hoped they could use that to get Ruth Ann to meet with Laura. If they sent it right away their ammunition would be depleted, and additional planning would be required. Max suggested Vera attempt to engage Ruth Ann in an email exchange about documents she had previously requested. He asked her to mention a specific FAA file that had been provided earlier, and suggested Vera ask if there was anything else in conjunction with that file that might be helpful. Vera sent the emails, and added a few personal touches that she hoped would endear her to Ruth Ann.

Both emails set off red flags to Ruth Ann's captors. The first was suspicious to them, but the second one, coming so soon afterwards, marked a definite change in the demeanor of the archive department's employees. The agency never responded that quickly or politely. This sudden willing assistance coming from that agency made them all nervous—it proved that something was amiss.

For the past several months, Ruth Ann had been cooperating with her captors. She realized that no one in the world knew where she was, and that not a soul knew she was missing. She felt vulnerable, and that caused her to realize she might be eliminated. Now the only positive responses in her life occurred when she helped her captors. She hated it at first, and was very much aware that the Stockholm syndrome was in play. She was starting to lose hope. She reflected many times on the stories she'd heard from her grandparents. What strength she was able to muster was a reflection of the determination she knew her grandparents exhibited in their efforts to gain freedom from Auschwitz. They eventually survived, but not without their scars and their tattoos.

As time passed, Ruth Ann was able to move about the basement at will. Her meals were brought to her, and she spent more and more time with Liv, who would interrogate her about her research on a daily basis. Ruth Ann knew they were starting to figure out the kind of data available on her hard drive. She also knew that her files would eventually lead them to the conclusion that the perpetrators of the 9/11 attacks were at severe risk of being exposed. Ruth Ann was not shocked when Jake would occasionally grill her about certain aspects of her research, like flight paths or radar data. It did surprise her when he questioned her persistently about who she thought might be responding to her archive requests. Ruth Ann had no idea, but she wasn't opposed to helping them find out. Jake and Liv decided to request another document to see if this Laura would comply.

Liv sent off a new request for a file. It was a file Max did not have. He immediately sent the request to Jerry Reitz, who had the file in Vera's email inbox the following morning. 'Laura' sent the document, hoping it would establish enough trust to encourage Ruth Ann to set up a meeting. When the email arrived in Liv's inbox, all hell broke loose. Ruth Ann's captors were absolutely certain that someone in the government was setting them up. They knew it was next to impossible for an archivist to respond that quickly to a FOIA request. Now their desire to set up a meeting with this archivist took on a critical dimension. It was imperative that they find out who was setting them up, and they had to make that person stop interfering. Their plan was to initiate a meeting at a coffee shop to go over the new document. Liv would explain to Laura that there was so much redacted content that she felt needed to be exposed, that she wanted to meet to discuss the possibilities. The meeting would allow them to surveil Laura, plant a tracking device on her, or kidnap her, much like they had done with Ruth Ann. They were not going to allow the government into their business. They had to avoid exposure at all costs, and they were willing to sacrifice Ruth Ann's life if necessary.

Liv sent back an email to Laura complaining about the redactions, and asked her how she could obtain a clean copy. When Laura's email arrived, suggesting they meet at a coffee shop in Bethesda, Maryland, they immediately begin to make plans to take Laura hostage.

Liv wrote back and told Laura that she would meet her at the Starbucks inside a Safeway store on Bradley Street, at ten o'clock the following morning.

Max was overjoyed when he heard the news. "Our plan is working. I thought there was less than a forty percent chance this would be successful, and here we are, right where we need to be. Great work, Vera. You're the best."

Immediately Max, Vera, Jim and Gordon went into strategic planning mode, to determine how they would persuade Ruth Ann to emerge from the shadows and start working with them. Excitement filled the room, except around Gordon, whose cautious nature could always be felt and was never infectious.

Max was of the opinion that once they determined it was Ruth Ann, they should surround her with a group of Secret Service agents and bring her in for debriefing. Jim felt that was overkill, and a full-on discussion commenced as to how to proceed. The conversation was heated at times, the close proximity of the goal increasing their sense of urgency. It was Vera who finally presented a plan, and insisted it be followed.

"Ruth Ann has no idea who I am. I mean, disguised as Laura Metcalf, no one knows who I am. It's imperative that I build substantial trust with this woman. Quite frankly, I'm shocked she suggested this meeting so quickly. She must be getting impatient or desperate, neither of which are great foundations on which to build trust. Let me go alone, meet with her, and try to assuage her fears. If I can do that, then I think within a day or two, she'll be willing to work with me in any way I suggest. It'll be her decision, and if it's her idea to help us rather than our demand to make her, we'll have the key to the gold mine Max thinks she has."

Gordon shook his head. "I don't like it. In fact, there is nothing about it I like. We can't have Vera exposed, not even for a second. I understand why we can't have a small brigade of agents on the scene, but even in a benign situation like this, we can't afford to leave her unprotected."

Jim finally weighed in. "Vera, I know you speak for the president more so than anyone here, but I don't think you're being fully objective. If he were here, I have no doubt he would veto your idea, and prevent it from ever being considered."

Ultimately, a compromise was reached. Vera would go dressed as Laura and arrive early, which would give Gordon sufficient time to check out the surroundings and feel confident Vera would be safe. The fact that the meeting was scheduled to be in a public place made him feel more comfortable about the whole idea. Gordon knew he could protect her from any possible scenario, and gave his consent.

On the morning of the meeting Vera dressed as Laura, and Gordon provided her with a wire so that he could listen in on whatever conversation occurred between the women. He provided her a map of the Safeway store, and showed her the location of the Starbucks near the front of the store. He suggested that she sit nearest the entrance, and position herself so that she would have a good view out the window. Gordon would be dressed as a Safeway store clerk and be stationed close to the coffee shop, allowing him easy access should something go wrong.

As planned, Gordon and Vera arrived early. Vera ordered her favorite vanilla latte, and selected a seat near the door as she had been instructed. Gordon scanned the immediate area for listening devices and anything else that might raise a concern. Then they waited.

Just before ten o'clock, a yellow SUV pulled up in front of the store. Liv knew that with her heavy accent, speaking with Laura was going to be a problem. She also knew she could never pass for Ruth Ann. Nevertheless, she wore a wig, and even dressed in some of Ruth Ann's clothes. As she exited the driver's side door and started to walk around the front of the vehicle, Vera noticed the woman had a cast on her right foot up to her knee. She also had a sign that read "Laura Metcalf." Immediately, Vera assumed that this must be Ruth Ann. Max had told her the car would be yellow, and no one knew the name Laura Metcalf except Ruth Ann. The woman opened the back door to the SUV and got a set of crutches out, and then reached in for what appeared to be a heavy briefcase. Vera instinctively rose from her seat to assist the woman. The moment she did, she could hear Gordon in her ear, warning her to sit down. She paid him no heed and raced to the car, reaching for the briefcase. The moment she had it in her hand, Liv put a gun in her ribs, pushed her into the back of the SUV and closed the door. Jake was sitting all the way in the back, out of view. Once Vera was inside, he put a black cloth bag over her head and handcuffed her. Liv jumped into the passenger seat and Jake made his way to the driver's side. When Gordon saw what was happening, he quickly pulled his gun and raced toward the yellow vehicle. Customers were coming and going from the store, obstructing his view, and impeding his progress toward the SUV. He was too late. Jake sped out of the parking lot with total disregard for people, cars or shopping carts. Liv climbed into the back and frisked Vera. She immediately found the wire Gordon had given her and ripped it from her clothing.

In her strong accent, she said, "I don't know who you are, but we sure as hell intend to find out. When we, do we'll put an end to your plans and then your life."

twenty six

*G*ordon put out an all-points bulletin for the vehicle. It went to every agency within a hundred miles: all local police, and the state police in both Virginia and Maryland, along with the FBI, Capitol police, the Secret Service, and even part of the military used for surveillance. He did not disclose that Vera had been kidnapped, or even the reason he wanted the car located and its driver and passengers apprehended. However, he left no question that it was a matter of national security, and was to be their primary priority under the command of the President of the United States. He couldn't believe he had let this happen. He knew in his gut he should not have allowed Vera to override his doubts and misgivings about the plan. Had it been the president that would have never happened, but because she was engaged to the president she carried full executive officer weight, even if she didn't carry his importance. It was that gray area into which Gordon had never before ventured, that had caused him to ignore his professional experience. The drive back to the White House was excruciatingly painful. He knew the president had been made aware the moment the bulletin had gone out, and though he had not contacted Gordon for details, it was likely he would have assumed the worst.

Once Gordon cleared through security he made his way to the Executive Offices. The weight he felt was unbearable. It caused his breathing to grow shallow and sweat to come from every pore. He had to face the president, and he had no excuses and no real answers. The president's secretary kept him waiting, which only intensified his anguish. Finally she announced to him that the president was in the residence and wanted to see him there. The long walk felt like a death march, as he made his way through the corridors of the Executive Offices, into the White House itself and up the elevator to the residence.

The president was standing in the doorway to the suites, waiting for him. Rather than say a word, he reached his arms towards Gordon and drew him to his chest in a prolonged embrace. It was something both men needed. Gordon could feel his emotions beginning to let go, and he fought with all his might to keep his composure. The president had tears in his eyes he could not begin to hide.

"I'm so sorry, Mr. President. I'm just so sorry," Gordon whispered.

"Come, follow me into the study and tell me everything," replied the president.

When the men had situated themselves, Joel asked, "Is she still alive?"

"I don't know, sir. Her abductors don't know who she is. As long as she maintains her disguise, they won't know for a while. I can't imagine their intent was to kill her—at least, not until they ascertained what it was she wanted and what she knew about them. Fortunately, Vera knows how to be tightlipped about facts. Her airline training and experience drilled that into her. Obviously these people have either kidnapped or killed Ruth Ann. Depending upon what she's told them, they probably assume the government is trying to infiltrate them and perhaps eliminate them."

"Just so I'm certain, Gordon, who is 'they'?" asked the president.

"These people are the same ones who tried to abduct Gil, and succeeded with Ruth Ann. They're the enforcement arm of the Octopus, and the protectors of the master secret. The secret of who is behind 9/11, and most everything else that works against this country and to its detriment. They are vicious, but they are not stupid. They took Vera for information, which means we have some time to find her," Gordon said.

"This is all my fault; you know that, don't you, Gordon? I should've never allowed her to get involved. You know it was against my initial instinct, but it's so difficult to say no to her, especially when her heart is so tightly wrapped around something."

"Don't blame yourself, sir. I knew the risks and ignored them. Blame me. I lost her and I'll find her. I promise."

"So she was able to persuade you, too, using her intensity and charm? We'll get her back. I can feel it inside. God may not be proud of me, but I can't imagine He'll allow me to suffer the loss of two loves while in this office. Keep your promise, Gordon, and I'll rely on God to keep His. So what's your plan to rescue her, and how can I best help?"

"For the immediate time being, the most important thing is to keep this quiet. If her identity gets out, we'll have multiplied our problems and complicated our options. As far as I know, only our tight circle knew Vera was going to this meeting. And I don't know if they even realize what has happened, at this point. I've not shared a reason for wanting information on the SUV, so no one can associate a crime with the request. I'll work with Jerry to coordinate the knowledge we have and come up with a plan. There are some things I need to have local agencies follow up on, which will help. For example, how do you get a yellow SUV? That's not going to come from a factory, and if it was painted, it had to have happened yesterday. So I have clues I'll follow up and add to the mix. I'm also going to talk with Jerry and see if some of our high-tech capabilities can help locate her. If we can do that, then we have to implement a rescue plan. You know I'll keep you informed before making any decisions," Gordon said.

"I have a tracking device which informs you where I am at any time. Was something like that provided to Vera?" the president asked.

"Unfortunately, the law dictates who is entitled to those types of implants and Vera, not having married you yet, did not qualify. Lawmakers just have no experience with a fiancée. Ultimately, though, that might be a blessing. I have no doubt they'll scan her for transmitting devices. If they were to find one, it would set off alarms with them, and intensify the risk to her life. So let's cross our fingers and hope they think she's a low-level nobody. That will play out to our advantage. We may have some other options that Jerry and I will discuss. If we can narrow the range of where we think she might be, I think we can zero in on her. We shall see."

"I was briefed on the technology I think you are referring to. It's in a testing phase, as I recall, and not fully proven. Is that correct?" Joel asked.

"That's right, Mr. President, but if we think it can help, we'll employ it—authorized or not. It can't hurt Vera, and might be exactly what we need to locate her."

"Enough from me. I'll let you go and do what you can to find her." The president stood up and walked over to hug Gordon again. "Don't blame yourself, my friend. I know you've come to love that woman. You can't give someone as much of your life as you have given her, and not care deeply. You'll find her and everything will be all right. Now go and do."

Gordon left the residence with a calmness running through his soul that was much needed and very welcomed. It was a gift President Sherman was able to convey to people, that was without precedence and without equal.

twenty seven

*T*he drive from the Safeway to the house where Ruth Ann was being kept was short and direct. It had been planned that way so that if Jake and Liv had to make a fast exit, they would be on the road for as short a time as possible. They even managed to find a route that avoided most of the traffic lights. They were aware that intersections had cameras. It was unclear if they were hooked up or not, but they didn't want to take any chances. They arrived at the house and pulled the SUV into the garage. The hood was removed from Vera's head, and as her eyes adjusted to the light she could see that the garage had been used to paint something yellow. On closer inspection it was obvious that the paint job on the vehicle was anything but professional. She was escorted outside, down a narrow path between the house and a high wooden fence. When they arrived at the back of the house, Jake held her arms until Liv could open the door leading down a stairway to the basement. Vera assumed they didn't want her in the house for a reason, but could not figure out why at this point. Jake pushed her forward through a darkened hallway and into a great room. She tried to ask a question, but was told to shut up. Liv opened a door to what looked like a bedroom, with two beds, and Jake pushed Vera inside. Sitting on one of the beds was another woman. "This is our Laura Metcalf," announced Liv. "See what she knows." Liv shut the door behind her, and Vera was left standing, looking at Ruth Ann.

Vera didn't say anything. She quickly glanced around the room, and couldn't help but notice the bars on the very small windows. She moved toward the second bed to sit down. "You wouldn't happen to be Ruth Ann, would you?" Vera asked, looking at the other woman and examining her from head to toe to determine her physical condition, and to ascertain how she had been treated.

The woman nodded, but chose not to speak.

"How long have you been here?" Vera asked.

"Two or three months," she said, glancing down at the floor.

"Has it been you I've been corresponding with through email, about documents at the archives?" Vera asked.

"Sort of. I didn't send any email. I don't have access to a computer, but Liv kept me informed as to what was happening. I kind of guessed they would take you and bring you here. They don't believe you really work at the archives. They want to know who you are, so—who are you?"

Vera didn't answer that question. Instead she asked, "Who do they think I am?"

"They don't know. They think you're a government agent, but they'll know soon. I'm sure they've taken your fingerprints, or will come down and get a pristine set. They'll send them off somewhere, and in a day or less they'll know everything about you. And for your sake, I hope they like what they find," Ruth Ann responded.

"Do you know who these people are?" Vera asked.

"At first I wasn't sure, but as time goes on I'm beginning to suspect. It's not hard to tell, with Liv's accent, that they're not part of our government. But they have access to all kinds of information that you don't just get from the internet. They have to be connected with some kind of foreign intelligence, and I think I know who."

"What makes you so sure?"

"Nothing they seem to be interested in has anything to do with United States government interests. They kidnapped me for my research, and my ability to lead them to those who are asking the same kind of questions I ask."

"What do you ask, Ruth Ann?" Vera asked.

"Of late, I want to know who pulled off 9/11 and why it's been systematically covered up ever since. I'd pretty much given up hope on finding answers to that until I heard the president's State of the Union address. That, combined with that Hanson lady and the Bowman guy, refueled my desire to dig into this with all I have. That is, until I was kidnapped. Now I'm just happy to talk to someone besides Jake and Liv," Ruth Ann explained.

"You mention Vera Hanson and Jim Bowman. Why are they so significant to you?"

"Oh, they figured it out. Their revelations coincided with what I was researching, but they figured it out and I couldn't. That Hanson lady is my hero. I would love to get a chance to pick her brain. The problem is, they nabbed me before I could reach out to her."

"You may still get your chance," said Vera.

"I don't know. Now that they have you, I'm not sure they have much use for me," Ruth Ann said.

"Do you fear for your life?" Vera inquired.

Ruth Ann reached into her blouse and pulled out what looked like dog tags, which were attached to a chain around her neck.

"What are those? Were you in the service?" Vera asked.

Ruth Ann laughed. "Not hardly. I doubt I would've lasted a week in the military. These are my special memories, and they give me strength to survive anything that comes at me, including death." She took them from around her neck and placed them in Vera's hand.

Vera looked down at them. They were in the shape of military dog tags, but they only had a long number embossed on them. "What are they?"

"Those are the numbers that were tattooed on my

grandparents' arms while they were at Auschwitz. They survived, and as a little girl I would sit on their laps and trace the numbers with my finger as they told me their stories of survival and perseverance. When they died I had these made, so that I could still trace the numbers and seek strength from them. They've never let me down, and I'm sure they won't now."

Vera looked up at Ruth Ann. "May I trace the numbers?"

"By all means; memorize them if you want. They were good people—Jewish in every sense of the word, but not those evil Zionists. There's a difference, you know."

Vera nodded, but kept tracing the numbers with her fingers.

"It was Zionist-loving Jews who had them picked up by Hitler's men and thrown into the concentration camps—you know, people like George Soros's father. Of course he went by the name of Schwartz in those days. My grandparents told me all the stories from before the war, and explained what they saw transpire after the war. They knew who the real enemy was. That's how I knew immediately who Liv was. She's one of them. And my research never goes too deep without one or more of them raising their evil head. They have infiltrated every aspect of this government, and it's they whom we need to fear and defeat."

Ruth Ann's rant caught Vera by surprise. She handed the necklace back and thanked her for sharing the tags. "It's unusual for someone of Jewish descent to point the finger at anyone from their homeland. That makes you unique, you know," Vera said.

"I'm not pointing fingers at people from my ancestral homeland. I'm shining the light on those who claim to be Jews, and yet they are not. They're nothing even close to being Jewish from the ancient tribe of Israel, and father Abraham. Tell me you know what I'm talking about, Laura. Don't make me think I've just shared with you something sacred to me, and now you'll turn your back and think me the fool."

Vera folded her arms across her chest. "Believe me, I know

what you're telling me is true. I may be a little new to its discovery, but I learn fast, and I'm surrounded by people who completely understand and seek to do something to expose it. In fact, that's why I'm here. Though this isn't quite how I planned on it playing out, nevertheless here we are, and we'll do like your grandparents did—persevere and survive."

Ruth Ann looked a little confused. "There's something you're not telling me. What is it?"

Vera almost laughed. "A while back you mentioned your desire to meet and talk with Vera Hanson. Well, this is your chance. I'm Vera, and I'm pleased to finally find you."

"No way," Ruth Ann gasped. "How can this be? You don't look a thing like the Vera Hanson I saw on television."

Vera lifted the wig and removed her glasses. "This is my Laura Metcalf disguise, and for our safety it's going to stay that way. I have been working with Max to try to find you and the other members of your team. We have Gil, but Bob was killed in Las Vegas. Max thinks you're mad at him, but he knew enough about you to help us search in the right direction. We just had no idea you'd been kidnapped and were unable to adequately respond."

Ruth Ann was in shock. She couldn't believe what she was hearing. "Vera Hanson, it's really you. And about Max, he's a sweetheart and this is the first I've heard for sure he survived the attack in Chicago. I do get testy with him from time to time. He can be exasperating, but he's like a father to me, so I never stay upset for very long."

"Max is a dear, and for several weeks Jim and I thought he was dead. That hurt a lot, because I had been with him the night before his car exploded. He was really the key to helping us discover all that we did. Now that he's back in action and poring over Bob's files with Gil and Jim, we're discovering amazing deceptions that have covered up much of what happened on 9/11. We need to get you back in the game and get you plowing through your data. I'm sure you'll be a huge help to the effort."

Ruth Ann smiled, but then her brow furrowed. "Do you have any idea how we're going to get out of here? I've spent months examining ways to break out, but this place is locked up tighter than you can imagine. Worst yet, Jake and Liv never leave this place at the same time. The only thing I'm grateful for is that they treat me decently. Of course, I must confess, as time has gone on I've been helpful to them."

"I don't suppose you're allowed to watch or hear any news coverage, are you?" Vera asked.

"None. I do hear them talking about some current events, but I never have the full context, so it never makes much sense," replied Ruth Ann.

"There's more you need to know. Not only am I Vera Hanson, but as of a few days ago I'm engaged to marry the president. So you could say I'm the First Lady in waiting. I'd show you my beautiful ring, but I removed it to keep to my disguise."

Ruth Ann just shook her head and stared at the woman she'd thought was an archivist for the government. "You're just full of surprises, aren't you?"

Vera's blush turned into a smile and she said, "You can imagine that the president and every arm of the United States government is going to be looking for me, and that now includes you. So don't worry. There's no doubt they'll find us and free us. Stay close to me at all times, if possible. We'll make your grandparents proud."

twenty eight

"*H*ow's the president?" Jerry asked, when Gordon walked into his office.

"Surprisingly strong, for someone going through this again, but this time he's confident we'll find her and they'll be reunited soon," Gordon said.

"I wish I had his conviction. At the moment, we're not even sure where to begin looking. The information you provided was pretty sketchy. It was a professionally designed plan: in, out, gone," added Jerry.

"Yeah, and it played right into Vera's only weakness—helping others in need. I suppose any woman might have done just what she did. I tried to stop her, but she wouldn't listen, and before I could get to her they were out of there. It's no question they're part of the same group that tried to abduct Gil."

Jerry had a set of files on his desk that he began to sort through. "So what do we have on them here in the D.C. area? Should we bring the CIA in to assist?"

"Look, you know as well as I do these foreign agents wind in and out of the CIA almost seamlessly. It's nearly impossible to tell them apart these days. If you have a contact there you know you can trust, it might be worth a shot, but if not, working with them could quite possibly allow our information to flow directly to Vera's captors. I also told the president that we'd keep this circle tight, as in only those who knew Vera was on assignment. Get my drift?" Gordon asked.

Jerry nodded that he did and kept looking at his files, hoping something would leap out and give him a place to start.

"You know, Jerry, there's one clue we might start following up."

"What's that?"

Gordon explained, "I keep coming back to that yellow SUV. It had to have been painted, and it would've happened in the last day or two. We can begin by calling every auto repair place in the area and see if they painted a Ford Expedition an ugly yellow color. If they did, we're on to them. I can get Gil to make those calls and report back anything he finds."

"That's better than the nothing we had," Jerry said.

Gordon left Jerry and went to brief Max, Jim and Gil. They were working in the West Wing of the White House. Max had somehow gotten wind of Vera's kidnapping and had shared it with the other two, but they were shy on any real details. Gordon explained everything to them and swore them to secrecy. He explained to Gil what he wanted him to do, and had a White House aide assigned to provide him with the numbers of all the automobile repair shops within a fifty-mile radius of the Starbucks.

He pulled Max aside and said, "There's always the outside chance that these goons painted that vehicle themselves—you know, masking tape and ten cans of yellow Krylon spray paint. I didn't get close enough to see and at that point I didn't care, but in the back of my mind I just can't figure out how you could get a big SUV painted in a day. Here's what I want you to do. Go around to the paint and auto parts stores, and see if anyone has purchased several rolls of masking tape and lots of yellow spray paint. I'll get you a Secret Service ID that you can show to look official. Keep in mind they have that information on their computers, so make them check. Then let me know what you find."

Max was all smiles. This kind of thing was right in line with his personality, and he couldn't wait to get started.

When Gordon was finished instructing Max, he said to Jim, "If we get lucky we're going to need your aviation experience, doing some surveillance work. What do you know about drones?"

"Big ones or little ones?" Jim asked.

"Not quite sure yet. It depends on what we find."

"I actually have experience flying the little ones—you know, the ones Max hates that have been harassing him for years. I have several of them, and fly them as a hobby. Of course I've never flown the big ones—never even seen one," Jim replied.

"Why don't you stick with me, and we'll work this out together as we learn more," Gordon said.

Shortly after noon, Gil reported to Jerry that four different auto body repair shops had received inquiries about a rush job on painting an SUV yellow. None of them had been able to meet the time requirements of the caller, and had turned down the job. They all said that when they told the man it would take a week or more, he just hung up the phone and wasn't interested in discussing other possibilities. Jerry asked Gil to locate these repair shops on a map, and come to his office. He then called Gordon and shared with him what Gil had discovered.

"That's great news, Jerry. My guess is he started calling places close to home, and when he got essentially the same response from each one, he realized that he was going to have to paint the beast himself. I'll call Max and give him the news. I'll also intercept Gil and find out what four places he called. Start positioning the satellite over that area, and keep it in a holding pattern until we can fill in some pertinent data."

"On it," replied Jerry.

When Jerry found Gil, not only did he have the locations of the repair shops, but he had asked to get a time confirmation on when the guy called. Three of them had automated phone logs and the times were accurate, but unfortunately the calling number had been blocked. Nevertheless, that gave Gordon what he was looking for, and with the time stamps his theory of calling close to home was proven correct. He called Max and gave him an idea of where to focus his paint purchase search. Max was appreciative for the help, and assured Gordon that he would find where the paint had originated.

It didn't take him long. Thirty minutes after talking to Gordon he hit pay dirt. A well-dressed man in a suit had purchased ten cans of yellow paint from a Sherwin Williams store on Auburn Avenue. It was a large order, and they had to have six cans brought in from a neighboring store. They asked the man if they could deliver it to him, but he declined. He came in two hours later to pick up the rest, covered in yellow paint. Unfortunately he paid cash both times for the paint, but it focused the area in which to search.

Gordon called Jerry. "Okay, buddy, you have search parameters. Focus the satellite to these coordinates and run a standard sweep. You're looking for yellow paint on driveways or on the street. I can't imagine they managed not to make a mess. From what Max tells me, the guy was no Michelangelo, so I'm sure you'll find a paint trail somewhere. When you do, Jim and I will be ready with the next stage of the plan."

Gordon and Jim loaded the small drone into the Secret Service SUV and headed over to Bethesda to await any information from Jerry.

"That's quite the contraption you have there, Gordon. It's not like anything I've ever seen. What exactly do you have attached to that drone?" Jim asked.

Gordon smiled. "Oh, you know—the usual presidential protection package that you can pick up at any Walmart."

Jim laughed. "Yeah, right. I'm pretty sure one of those devices is a thermal imaging camera, but the other one is a mystery."

Gordon looked over at Jim and said, "You can still fly it with all the added features, right?"

"I'm sure I can, but what is that other thing?"

"Jim, I'm going to tell you only because you deserve to know, but you didn't hear any of it from me. It's a DNA analyzer. The president gave me authorization to employ it today if we needed it. It isn't fully tested and issued for service yet, but it may come in handy."

"What the hell is a DNA analyzer?" Jim asked.

"You're probably not going to believe this is even possible, but you know how technology is—it never stops churning out amazing inventions. When you breathe, of course you exhale, and that exhalation contains carbon dioxide. Of course, since the air has come in contact with your lung tissue, that particular specimen of carbon dioxide can be identified. Now, you can't fly this contraption over FedEx Stadium and tell me everyone who is in attendance at a Redskins game, but in isolated locations with relatively few subjects, you can identify them. Of course you need to have a DNA sample of the person you're looking for, and it just so happens I've loaded a sample of Vera's DNA into the analyzer's computer."

"I'll be damned," replied Jim. "So you're telling me if we fly this drone over a house and use the thermal imaging camera, we can tell how many people are in the house and where they're located. Then if we use the DNA analyzer, we can tell who they are?" he asked, just to make sure he understood what Gordon had tried to explain.

"If all goes well, that's exactly what I'm telling you."

A few minutes later Gordon's phone rang. It was Jerry. "Nailed them. The satellite found two houses next to each other, with yellow paint in the driveways. I'm running checks on them now to see who owns them. Here are the addresses. I hope you're close by. Do your thing."

Gordon turned to Jim. "I think we've found them. Punch this

address into the GPS and we'll soon know what we have."

"Awesome," responded Jim.

A half a block down from the address was a small community park, the perfect place from which to launch the drone. Gordon pulled up onto the lawn, but before he did he called the Bethesda police department and explained he was running a Secret Service investigation and to ignore any reports coming in from neighbors in the area. Jim helped him get the drone out of the back, and together they assembled the pieces necessary to launch it and maintain flight. Fortunately Jim knew this drone and its flight commands very well, and so it was no problem getting it over the targets. As the drone began to relay information, Gordon began to monitor the screens from his position in the back of the SUV.

"Let's run a test first and see if everything checks out. Fly it directly overhead; we'll see if it recognizes us," Gordon instructed.

Jim directed the drone to hover over them, and it indeed recognized two men and identified one of them as Gordon Garcia. "Looks good. Sorry, I didn't have time to put your DNA in the computer. Now fly it over those two houses and let's see what we find. Keep the altitude to at least eight hundred feet. That's well within range for getting an accurate reading, and high enough to avoid detection."

Jim did as he was told, and it was determined that the first house contained four adult men congregated in the living room.

"Four men, huh?" said Gordon. "That's probably not your standard mom and pop with two kids kind of house. I'd guess that's a safe house for agents assigned to the area. Check the next house."

Jim flew the drone over the neighboring house and identified three females, one on the ground floor and two in the basement— one of which was Vera. Gordon clenched his fists and shook them in front of him in a short double burst. "Found her. Bring it back, Jim. Now the real work begins."

Gordon called Jerry with the news and instructed him to tell the president. "I'm wondering who those females are, in the house with Vera. My guess is that one is the woman who lured Vera into the SUV, but I'm wondering if the other one might be Ruth Ann. If not her, then it's probably another agent assigned to guard Vera. That'll make things more difficult. Is there any way you can get us a DNA sample for Ruth Ann?"

"Not in a timely manner," replied Jerry. "You might try Max and see what he can do."

"Good idea," Gordon said.

He called Max with the good news, and asked him if he had any way of identifying Ruth Ann, more specifically if he had anything with her DNA on it to load into the computer.

Max thought for a moment and then asked, "Would a hairbrush work?"

"A hairbrush would be perfect. Do you have one of hers?"

"Well, funny you should ask. I do. She left it in Minneapolis months ago, and I've been carrying it around hoping to give it back to her when we meet up. It's in my bag back at Blair House," Max responded.

"Terrific! Head back to Blair House and get the brush over to Jerry, and he can have her DNA coded and sent directly to this computer. Hurry."

Gordon turned to Jim and said, "It's happening. We're going to free her sometime tonight. Let's go grab a bite to eat while we wait for Max to get Ruth Ann's DNA to Jerry. I've been doing this a long time, and you get to the point where you can just feel it start to all come together. I have to say you're a pretty good partner. Have you ever thought of a second career as a Secret Service agent?"

"I wouldn't mind piloting one of those Gulfstreams for you, but I could never take this kind of excitement on a regular basis. Look at me, Gordon—what you see is the beginning of an old man."

Gordon laughed. "The food's on me tonight, gramps."

Gordon received word that Ruth Ann's DNA had been loaded into the computer and that another flyby would verify her presence. Once again they headed to the park and launched the drone. In just a few minutes it was at the correct altitude and running its scan. To their delight, the preliminary reading confirmed that indeed it was Ruth Ann, and she and Vera seemed to be inseparable. That was a good thing, because it made rescuing them much easier. In the process of scanning, Gordon noticed what appeared to be a tunnel that led underground between the basements of the two houses. The unidentified woman had left the house Vera and Ruth Ann were in, through the tunnel, and made her way to the living room to meet with the men.

"This is perfect. It couldn't be better," exclaimed Gordon.

"What?" Jim asked.

"There's a tunnel between the homes, which means we're certain that the men in the other house are part of the group that kidnapped the women. If we can get all five of them in the one house like they are now, we can take that house out and just walk right in to where Vera is, game over," Gordon explained.

"What do you mean, game over? You said take out that other house. Are you saying what I think you're saying?" Jim asked.

"Probably, but we'll leave that for the president to decide. We need to get back to the White House and plan the rescue."

In the Oval Office, the president and Jerry were already waiting for the others to arrive. Max showed up first, followed by Jim and Gordon. The president stood and welcomed them, and invited them to sit on the couches in the center of the room. "We're waiting for the attorney general; as soon as he arrives we can get formally started. In the meantime, great work today, gentlemen. Tonight she'll be back home where she belongs, and this nightmare will be over."

"If I might ask, sir, why is the attorney general coming?" Max asked.

"We may have some legal issues that require an opinion from him. I think that's him now."

"Rudy, it's good to see you my friend, thanks for coming over on such short notice," the president said, extending his hand to the attorney general.

"My pleasure, sir."

"Let me see if I understand the facts," said President Sherman. "And correct me if I'm missing anything. You have located the house in Bethesda where both Vera and Ruth Ann are imprisoned. Adjoining that house is another which contains somewhere between four and five enemy agents. If that is correct, how do you plan to rescue Vera and Ruth Ann?"

Jerry Reitz motioned that he had something to add. "We were able to collect DNA samples from all the agents in those two houses. I've run them through FBI databases—and you can confirm this, Rudy—they're all Mossad agents who have lived here for several years."

Max interjected up, "Does that come as a surprise to anyone? I've been chasing the tail on that dog for years, and the bark always comes out Yiddish. Mr. President, I can't prove this, but I think this group bears some responsibility for the plane that crashed into the Patriot Hotel. If that's true, you can't allow them to hurt you again."

"Thank you, Max. Gordon, how do you see this going down?" the president inquired.

"This is what I'd suggest. Jim and I go back to the park and launch the small drone over the houses. When only Vera and Ruth Ann remain in the one house, we take the other out," Gordon answered.

The president turned to Rudy. "Can we do that?"

Rudy handed the president a document he had prepared. "My

opinion is explained in this brief. The bottom line is that none of them are American citizens, they have committed a capital crime that we can prove, and if they're killed in a rescue attempt, that would be unfortunate at best."

The president turned to Jerry and asked, "Can you get access to a military drone?"

"The NSA has military drones independent of the armed forces. I can have one in the air circling that location within an hour," Jerry replied.

Jim, who was sitting next to Gordon, whispered, "Are you going to do what I'm thinking?"

Gordon nodded.

Jerry said, "The decision is yours, Mr. President."

Joel did not hesitate for a second. "Do it!"

Gordon pointed to Kelli and said, "We're going to need the dog."

"What on earth for?" the president asked.

"If we can send Kelli onto the property at night, she'll be able to pick up Vera's scent. If she's able to press her face up against the window, that will be a sign. When Vera sees her dog, she'll know we've located her and are about to launch a rescue. Instinctively, she'll go into 'brace for impact' mode and when we see that from the infrared, off goes the 'hellfire' missile."

The president rose and with perfect resolve in his voice instructed, "Gentlemen, you have your orders. May God be with you, and I'll be here when you bring my Vera back to me."

Gordon, Jim, Max and Kelli headed to the Secret Service vehicle. Jerry made his way to the armed weapons works in the NSA bunker, and the president and Rudy remained in the White House, awaiting word of their success.

"Don't we need something with Vera's scent on it for the dog?" Jim asked.

"Yeah, we do. Can you call Mike and ask him to bring an

article of her clothing down? Tell him we'll be waiting in front of the portico," Gordon said.

Gordon took his time driving to Bethesda. He needed to give Jerry a chance to get the drone in alignment and the target locked into place. "Well, Max, we're about to get revenge for that Range Rover, I think."

"It won't matter. That was a sweet ride, and this'll only help a little. I'm anxious to see Ruth Ann again and find out how long she's been a prisoner. I can't imagine that's gone well with her demanding personality, but who knows—maybe in the end it'll help to make her a better researcher," Max replied.

Jim kept petting Kelli and reassuring her everything was going to be all right. He let her smell the blouse that Mike had provided. "We're going to find your momma, Kelli," he kept saying over and over to her. Kelli responded as if she knew what Jim was saying, and sat at alert the whole time they were driving to the park.

When they arrived, Gordon explained to Max how everything worked. His job was to take Kelli for a walk over by the house, and instruct her to find Vera at the appropriate time. Jim flew the small drone up over the houses, and Gordon recorded the data as it came into the monitors. Again, the male agents were in the neighboring house, and all three women were in the house where Vera and Ruth Ann were imprisoned. Gordon phoned Jerry and gave him the report. Jerry explained that the drone would be in position in ten minutes. It was a dark and quiet night, which would allow for the operation to proceed without interference. Almost exactly ten minutes later, Jerry phoned. "The drone is in position," he said, "circling at ten thousand feet. The target is acquired and locked in place, awaiting your word."

"Roger," replied Gordon.

He phoned Max to see where he was in relation to the house. The report back was that he was there, pacing up and down in front of both houses. "Excellent," Gordon said. "Now we wait for the woman to move through the tunnel."

Thirty minutes later, Liv made her way through the tunnel and into the living room to join the men. Gordon phoned Max and told him to release Kelli. He gave the dog one last sniff of Vera's blouse and told Kelli to find her. The dog shot off down the side of the house, along the path that Vera had been led down when she arrived. Gordon was watching on the monitor, and could see where Kelli was going. The dog ran toward the small window of the room where Vera and Ruth Ann were being held. The dog began to paw at the window. Vera looked up and saw Kelli. At first she was shocked to see her dog, but quickly she understood what it meant. When Gordon could sense that a connection had been made, he called Max. "Call the dog back and get the hell out there as fast as you can."

Max called Kelli's name and the dog immediately came running.

Ruth Ann had fallen asleep on her bed. Vera shook her gently to wake her up. "Ruth Ann, I have great news. My golden retriever Kelli was just at the window. That means they know where we are and will begin a rescue attempt shortly. We need to get into protection mode to be prepared for anything they might attempt to do. Get under the bed and pull the mattress down around you."

Ruth Ann did not ask any questions, just did exactly as she was told.

"Smart girl," shouted Gordon to Jim, seeing what Vera was doing. "She figured it out immediately."

Jim replied, "Again, that's why we love her."

Max and Kelli arrived back at the vehicle. "We're good to go. I'll call Jerry."

Gordon phoned Jerry and gave him the 'all clear.'

Jerry pressed the ignition button on the hellfire missile.

Within seconds it hit its target, going right through the living room window to where the group was seated and exploding the house into a million pieces.

Jim had already brought the little drone back and landed it in the park. Gordon shut down the monitoring system, and Max and Kelli jumped into the back seat. "Let's get them," shouted Jim.

Gordon whipped the SUV off the lawn and raced toward the house that had burst into flames. The heat was intense. He parked several houses past the one Vera was in, and hoped they could get this part of the job done before the police and fire departments arrived. "There's a small battering ram in the way back," he said. "Get that, Max, will you, and let's go. Follow me."

Gordon knew right where the outside door was and when they arrived in front of it, Jim and Max had the battering ram cocked and ready to swing. "Now," he commanded.

Two swings were all it took before the door popped open. "Vera," called out Jim, as loud as he could. From the other room both Vera and Ruth Ann came running through the smoke that was starting fill the house from the explosion and fire next door. Vera ran up the stairs into Jim's arms, and when Ruth Ann realized Max was there, she ran into his.

"Come on, folks, we've got to get out of here fast," ordered Gordon.

They ran in single file behind Jim, up the path and out to the sidewalk. What was left of the neighboring house was in flames, and sirens could be heard approaching. They raced to the SUV and before all the doors were completely shut, Gordon gunned the engine, and out of the neighborhood they flew. Vera reached into the back and hugged Kelli with both arms. "You saved me, girl, you did it! You saved your momma, and you're going to make your new daddy very happy."

twenty nine

*W*hen the good news was conveyed to the White House, the excitement completely dispelled a foreboding gloom that no one had wanted to recognize. Mike had joined the president in the Oval Office, wearing his lucky Philadelphia Eagles shirt. After he heard the results of the rescue, the smile on his face had no "off" switch. The president slapped a high five with Rudy, and then hugged Mike for all he was worth.

"You did it, sir," whispered Mike in the president's ear.

"I can't wait to get the details and hear the debriefings, but yes, Mike, we did it, and I have so many people to thank. They'll be here shortly. See if you can get the kitchen staff to fix up some sandwiches or something. I'm sure they'll be hungry, and we all have a lot to talk about."

"That's already been taken care of, sir. I had no doubt that Gordon's plan would be successful, and I talked to the staff an hour ago. Everything will be in order upon their arrival."

"No doubt, huh," responded Joel, pointing to Mike's shirt.

Mike smiled. "Never doubt the bird, sir."

"You may have convinced me, my friend."

When the president was informed that Gordon's SUV had passed through the security gates, he personally went out to meet the group. He opened the door for Vera, helped her out, and embraced her as if he never wanted to let go.

"I'm so sorry, sweetheart," she said.

"Hush, sweet girl. No apology is necessary."

Kelli barked when she saw the president and Vera hug, and

together they went around to the back of the unit to let her out. She was overjoyed to see them together. Max and Ruth Ann had been talking between themselves the whole way back to the White House, and were both still talking nonstop, hoping the other was listening. Ruth Ann filled him in on all that had happened to her since she left Minneapolis. Max shared with her what had happed to Gil and Bob, and assured her that moving forward with all the research was in everyone's best interest. The president shook Jim's hand and thanked him for all he had done to save Vera. Words were not necessary between them. Jim knew better than anyone what Joel was feeling inside, and Joel appreciated his understanding. The president saved Gordon for last. His favorite and most trusted agent was still standing near the car door when the president approached. Joel looked Gordon in the eye and saluted him.

"Words of appreciation will never convey my gratitude to you. The fact that you were in charge of this operation gave me the confidence needed to instill hope in everyone involved. You are an exceptional human being, and I'm honored to serve this country with you. More importantly, I'm proud to call you my friend."

Gordon just smiled in his humble way and said, "Thank you, sir. If you were a lesser man, I could not have done it."

When Max finally stopped talking he made his way towards the president to introduce Ruth Ann to him. Joel put his arm around Max's shoulders and drew him near. "Adventure never stops with you, does it, Max?"

"No, sir. It seems to chase me wherever I go, but I always stay one step ahead."

"Evidently that's true. Even a good burial couldn't keep you down," replied the president.

Max laughed. "Mr. President, may I introduce to you Ruth Ann Lowy. From what I understand, she's now a wealth of information, having spent several months with those freaks."

The president put out his hand and shook Ruth Ann's. "Welcome to the White House. I'm sorry it couldn't be under more pleasant circumstances, but we're all thrilled that you were part of the rescue, and I'm anxious to hear all you have to tell us."

"Thank you, Mr. President. You're not nearly as happy about it as I am. I didn't think I was ever going to see my freedom again, so these circumstances suit me just fine."

The group made their way into the White House, talking and laughing as the tension of the day began to dissipate. As Mike had promised, food and drink awaited them in the dining room. When everyone had had an opportunity to relive and share their experiences, the president rose and announced that the following morning at ten o'clock, a meeting would be held in the Cabinet room to discuss all the events leading up to the rescue and reunion of Max's team. The meeting would serve as both a debriefing, and an examination of all the intelligence that had been acquired to date regarding 9/11. He encouraged all of them to come expecting to discuss strategies to force the Congress to open a new investigation. He also wanted them to explore ways to present information to the public that had been hidden and disguised by the perpetrators of that horrible event.

The president closed by saying, "The presence of every one of you is required at that meeting tomorrow. Come without fear, and be prepared to leave with a renewed hope that his country will do all that is necessary to ensure life, liberty, and the pursuit of happiness for its all its people"

thirty

The door to the Cabinet Room was already open when Gil, Ruth Ann and Max arrived. The president was seated at the center of the large oval table with his back to the windows. He stood and welcomed them and invited them to sit directly across the table from him. Vera and Jim were already seated to the left of him and, Jerry Reitz and Gordon Garcia were seated to his right.

President Sherman began the meeting, "Good morning. I want to thank you all for coming and being so punctual. We have a great deal to discuss, so let's get started. Vera and Jim each smiled and nodded to Max and his team.

The president said, "Jerry, let's begin with you."

Jerry Reitz began, "I first want to thank you all for your research and perseverance. Without fearless researching, the truth of what happened to our country would have remained hidden forever. I'm aware that it's no easy task to unravel and prove a covert action was methodically planned and executed. And worse, falsely blamed on innocent parties. In fact, with the media's full compliance in propagating the illusion, your job has been made more difficult. So, Max, what have you found on Bob's hard drive that will shed more light on your past discoveries?"

"This isn't earth shattering, but I find it to be very troubling. I uncovered a document from the U.S. Air Force dated September 13, 2001, that claimed Flight 93 was a 747 aircraft. At first I thought it was a type error, by then everyone knew that plane was a 757. Upon deeper review, I noticed that the same mistake was made more than once in the document. This type of incompetence makes it difficult to trust any information coming from the Air Force. These are the same people that produced the radar data for NORAD."

"Is this a common occurrence?" the president asked.

"Not particularly with the Air Force, but I have noticed over the years that the data from NORAD and the FAA are not always in sync," Jim added.

The president furrowed his brow and looked at Max, "Can you explain this?"

Max replied, "Not directly but it jives with some of the other things I have found that are more disturbing. One of Bob's files named ATTABOY reveals the only photograph on record from 9/11 of Mohammad Atta and his alleged co-pilot. It was taken at the Portland, Maine airport and shows two men entering security. The problem is the security camera shows two conflicting time stamps. How can you explain that?"

"Photoshop could explain that. Security cameras only have one time and date stamp embedded."

These time stamps were 8 minutes apart, one of which was only 6 minutes prior to their flight taking off to Boston. Not only are there two different time stamps on the security camera photo, which raises suspicion, but the picture is so grainy that it's impossible to tell a definite identity. The photo could be of anyone with dark hair and a blue shirt. The man's hairline appears to be slightly different that the photo the FBI routinely shows of Atta. Another problem is that the ticket agent at Boston, when interviewed by the FBI, reported that Atta and al-Omari were wearing suit jackets and ties, not casual dress shirts and pants. To me, it looks like they have taken a photograph of two dark haired men and doctored it to fit their contrived story and their FBI photos. I'm going to pass these photos around, look at the hairlines, they don't match, and they could be anyone."

As the tablet was handed to Ruth Ann, she stared at one of the faces on the screen. "Wait, this is supposed to be one of the hijackers on Flight 11?"

Max answered back, "That's what the FBI would like us all to believe, however, his father said he spoke to him the day after the attacks, and he was very much alive. The FBI claims this was the ring leader of the event. And Al Omari, he's still alive and working as an engineer in Saudi Arabia. He's never been to the United States so, I'm sure that's not a photo of him in Portland, Maine."

"I think this guy in the photo visited the house in Bethesda. If it wasn't he, it was someone that looked exactly like him," Ruth Ann said. "There were several other foreign agents that shuffled through that house in the time I was there. Often I was able to hear their conversations through the heater vents late at night and sometimes in the early morning. I didn't see all their faces, but the ones I did see, are well ingrained in my memory in case that was the last face I ever saw."

Jerry Reitz spoke, "May I see that photo again?"

Ruth Ann handed the tablet across the table to Jerry, "This is a familiar face, as unclear as it is, I can see a difference from the FBI photo. I know this sounds crazy but this guy in the airport security photo could have been one of the Israeli IT guys that Bush hired immediately after 9/11. The more I look at this guy, the more familiar his face is. I might have seen him right here in D.C." Jerry handed to photo back to Max.

President Sherman asked, "Ruth Ann, you mentioned overhearing them, what do you remember?"

"I often heard them laughing at the stupidity of Americans, they joked about Texans for some reason. There was some talk about the old Sears Tower in Chicago, but I couldn't quite make out what they were planning. Then, I heard one of them mention something about the Twin Towers and art or artists, but that made no sense to me. Have any of you heard about Israeli art students traveling around the country visiting Federal government employees at their homes and offices? There were often visitors to the house that talked about art and selling art. What didn't make sense was that talk was always in conjunction with visiting different government facilities. At first I thought the word art was a code word for some type of illegal drug they were dealing. By the way, only two of these guys spoke perfect English, the rest of them spoke with a distinct Israeli accent."

Max interrupted, "I found this file last night, it's codenamed: WARHOL. I wasn't sure if it was an acronym or if Bob was a closet art collector. When I opened it, I discovered a classified document out of the DEA, from 2002. This sixty-one page report is now starting to make more sense. In light of what you overheard Ruth Ann, I would like to interrupt here and brief the group on the contents of this file. Someone at the DEA thought it suspicious that groups of Israelis claiming to be art students were traveling around the country selling artwork but mostly asking questions about security, phone systems and cameras. What caught the attention of some federal employees was that even the addresses to non-public buildings and agents personal residences were visited. A bulletin went out to several federal offices warning about these art students' suspicious behavior. After the bulletin went out, several agents started interrogating these art students. Their identification showed they were involved with Israeli intelligence or Israeli Defense Forces. Some of them were explosive specialists and others had backgrounds in communication surveillance. The majority of these foreign art students resided in Florida, but they were reported in almost every state. Some of them showed addresses that were a block or two away from the reported 9/11 hijackers. Coincidence?" Max let out a slight chuckle, "So, as I'm reading through this once classified document, I'm asking myself, why would no one at the

FBI think this might be worth looking into? This ended up being labeled an Israeli spy ring, and still no investigation. No federal agency would have reported this had it not been for the public's concern for anyone with an accent. As it turns out, some of them were associated with an Israeli owned moving company. We all remember reading about the now famous Urban Movers and their vans painted with murals of a plane flying into the Twin Towers. The CEO of the moving company quickly fled to Israel after the attacks."

Jim interrupted, "Max, did you just say communication surveillance specialists? Perhaps it was these agents who were responsible for tapping the airlines' phone and computers systems."

Max pointed at Jim and nodded.

Jerry Reitz was taking notes, "It's starting to look like people had a reason to say 9/11 was an inside job. How can anyone not pay attention to this type of espionage? Israel has a reputation for spying on America; we all remember the Jonathan Pollard spy case in the mid-eighties."

Max nodded and continued, "Somebody at the top of the pig pile as they say didn't want anyone to get dirty and kept this document classified until someone in the DEA managed to leak it. Naturally, they demonized the guy and claimed he was a disgruntled employee, but the only thing he was unhappy about was that nobody in the federal government was concerned about an obvious national security issue. It also became known that these Israelis were arrested for their activities around some nuclear power plants. Several of them were arrested but you didn't' hear about that in the media did you? This spying has been going on since before 9/11 and is still going on today."

Ruth Ann added, "I distinctly remember one night, I overheard them talking about a nuclear power plant somewhere in Pennsylvania, it sounded like things got a little dicey there."

Max continued, "It gets even crazier here, listen to this. There was a group of artists living inside the Twin Towers, Bob managed to find a copy of one of their temporary construction passes. Each artist had a pass which gave them complete access to both towers. The group was sponsored by the Lower Manhattan Cultural Center. They were actually living on the ninetieth and ninety-first floors. One group of these artists removed an exterior window from the North Tower on the ninetieth floor and placed a platform they called the balcony outside. At the same time an art sponsor rented both the top of the Millennium Hotel and a helicopter to photograph the balcony and individual art students standing on it."

Jim questioned, "How in the world did security ever allow that to happen?"

Max raised both eyebrows, "Good question Jimbo, it gets worse. This group of artists called themselves, Gelatin. My uncle owned a demolition company. During summers between college quarters, I worked for him. In the explosives world, there's something called blasting gelatin, sometimes we called it Jelly, but you get my drift. Two very important details I need to point out are contained in this photo. The first is, the cardboard boxes surrounding the men in the photo. The label on the boxes: BB18, designates a remote control detonation fuse bar and is from a demolition company. Take note of the number of boxes surrounding the men and the international symbol for no smoking on the boxes. Now, second is the fact that at least one of these Israeli art students was trained as a bomb expert by the Israeli military. He was also arrested in Texas months earlier and apparently released. Now, what are the chances that this is all a coincidence? We have at least one explosives guy pretending to be an artist with a whole lot of demolition equipment, and the group he belongs to calls itself Gelatin, as in the explosive jelly gelignite?"

"That's inconceivable." Vera whispered so that only Joel could hear.

Max added, "These traveling artists were deported after 9/11, most of them for immigration violations, but they have been replaced by others. If you do a google search you can find them."

Jerry Reitz joined the conversation. "I'm particularly troubled by the total disconnect between those government employees who recognized a problem and their superiors who are intent on covering it up. Max, this example you've just shared is not isolated to the DEA, I'm beginning to see it across the entire government spectrum. I'm of the opinion that if we discover something suspicious or threatening we need to take action, no matter the color of their skin or their passport."

"That's exactly why I selected Rudy Rathburn as the attorney general. He has the clarity of vision to prosecute and deport those who are here illegally or who have a clandestine agenda," said the president.

"It's unthinkable that obvious espionage activity wasn't investigated by the FBI." Jim added.

"I will instruct Rudy do some investigating to determine whose decision it was to ignore Israeli military intelligence agents residing in the World Trade Center completely unsupervised. The report of foreign agents arrested at nuclear reactors is even more concerning. It indicates a vulnerability that we must address and eliminate," the president said.

Jim added, "When Vera and I made our Westover discovery public, people began contacting us expressing their doubts about the official 9/11 story and sharing with us facts that had previously not been reported about 9/11. I think if we can motivate the public and get them to understand that there needs to be a new investigation, they will come forward in droves with additional information and support."

"That's exactly what we're trying to achieve with this research and the actions that we will employ," the president said.

"Hold on one minute. I think I have a perfect example of what Jim is talking about. In one of Bob's files marked OTIS, I found the most incredible affidavit. I hadn't paid much attention to the file, thinking it was just more military's excuses for not scrambling jets. This statement is from an eyewitness and it's recorded on an mp3 audio file. Let me play it for you," said Max.

"My name is Sara Swain and I was living in Otis, Massachusetts on September 11, 2001. At approximately 8:30 - 8:35, I saw a United Airlines plane fly over my residence at the time, and I was shocked because the plane was very low. I could see the people in the windows. I was standing on a deck on the second floor and I was watching the plane fly over the top of the house and I lost track of it because of the way the building was, but I do think it was going north when it flew over the house and after I lost sight of it, I was speaking with my neighbor and we were just amazed at the height of the plane, it was so low, shouldn't say height, meaning altitude, it was so low, we were flabbergasted. Now I know that it was approximately 8:30, I would say 8:45 at the latest, because I had to go to an appointment in the next town over at 9:30 and I left, maybe five minutes after I saw the plane and headed to Great Barrington."

President Sherman was first to speak, "I would like to speak with this woman."

"Max, if you don't have her contact information in Bob's files, let me know. I'll have the NSA get that to give to the president." Jerry Reitz stated.

Ruth Ann exclaimed, "I knew it, I knew someone had to have seen something that morning. I've been waiting for this for over a decade. We now have an eyewitness that was willing to go on the record to confirm what you two discovered about Westover."

Vera joined the conversation, "This poor woman, she must've thought she was out of her mind to see a commercial 767 flying so low. That's a large aircraft, and to see it flying so low, she had to question her sanity. And what's worse, she had to have been ridiculed when she told friends and family about what she saw, especially when she found out later that the plane she thought was going to crash up the road crashed in New York. She knew that was impossible."

Jim opened his laptop to a Google map of Massachusetts and found the exact location where Sara claimed to have seen the plane. "This would be exactly correct, Flight 175 lost its transponder just south of Westover and would have circled around to land to the south, so of course she would have seen the plane headed north. Her story fits the timeline perfectly! We now have a civilian eyewitness in conjunction with the reservists that reported being locked out of their base. This is a real game changer."

Gordon asked, "Mr. President, do you think this woman needs Secret Service protection?"

President Sherman answered, "No, not at this time, but I'll know more after I've had a chance to talk to her. If she feels threatened or if we feel her life is in danger, it might be a good idea, because Jim's right, this is a game changer."

Gil interjected, "I have something to add, I found some audio wav files labeled 'terrorist', 'terrorist1', 'terrorist2' and so forth. This one claims to be one of the hijackers. Listen to this: "We have some planes, just stay quiet and you will be okay, we are going back to the airport." The next one is marked Terrorist 1, "Nobody move, everything will be okay, if you try to make any moves you will injure yourself and the airplane, just stay quiet." The weird thing is the air traffic controllers don't seem to hear the hijacker's voice, which means the tapes were undoubtedly doctored. And the most confusing part, in the metadata for one particular file, the FAA has copyrighted it. Why would they do that?"

"What? Jim asked. "The FAA put a copyright on a voice file

of a hijacker?"

"That's right Jim, every electronic file is stamped with metadata, indicating when the file was created or modified. It also provides space to indicate a copyright. If what Gil has told us is true, the FAA has some serious explaining to do," Jerry explained.

Ruth Ann interjected, "That isn't even an Arab accent. If I listen to it several more times I will be able to tell you which Israeli town it comes from."

Vera added, "It's also very interesting that the FAA would label the voice as belonging to a terrorist because prior to 9/11, such a voice would have been labeled as a hijacker. Terrorist was not a term used by the FAA or the aviation industry until well after 9/11."

While the others were discussing voice files, Max was searching for a file he had seen earlier on Bob's hard drive, it was labeled: TAGURIT. "I'm reading this one as tag you're it." Max chuckled. "Bob isolated several FAA and NORAD radar files that indicated the altitude, latitude and longitude of the four planes that morning. Now, you'd think this information from those two agencies would exhibit the exact same data. But, Bob's research clearly indicates those files have discrepancies by as much as seven thousand feet and thirty-five miles. If that information isn't the same what kind of problems might that create, Jim, for an airliner anywhere around the New York area?"

Jim looked shocked, "You have to be kidding me, those altitudes are that far off? Something is very wrong."

Max continued, "And this will blow you completely away, Bob took screenshots of information that was uploaded to the FAA computers detailing accounts of all four airplanes. It's a combination of radar locations, voice files, text and word documents pertaining to those flights. He noted at the top of the screenshots metadata and circled the upload times. The circled times show the files were uploaded to the FAA prior to the airplanes even taking off, in some cases as early as 5:57AM that morning, nearly two hours before departure. Only one file appears to include the authentic radar data for the take-off times for Flight 11 and 175, the rest of the information has to be counterfeit."

Gil chimed in, "Remember those two companies MITRE and Ptech that were working in the basement of the FAA Headquarters before 9/11? It looks like they were busy creating plenty of fake flight paths. Once the real planes pushed back, radar data sets were chosen that best fit the actual departure times. Bob had mentioned there were sixteen to eighteen minutes of radar data completely unaccounted for, but he didn't want to tell me over the phone. It looks like these radar specialists forgot one critical detail; computers always time and date stamp files."

Vera looked across the table at Max's team, "This explains a lot and mostly it explains why the details of the official story changed so often, they were making up scenarios to explain their illusion. Now that we know the radar data was uploaded early and the planes were really taken to Westover, it's easy to see that everyone was lying to us and using fake data to substantiate it. They needed us to all believe in their false flag, so that as a nation we would support their preplanned wars in the middle-east. No wonder the callers used the words middle-eastern descent to describe the hijackers. That's who they wanted us to hate."

Gil's eyebrows rose as he looked at his computer screen. "Max, the metadata time stamp on some of these wav files I mentioned is stamped before departure too. One of them is marked at 6:37am on the morning of September 11th."

"A word I keep hearing Vera use when she speaks about 9/11 is illusion, she sometimes reinforces that by comparing it to a magic trick." President Sherman said.

Max laughed, "Like a magic trick where the audience sees

through the illusion, but the announcer keeps telling them that they didn't see what they saw."

Jerry Reitz added, "That's apparently what the government and the media have done for all these years. They have lied and told the people what they saw and never allowed them to think otherwise."

"And that deception permeated everywhere," Vera explained. The perpetrators completely ignored the FAA protocols when executing the in-flight scenario. If they had consulted a flight attendant the whole story would have been completely different. I was also amazed that never once, in any of the passenger phone calls, did one of them mention the rapid decent of the airplanes. How could they have overlooked that unless it never occurred? That kind of decent warrants fear and screaming on the part of passengers. And yet, when all the calls were made, the recipients of those calls often mentioned the lack of background noise. But the best part of all, that blows their deception out of the water, is the fact that everyone knew cell phones didn't work at altitude. So they were performing the illusion with the curtain down. Those of us who had eyes to see saw and the rest had the curtain pulled over their head."

Max nodded and added, "They have had control of the message since the very first impact. The media wasn't enough for them. They have infiltrated every group that questioned any aspect of the official story from the physics of the towers' collapses to the weather. They appear everywhere on social media prepared to refute and castigate anyone who dares speak the truth. If the general public ever opens their eyes and learns the full story about this manipulation, angry won't even begin to describe how they'll react."

Silence filled the room for the first time since the meeting commenced. President Sherman asked, "Is there any more you wish to reveal?"

Ruth Ann responded, "Mr. President, with all the information we have at our disposal just on this terabyte we could go on for months, but I think we have exposed the more salient points and presented you what formed the basis of this grand deception."

"I have been mostly quiet listening to all of you. I would like to say that I have been shocked at your revelations, and though much of what you have shared has been new to me; I'm not surprised by the depth of the malicious wickedness that has been presented here. I believe you have given me sufficient information to go before the American people and attempt to pull that curtain from off their heads and show them what it was they really saw on 9/11. If done correctly, they will be angry, as Max said, and demand we investigate the entire event. I see my responsibility, before I leave this office, to expose, to charge and to convict all those responsible for the crime, the complacency, and the cover up that was 9/11."

thirty one

For several days following the meeting in which so many of the details of the 9/11 research had come to light, the president met with only his closest advisors—including Vera—to determine how to move forward. He knew that what had been revealed to him needed to be condensed, but had to be sufficiently powerful that the public could understand the magnitude of the message. After his State of the Union Address, he had developed a reputation for being able to communicate effectively to all the country's citizens, regardless of their political affiliations. Unfortunately, one address—though formidable—was insufficient to motivate the people to demand a new investigation of 9/11. The consensus from his advisors was that another prime time address needed to be scheduled, in which the president would focus only on the planning, preparation, execution and cover-up of the terror attacks. The thinking was that if the evidence were cogently presented, with enough examples, the people would begin to wake up and realize that they been lied to and cleverly deceived on a massive scale. He hoped that such enlightenment would lead to resentment that could be harnessed and directed at Congress to demand action.

A date was selected which did not conflict with any sporting events, music awards or popular reality television programming. The president's communications director presented the proposed plan to the networks, and the date was scheduled for a one-hour prime time address to the nation from the Oval Office. The television executives' enthusiasm for the speech was tepid at best. As the date approached for the scheduled event, many of them demanded an advance copy of the speech. When they were denied copies, they insisted upon a general outline of the points the president intended to cover. That too was held in abeyance, and only a mention of 9/11 as the subject of the speech was shared with them, in the hope that would be sufficient. That revelation sent them into orbit, and one by one they began to refuse to air the speech. Every network that declined to cover the speech conveyed to the president's office that they did not feel that such a message, fifteen years after the fact, was important enough to sacrifice revenue-producing air time. It was curious that each message sent to the president stated the exact same thing, using almost the exact same words. The president's communications staff sought direction as to how to proceed. At each inquiry, President Sherman reassured them that all was well, and that they should plan to proceed as though nothing had changed.

On the afternoon of the scheduled speech, lighting, Teleprompters, and communication relays were moved into the Oval Office. Everyone complied with the president's orders, but none of them could figure out why they were moving forward with all the preparations for an event they knew was not going to occur.

Thirty minutes prior to the scheduled starting time, Joel was getting dressed in the residence. When all was in order, he found Vera and asked her to step into the study. He closed door behind them and asked her if she would kneel in prayer with him. She was surprised, but she could feel his spirit supplicating her to join him. She nodded in agreement and knelt beside him.

The president offered these words: "Our beloved Father in Heaven, humbly we kneel before Thee and express our gratitude for the magnificence of this country that was formed from your inspiration, and by the hands of wise men that heard your voice and brought forth, out of obscurity, a nation built on the principles of freedom and liberty. One of this land's basic tenets is trust in Thee. As a country we have fallen short in meeting that expectation, but Vera and I still believe and trust in Thee, and we need Thy help this night as I address the nation in an effort to help them see the light and shine it into the darkness that has separated us from Thee. Help me to express the words in a way that will touch the hearts of those who still hearken to Thy voice. Bless them that in hearing Thy voice, they will move forward to reclaim these United States from the grasp of the evil one whose desire it is to destroy and enslave the minds, hearts and will of this people. Bless us, Father, with the understanding to lift rather than to push, and to lead rather than to drive. Again we are thankful for the opportunity and the responsibility we have to be of service to Thee, this nation and its people, and we say these things in the name of Jesus Christ. Amen."

Tears fell from their cheeks as they rose to their feet and embraced one another. Vera kissed Joel and whispered to him, "All is well. Go with God."

Joel thanked her and squeezed her hand as he began the walk from the residence to the Oval Office, to deliver what would be the most important speech of his presidency.

When he arrived, everything was set up as he had directed, and he took his place at his desk to complete a sound check and make sure the Teleprompter was working properly. The staff was still confused, and from the looks on their faces, they thought they were running through a futile exercise. Jerry Reitz arrived at the office right on schedule, and nodded to the president. He took his seat out of camera view, and waited for the president to commence.

Just before nine o'clock eastern time, the president signaled Jerry, who gave word to his subordinates to engage the EBS. Immediately, the emergency broadcast system was activated with its familiar tone. When it went live every television station, radio station, tablet, computer and smart phone in the country was connected to the president, who began his speech.

"My fellow Americans, I am coming to you through the Emergency Broadcast System tonight because the media deemed that what I have to share with you was not important to them. I can assure you that what I am about to say is important, and it is an emergency.

"We as a people are on the precipice of losing our country and our freedom. We have not assumed the responsibility that freedom demands, and have left that duty to others who do not have our best interests in mind. We can feel it in our states and in our cities, in our schools and in our places of employment. It winds its way into government regulation, and ultimately it makes its way into our wallets. What we knew to be the American way of life is slowly slipping away into darkness. And we seem to be blinded, so we do not notice or take action.

"My purpose tonight is to flood our minds with light that has come from hours of research and investigation into an evil that has usurped our freedoms and as a result is choking the life out of us. To begin with, not much of what we see or what we hear in today's media is real. It is designed to make us think it is real, but it is all a carefully crafted message to distract us from the truth, and from seeing the illusion through which we are being led. That illusion does not satisfy—it destroys.

"Let me give you some quick examples:

"In June of 1967, the six-day war broke out between Egypt and Israel. The USS Liberty was in the Mediterranean Sea when the Israeli Defense Force's jets attacked the ship. Simultaneously, torpedo boats fired their payloads into its hull. The jets continued to attack for over an hour, with the intent to sink the Liberty and kill all the crew. Israel's plan was to blame the attack on Egypt. The United States government was aware of the attack and who was responsible, but it covered it up and threatened the survivors if they ever told the world what actually occurred. This event established a pattern that prevails to this day, and must be stopped.

"In April of 1995, half of the Murrah Federal Building in Oklahoma City was blown to rubble and 168 people were killed. Timothy McVeigh and Terry Nichols were quickly arrested, charged, convicted, and in McVeigh's case, executed. However, there was much more to the story, concerning who was involved in the planning, implementation and execution of that tragedy. Almost immediately, Congress passed the Antiterrorism and Effective Death Penalty Act, which began a process of limiting American citizens' freedoms. Congress' unwillingness to fully investigate the bombing, which would have uncovered all those responsible, also established a pattern which is reprehensible and must be eliminated.

"More recently, the Sandy Hook school shooting raised many unanswered questions and contained many unexplained anomalies that a prudent person is forced to question. Even the slightest investigation into that event yields so many disturbing facts that a conclusion can be drawn that the shooting was staged to take away the gun rights of individuals. Again, the easy patsy was identified, blamed, and eliminated. No significant or substantial investigation was deemed to be warranted, but legislation was ready to be passed, signed and implemented, limiting liberty.

"Of course, 9/11 was a well-planned and well-orchestrated disaster, designed to instill fear in the public, thereby allowing the government to usurp constitutional rights from the individual. Without those rights, the masses become more easily controlled. With fear that lingers and is magnified daily by the media, wars and rumors of war infiltrate every corner of the world. We now have proof of what actually happened on 9/11, how it was done and who is responsible. Worse, we have evidence of how the facts have been obscured, ignored and altered to fit the needs of those degenerates whose evil knows no limits.

"I am calling on you this night as a people, to demand an investigation by your elected representatives in Congress into the event referred to as 9/11. There are people waiting at the edge of the light to testify, demonstrate and prove to the American people all the truth of that horrible day. Your representatives do not want this to happen. They have demonstrated for decades, be they Republicans or Democrats, that they believe that seeking the truth is not only a burden, but it conflicts with their primary interest. They will avoid, delay and obscure any attempt to reveal the truth because they are controlled by those who reign with blood and horror on this earth.

"I am addressing you tonight to remind you that it is your responsibility as a people who cleave to freedom, to insist that your representatives yield to the will of the people. This is not a political issue. It is a survival issue. If you choose to ignore my message and continue to have your thoughts about these events shaped and molded by those who inflicted them upon you, those individuals standing at the edge of the light will be shoved back into the darkness and you with them. Should that occur there is no escape. Lovers of darkness will grind you into dust, and your posterity with you.

"Only you can bear the burden of freedom. Never can you delegate it to Congress or to anyone else. Our founding fathers knew this, and I am here tonight to remind you. Allow me to conclude by repeating the last lines of my State of the Union Address:

"We stand on the precipice of decision. We can choose to be free, based upon the principles this nation was founded upon, or we can be forced into the den of destruction, forever serving the masters of evil who are consumed by their own lusts. Join me and rise above such evil. Throw off the scales that blind your eyes from truth. Look to liberty and live. May God bless each and every one of you, and may God once again be sufficiently trusted in, to bless the United States of America."

thirty two

*T*he camera pulled back just far enough to focus on two hands resting atop the leather-bound Bible, symbolizing their commitment to one another and their trust in the Almighty. The image froze there for a moment for the entire world to see, and then pulled back even farther, so that the radiant faces of Vera Hanson and Joel Sherman could be shared with those witnessing the first wedding in the Oval Office of a President of the United States. The Chief Justice, in his black robe, was presiding. The president was beaming. Vera's gown was gorgeous; its flowing white train swept across the Presidential Seal that was emblazoned on the carpet. Jim was standing off to the side in his tuxedo, acting as best man, and Vera had asked Mari to be her Matron of Honor. The flowers had been selected from various parts of the country, and were positioned elegantly throughout the room. Vera's bouquet had come from the state of Washington, and had been personally delivered by her friend Jenny, whose excitement knew no bounds. Max, once again, had to find his way into a tuxedo, but wasn't heard to complain. Kelli was curled up in her doggie bed near the president's desk, which had been moved off to one side.

Their vows were simple: each pledged their life and their love to the other. Their hands together symbolized a unity bound by God and forged in trust. The Chief Justice began the ceremony, and concluded with the words, "I now pronounce you man and wife, President and First Lady of the United States of America."

Joel sweetly kissed his bride, and together they glanced over at Kelli, who was fast asleep. The few invited guests warmly applauded, as Hope and Change filled the White House.

Rebekah Roth

"*The light at the end of the tunnel is not an illusion.
The tunnel is.*"
Unknown

ACKNOWLEDGEMENTS

A Special Thanks To:

The hosts and listening audiences from:
Coast to Coast am, Caravan to Midnight,
The Hagmann & Haggman Report, The Kev Baker Show,
Truth Frequency Radio,
The many citizen journalists, bloggers and radio hosts.

Lauren Sweet for her excellent editing work.
Landon Meikle at Alphagraphics for his design work
Keith Kintner and all my fans on Facebook.
Jonathan Anderson for his incredible artwork.
www.andersonpetportraits.com

And
To my husband for all his patience and help.

APPENDIX

U.S.A.F. Memorandum for the FBI

Israeli Spies/DEA Metapedia (3 pages)

Fox news Article Israeli Spy Ring

Gelatin ~ The B Thing

NY Times Balcony Thing article 8/18/2001

Temporary Construction ID for WTC

FAA files from 9/11/2001 (7 pages)

Chronology FAA 9/11/2001

FAA Daily Log 9/11/2001

Israeli Spies at Nuclear Sub base 2004

DEPARTMENT OF THE AIR FORCE
84TH RADAR EVALUATION SQUADRON (ACC)
HILL AIR FORCE BASE, UTAH

13 Sep 01

MEMORANDUM FOR FEDERAL BUREAU OF INVESTIGATION (FBI)

FROM: 84 RADES/CC
       7976 Aspen Ave
       Hill AFB UT 84056-5846

SUBJECT: Radar Data Analysis of East Coast Terrorist Activities, 11 September 2001 (World Trade Center, Pentagon, Pittsburgh PA).

1. **Introduction.** At the request of the Federal Bureau of Investigation (FBI), the 84th Radar Evaluation Squadron (84 RADES) analyzed data from US Air Force (USAF) radar sites with coverage on the four commercial aircraft used in the recent terrorist activities against the United States. Table 1 provides a mishap outline.

Table 1 Mishap Outline

Location	Airline/Flight	Aircraft Type	Crash Time	Tracking Radar		Radar ID	
				Location	Type	USAF	FAA
World Trade Center A/C #1	American Airlines (AA) – 11	Boeing 767	08:46 ET	Riverhead NY	ARSR-4	J-52	QVH
				North Truro MA	ARSR-4	J-53	QEA
World Trade Center A/C #2	United Airlines (UA) – 175	Boeing 757	09:02 ET	Riverhead NY	ARSR-4	J-52	QVH
				The Plains VA	ARSR-3	J-50	QPL
Pentagon	AA – 77	Boeing 757	09:37 ET	Gibbsboro NJ	ARSR-4	J-51	QIE
				Oceana VA	ARSR-4	J-01	QVR
				Detroit MI	ARSR-1E	J-62	QDT
Pittsburgh, PA	UA – 93	Boeing 747	10:00 ET	Riverhead NY	ARSR-4	J-52	QVH
				Gibbsboro NJ	ARSR-4	J-51	QIE

From: http://en.metapedia.org/wiki/Israeli_Art_Students

Targeting the DEA and Defense Locations

In January 2000 persons claiming to be Israeli art students began appearing at the offices of the Drug Enforcement Agency (DEA) wanting to sell art work.[1]They were divided into teams of eight to ten individuals with a designated team leader. Art student teams appeared in 42 towns and cities across the United States, mostly the southeast and southwest parts of the country. The art they were selling appears to have been made in China. [2]

Many of them claimed to be students at Bezalel Academy of Arts in Jerusalem or the University of Jerusalem. Their enrollment at Bezalen Academy was never confirmed and the University of Jerusalem doesn't exist. Their sales pitch would at times involve promoting a new art exhibit and they would ask for business cards so information on the upcoming exhibit could be mailed to the interested buyer.

The Israelis appeared to be targeting the offices and homes of individuals working at the Drug Enforcement Agency. In addition, they were reports of them at 36 Department of Defense locations.[3] Around 140 Israelis were arrested or detained between March 2001 and September 11, 2001.[4] Although suspected of espionage, many were deported on visa and work violations. After 9/11 an additional 60 Israelis (most working a shopping mall kiosks) were arrested and deported after intensive interrogations. It was determined some of these were on active duty serving the in Israeli military.

DEA Report

Officials at the Drug Enforcement Agency began assembling a report on activities of Israeli art students appearing at the homes and offices of DEA officials. Reports came from various parts of the country indicating a similar pattern. The report is quite detailed and provides the names, dates of birth and other identifying information on the Israelis that were stop and interrogated by the FBI and other security officials.[5]

The report revealed a majority of the Israelis interviewed by US investigators had military backgrounds with expertise in intelligence, electronic surveillance and explosives. One "art student" was the son of a two-star Israeli general while another had provided security to the head of the Israeli Army. The report concluded, "That these people are now traveling in the U.S. selling art seems not to fit their background."[6]

The report was leaked to the media and placed up on the Internet.

Timeline

- March 2001: The Office of the National Counterintelligence Executive, a branch of the CIA, issues an alert urging federal agencies to report any activities or appearances of individuals claiming to be Israeli art students.

- June 2001: US Drug Enforcement Administration (DEA) compiles a report on the suspicious activities of Israeli Art Students appearing at DEA offices. In December 2001 the report is leaked to the media. [15]

- October 2, 2001: Anna Werner of channel 11, KHOU-TV news in Houston, Texas is the first reporter to discuss the appearance of Israeli Art Students at government offices. In her reporting she reveals 15 individuals claiming to be art students were arrested in Dallas, Texas back in March 2001. They seemed to be targeting the Drug Enforcement Administration and had floor plans of the building. Some of those arrested had home addresses of federal employees. All 15 were deported. [16]

- December 12, 2001. Carl Cameron (Fox News) begins his first report of a four-part series on Israeli spying. Cameron reports on the Israel Art Students arrested before 9/11 and 60 other Israelis later arrested and held for interrogation. [17]

- December 13, 2001, Carl Cameron presents his second report on the Israeli Spies. [18]

- December 14, 2001, Carl Cameron third report. [19]

- December 17, 2001. Carl Cameron final report on Israeli spying. [20]

- February 28, 2002: The Paris based *Intelligence Online* reports on the Israeli Art Students. Their reporting appears to be based on the leaked DEA Report.

  - March 5, 2002: An article appears in the French magazine *Le Monde*.

  - March 5, 2002: News agency Reuters reports, "U.S. Busts Big Israeli Spy Ring."

  - March 6, 2002: "U.S. Deports Dozens of Israelis," by Ted Bridis, Associated Press[21]

  - March 6, 2002: The *Washington Post* attempts to kill the story with the article, "Reports of Israeli Spy Ring Dismissed."

  - March 8, 2002: CAMERA (a news watch group concerned with presenting Israel in a positive light) claims the recent reports on Israeli espionage activities are false. [22]

  - March 11, 2002: The *South Florida Sun-Sentinel* reports on Israeli Art Students suspected of spying in south Florida. [23]

  - March 20, 2002: "The spies who came in from the art sale," by John Sugg, *Creative Loafing*. [24]

  - March 27, 2002: "Urban myth, my ass!" by John Sugg, *Creative Loafing*. [25]

  - April 1, 2002: Paul Rodriquez with *Insight* magazine writes the article "Intelligence agents or art students?" [26]

  - May 7, 2002: The first comprehensive article on the Israeli Art Students appears online at Salon.com. [27]

  - May 13, 2002: the Israeli newspaper *Haaretz* reports on the Israeli Art Students arrested in America. [28]

  - September 19, 2003: The *Ottawa Sun* reports nine Israeli art students are arrested and face deportation with the suspicion that they may be foreign agents. [29]

  - March 7, 2007: CounterPunch a Internet web site publishes an updated article on the Israeli Art Students. [30]

Saturday, January 22, 2011

FOX News 4 Part Series on Israeli Spying in America - Around 200 Israelis were arrested or detained in connection with 9/11

"Investigators within the DEA, INS and FBI have all told Fox News that to pursue or even suggest Israeli spying ... is considered career suicide."

-- Carl Cameron, as quoted in "The Spies Who Came In From The Art Sale"

"Evidence linking these Israelis to 9/11 is classified. I cannot tell you about evidence that has been gathered. It's classified information."

-- US official quoted in Carl Cameron's Fox News report on the Israeli spy ring and its connections to 9-11.

CORNERHOUSE
NEW TITLE INFORMATION

GELATIN
THE B-THING

essay by Tex Rubinowitz

In June 2000, before what are now coyly being termed the 'events of September 11th', a group of artists set about on a covert mission to build a temporary balcony on the 91st floor of the World Trade Centre (1) in New York. The group of four, called Gelatin, had a studio space on the 91st floor, provided by the lower Manhattan Cultural Council and they secretly drew up their plans. Nobody, including the other artist sharing the same studio space, knew anything of their plans. By smuggling in materials under their pullovers the balcony was prefabricated, made to hold just one person at a time, and their aim was to leave no visible traces:

'...In a complicated process they scratched out the putty around the tall and heavy windows - which were not intended to be opened - lifted them out using suction pads, shunted the balcony out, posed on it at 6 in the morning and had their photographs taken from a helicopter for their nearest and dearest back home.' [Tex Rubinowitz] The book includes Gelatin's own written plans for the project and is beautifully illustrated throughout.

artists: Gelatin

Walther Koenig
£20.00
ISBN 9783883755076
hardback 62 pages
illustrated in colour and b&w
275mm x 185mm

Keywords: Installation

DISTRIBUTED BY

tel: +44 (0)161 200 1503
fax: +44 (0)161 200 1504
email: publications@cornerhouse.org
www.cornerhouse.org/books

Cornerhouse Publications
70 Oxford Street
Manchester M1 5NH
England

The New York Times

N.Y. / Region

WORLD | U.S. | N.Y. / REGION | BUSINESS | TECHNOLOGY | SCIENCE | HEALTH | SPORTS | OPINION

AUTOS

Balcony Scene (Or Unseen) Atop the World; Episode at Trade Center Assumes Mythic Qualities

By SHAILA K. DEWAN
Published: August 18, 2001

The affair of the balcony ended, if indeed it ever began, with the appearance in July of a slender book of curious title, obtainable in very few places, one of them being an art gallery in a frosted storefront on Broadway near Franklin Street.

Called "The B-Thing" and produced by four Vienna-based artists known collectively as Gelatin, the book is demure to the point of being oblique. What little explanation it contains appears to have been scribbled in ballpoint. Among the photos and schematic drawings, there are doodles of tarantulas with human heads.

In short, the book belies the extravagance of the feat it seems to document: the covert installation, and brief use, of a balcony on the 91st floor of the World Trade Center, 1,100 feet above the earth. Eight photographs -- some grainy, all taken from a great distance -- depict one tower's vast eastern facade, marred by a tiny molelike growth: a lone figure dressed in a white jacket, standing in a lectern-size box.

The contemporary art world, of course, is rife with acts of subversion followed by boasting, which is known as "documentation." In that context, the beauty of the balcony was that it so literally pushed the envelope. Yet since that Sunday morning in March 2000, when the balcony was allegedly installed and, 19 minutes later, dismantled, the affair has taken on the outlines of an urban myth, mutated by rumors and denials among the downtown cognoscenti.

121001

WORLD TRADE CENTER
TEMPORARY CONSTRUCTION ID

MAY 0 1 2000

EXPIRATION
DATE:

LOCATION: 1 WTC / 90 FLOOR

NAME: ALEXANDER JANKA

COMPANY: PAL LMCc

AUTHORIZED SIGNATURE:

VALID 7:00 AM – 3:00 PM MONDAY – FRIDAY – SAT – SUN
** NOT VALID WITHOUT ACCOMPANYING PHOTO ID **

Name	Date modified	Type	Size	Folder	Authors
3 AWA 711 AAL11_...	9/11/2001 5:46 AM	Text Document	22,865 KB	(d) Radar (F:\FAA\...	
3 N90 62 AAL11_E...	9/11/2001 5:46 AM	Text Document	22,865 KB	(d) Radar (F:\FAA\...	
4 N90 62 AAL11_E...	9/11/2001 5:46 AM	Text Document	22,865 KB	(d) Radar (F:\FAA\...	
3 N90 62 jfk_nyt	9/11/2001 5:51 AM	Text Document	21,372 KB	(d) Radar (F:\FAA\...	
4 N90 62 jfk_nyt	9/11/2001 5:51 AM	Text Document	21,372 KB	(d) Radar (F:\FAA\...	
2 N90 62 AAL11_SWF	9/11/2001 6:13 AM	Text Document	37,429 KB	(d) Radar (F:\FAA\...	
3 AWA 711 AAL11_...	9/11/2001 6:13 AM	Text Document	37,429 KB	(d) Radar (F:\FAA\...	
3 AWA 711 AAL11s	9/11/2001 6:13 AM	Text Document	37,429 KB	(d) Radar (F:\FAA\...	
3 N90 62 AAL11_SWF	9/11/2001 6:13 AM	Text Document	37,429 KB	(d) Radar (F:\FAA\...	
4 N90 62 AAL11_SWF	9/11/2001 6:13 AM	Text Document	37,429 KB	(d) Radar (F:\FAA\...	
3 AWA 732 AAL11	9/11/2001 6:37 AM	Wave Sound	577 KB	(e) Other (F:\FAA\...	
2 N90 62 acft2_swf	9/11/2001 8:26 AM	Text Document	66 KB	(d) Radar (F:\FAA\...	
3 N90 62 acft2_swf	9/11/2001 8:26 AM	Text Document	66 KB	(d) Radar (F:\FAA\...	
4 N90 62 acft2_swf	9/11/2001 8:26 AM	Text Document	66 KB	(d) Radar (F:\FAA\...	
2 N90 62 acft2_ewr	9/11/2001 8:29 AM	Text Document	343 KB	(d) Radar (F:\FAA\...	

Name	Date modified	Type	Size	Folder	Authors
3 N90 62 ual93_ewr	9/11/2001 9:09 AM	Text Document	337 KB	(d) Radar (F:\FAA\...	
4 N90 62 ual93_ewr	9/11/2001 9:09 AM	Text Document	337 KB	(d) Radar (F:\FAA\...	
2 N90 62 acft2_swfa	9/11/2001 8:59 AM	Text Document	422 KB	(d) Radar (F:\FAA\...	
3 N90 62 acft2_swfa	9/11/2001 8:59 AM	Text Document	422 KB	(d) Radar (F:\FAA\...	
4 N90 62 acft2_swfa	9/11/2001 8:59 AM	Text Document	422 KB	(d) Radar (F:\FAA\...	
2 N90 62 UAL175_e...	9/11/2001 8:56 AM	Text Document	583 KB	(d) Radar (F:\FAA\...	
3 N90 62 UAL175_e...	9/11/2001 8:56 AM	Text Document	583 KB	(d) Radar (F:\FAA\...	
4 AWA 711 UAL175 ...	9/11/2001 8:56 AM	Text Document	583 KB	(d) Radar (F:\FAA\...	
4 AWA 711 UAL175...	9/11/2001 8:56 AM	Text Document	583 KB	(d) Radar (F:\FAA\...	
4 AWA 711 UAL175a	9/11/2001 8:56 AM	Text Document	583 KB	(d) Radar (F:\FAA\...	
4 N90 62 UAL175_e...	9/11/2001 8:56 AM	Text Document	583 KB	(d) Radar (F:\FAA\...	
5 AWA 711 atc01		...ment	5 KB	(d) Radar (F:\FAA\...	
2 N90 62 acft2_ew...		...ment	343 KB	(d) Radar (F:\FAA\...	
3 N90 62 acft2_ew...		...ment	343 KB	(d) Radar (F:\FAA\...	
4 N90 62 acft2_ew...		...ment	343 KB	(d) Radar (F:\FAA\...	
2 N90 62 acft2_swf	9/11/2001 8:26 AM	Text Document	66 KB	(d) Radar (F:\FAA\...	

4 N90 62 UAL175_ewr
Type: Text Document
Size: 582 KB
Date modified: 9/11/2001 8:56 AM

1.25 MB

Name	Date modified	Type	Size	Folder	Authors
4 AWA 711 BOS091...	9/11/2001 9:09 AM	TG File	20,165 KB	(d) Radar (F:\FAA\...	
2 AWA 711a ual93 ...	9/11/2001 9:09 AM	Text Document	337 KB	(d) Radar (F:\FAA\...	
2 N90 62 ual93_ewr	9/11/2001 9:09 AM	Text Document	337 KB	(d) Radar (F:\FAA\...	
3 N90 62 ual93_ewr	9/11/2001 9:09 AM	Text Document	337 KB	(d) Radar (F:\FAA\...	
4 N90 62 ual93_ewr	9/11/2001 9:09 AM	Text Document	337 KB	(d) Radar (F:\FAA\...	
2 N90 62 acft2_swfa	9/11/2001 8:59 AM	Text Document	422 KB	(d) Radar (F:\FAA\...	
3 N90 62 acf		Text Document	422 KB	(d) Radar (F:\FAA\...	
4 N90 62 acf		Text Document	422 KB	(d) Radar (F:\FAA\...	
2 N90 62 UAL175_e...	9/11/2001 8:56 AM	Text Document	583 KB	(d) Radar (F:\FAA\...	
3 N90 62 UAL175_e...	9/11/2001 8:56 AM	Text Document	583 KB	(d) Radar (F:\FAA\...	
4 AWA 711 UAL175 ...	9/11/2001 8:56 AM	Text Document	583 KB	(d) Radar (F:\FAA\...	
4 AWA 711 UAL175...	9/11/2001 8:56 AM	Text Document	583 KB	(d) Radar (F:\FAA\...	
4 AWA 711 UAL175a	9/11/2001 8:56 AM	Text Document	583 KB	(d) Radar (F:\FAA\...	
4 N90 62 UAL175_e...	9/11/2001 8:56 AM	Text Document	583 KB	(d) Radar (F:\FAA\...	
5 AWA 711 atc01	9/11/2001 8:49 AM	Text Document	5 KB	(d) Radar (F:\FAA\...	
2 N90 62 acft2_ewr	9/11/2001 8:29 AM	Text Document	343 KB	(d) Radar (F:\FAA\...	

Type: Text Document
Size: 336 KB
Date modified: 9/11/2001 9:09 AM

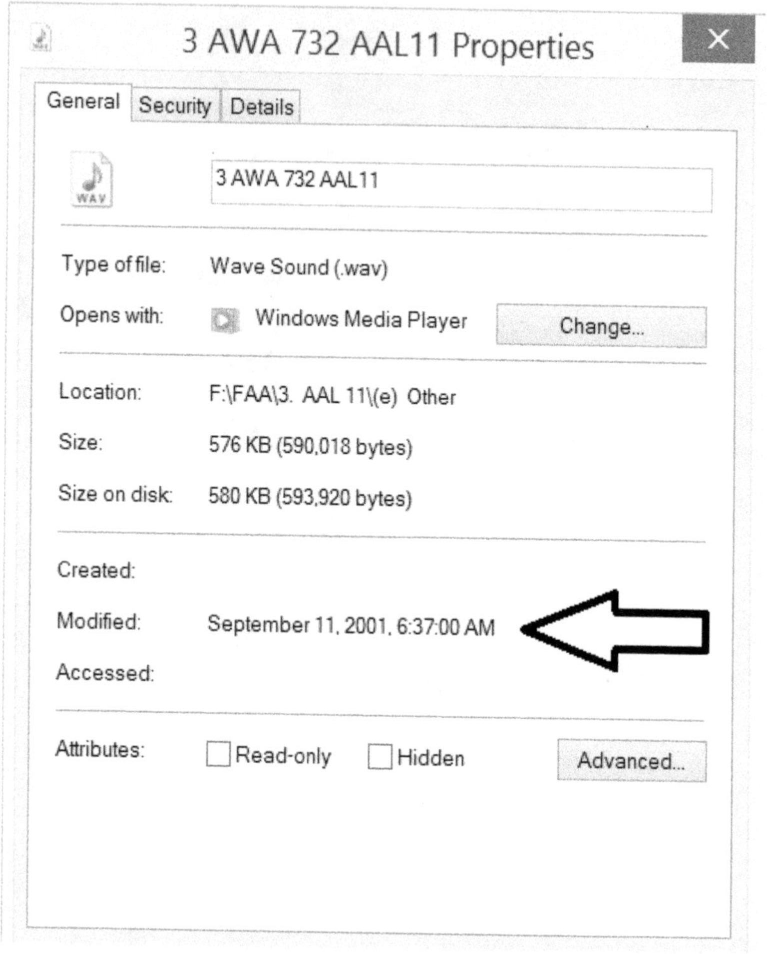
3 AWA 732 AAL11 Properties
General
Security
Details
3 AWA 732 AAL11
Type of file: Wave Sound (.wav)
Opens with: Windows Media Player
Change...
Location: F:\FAA\3. AAL 11\(e) Other
Size: 576 KB (590,018 bytes)
Size on disk: 580 KB (593,920 bytes)
Created:
Modified: September 11, 2001, 6:37:00 AM
Accessed:
Attributes: Read-only Hidden
Advanced...

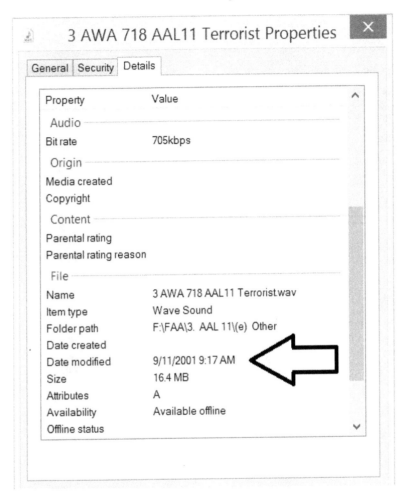

3 AWA 718 AAL11 Terrorist Properties ✕

General | Security | Details

Property	Value
Audio	
Bit rate	705kbps
Origin	
Media created	
Copyright	
Content	
Parental rating	
Parental rating reason	
File	
Name	3 AWA 718 AAL11 Terrorist.wav
Item type	Wave Sound
Folder path	F:\FAA\3. AAL 11\(e) Other
Date created	
Date modified	9/11/2001 9:17 AM
Size	16.4 MB
Attributes	A
Availability	Available offline
Offline status	

← → ↑ 🔎 ▸ Search Results in TOSHIBA EXT (F:)

Name	Date modified	Type	Size	Folder
SkyDrive				
Downloads				
3 N90 62 acft2_swfa	9/11/2001 8:59 AM	Text Document	422 KB	(d) Radar (F:\FAA\...
OneDrive				
4 N90 62 acft2_swfa	9/11/2001 8:59 AM	Text Document	422 KB	(d) Radar (F:\FAA\...
2 N90 62 UAL175_e...	9/11/2001 8:56 AM	Text Document	583 KB	(d) Radar (F:\FAA\...
3 N90 62 UAL175_e...	9/11/2001 8:56 AM	Text Document	583 KB	(d) Radar (F:\FAA\...
This PC				
4 AWA 711 UAL175 ...	9/11/2001 8:56 AM	Text Document	583 KB	(d) Radar (F:\FAA\...
Desktop				
4 AWA 711 UAL175...	9/11/2001 8:56 AM	Text Document	583 KB	(d) Radar (F:\FAA\...
Documents				
4 AWA 711 UAL175a	9/11/2001 8:56 AM	Text Document	583 KB	(d) Radar (F:\FAA\...
Downloads				
4 N90 62 UAL175_e...	9/11/2001 8:56 AM	Text Document	583 KB	(d) Radar (F:\FAA\...
Music				
5 AWA 711 atc01	9/11/2001 8:49 AM	Text Document	5 KB	(d) Radar (F:\FAA\...
Pictures				
2 N90 62 acft2_ewr	9/11/2001 8:29 AM	Text Document	343 KB	(d) Radar (F:\FAA\...
Videos				
3 N90 62 acft2_ewr	9/11/2001 8:29 AM	Text Document	343 KB	(d) Radar (F:\FAA\...
OS (C:)				
4 N90 62 acft2_ewr	9/11/2001 8:29 AM	Text Document	343 KB	(d) Radar (F:\FAA\...
TOSHIBA EXT (F:)				
2 N90 62 acft2_swf	9/11/2001 8:26 AM	Text Document	66 KB	(d) Radar (F:\FAA\...
3 N90 62 acft2_swf	9/11/2001 8:26 AM	Text Document	66 KB	(d) Radar (F:\FAA\...
Network				
4 N90 62 acft2_swf	9/11/2001 8:26 AM	Text Document	66 KB	(d) Radar (F:\FAA\...
3 AWA 732 AAL11	9/11/2001 6:37 AM	Wave Sound	577 KB	(e) Other (F:\FAA\...

Chronology ADA-30, Operations Center
Terrorist Attacks NY-DC 9/11/01

TIME	Remarks
0835	Received call ANE/Barry of possible hijack AAL11, B767, Bos-Lax, pilot keying mike and intruder in cockpit," stating Don't move or I'll kill you.
0836	ACI/Smith conf with ANE ROC and command center.
0840	Received via conf with ANE/ROC Acft heading toward JFK.
0842	Via conference with ANE ROC reported a flight attendant has been stabbed.
0844	Via conference with ANE ROC reportedly a passenger had been shot.
0845	Received a report via conf with ANE ROC that an aircraft had hit the World Trade Center in New York City.
0850	ACC activated. Tactical Net requested by ACO Weikhert.
0852	MOC activated.
0854	CNN televised that an a/c had hit the World Trade Center in New York.
0859	CNN televised that 2 a/c had World Trade Center.
0920	Primary NET activated. Request by ACO Wiekhert.
0924	AGL ROC reported AAL77, b752, from IAD to LAX, 10E York, Ky at FL350 disappeared from radar at 1256Z.
0930	Smith on duty.
0940	Computer room activated.
0935	Channel 9 televised that an a/c had hit the Pentagon.
0915	Contacted Smith to come in for assistance.
0945	Contacted Corcoran/Lewis to come in for assistance.
0946	Computer # 2 OTS,
1036	National COOP has been activated/Coop ANS activated.
0935	Johnson in facility.
0945	FAA Building Evacuated.
0958	Lewis/Corcoran in facility.
1045	Gordon/Corcoran relocating to RTS. Ground stop on all US Air Carriers @ 1017
1040	Alt ACC ACTIVATED.

DAILY RECORD OF FACILITY OPERATION				Page No. 1
				Date: September 11, 2001
Location:	Identification:	Type Facility:	Operating Position:	Checked By:
Des Plaines, IL.	AGL-6	ROC	Duty Officer	Chief: Tom Brand, Acting Manager

TIME (GMT)	REMARKS	INIT
0500	OPENING LOG.	RH
0527	DETROIT METRO AFCT REPORTED NORTHWEST 60 INCIDENT.	RH
1040	CLEVELAND ARTCC REPORTED UNITED EXPRESS 4044 INCIDENT	RH
1253	ACFT CRASHED INTO WORLD TRADE CENTER	GM
1304	SECOND ACFT CRASHED INTO WORLD TRADE CENTER	GM
1309	ZID: AAL77 OFF RADAR YKK050010	GM
1323	WOO/FBI TELECON	GM
1339	ZOB: UAL93 B752 EWR SFO SCREAMING/BOMB STATEMENT HEARD ABOARD	GM
1339	ACFT HIT W SIDE OF PENTAGON	GM
1345	UAL93 DESCENDING OVER CLE	GM
1354	DAL1989 B763 BOS-CLE HIJACKED	GM
1401	1 BLDG OF WTC COLLAPSED	GM
1410	CLE AFSS ATC 6 BLDG EVAC BOMB THREAT	GM
1412	BLOOMINGBIRD REQUESTED PG. ORDERLY EVACUATION OF RO	GM
1420	MALY REQ: EVAC OF NON-ESSENTIAL RO	GM
1420	NY/DC FED BLDGS EVACUATED. ALL ACFT INSTRUCTED TO LAND. NO DEP.	GM
1421	DAL1989 LNDD CLE WOI	GM
1425	CAR BOMB AT STATE DEPT. DC	GM
1425	WHITE HOUSE EVAC	GM
1425	2ND BLDG OF WTC COLLAPSED	GM
1435	UAL93 HIJACKRD	GM
1445	ALL RO NON-ESSENTIAL PERSONNEL SENT HOME	GM
1447	UAL93 CRASHED 10 NE IHD/60 SW JST SOMERSET, PA	OM
1509	CLE: NON-SPECIFIC BOMB THREAT TO FBO	GM
1522	ANE: SECON LEVEL BRAVO. REVIEW LEVEL C AND D	GM
1530	PRANK CALLER SAID "BOOM" AND HUNG UP	GM
1540	ACFT CRASHED INTO PENTAGON	OM
1540	UAL182 UNACCOUNTED FOR	CIM
1551	WOC: NATL CCOP ACTIVATED	GM
1645	DAL1989 DEPLANED CLE	GM
1646	IL NATL GUARD ON CALL	GM
1817	RENOT 1/03 SENT SBCON D	GM
1946	KOREAN AIR O.O W.O.I. WHITE HORSE, CANADA	TR
2212	RACER12 F16 UNSCHED LNDD FFO	TR
0500	LOG CLOSED	TR
TIME (GMT)	DATE	CARRY FORWARD TO NEXT DAY TITLE??	GM

The Florida Times-Union

Home

Published Saturday, May 22, 2004

Security scare shuts Kings Bay

By LIZ HAMPTON
Times-Union correspondent,

ST. MARYS, Ga. -- Kings Bay Naval Submarine Base was locked down for security reasons Friday after two Israelis were detained for questioning.

Base spokesman Ed Buczek said two Israeli men attempted to enter the base about 10:30 a.m. They were hired by a moving-and-storage company to pick up some household goods in base housing, he said.

One occupant of the vehicle was unable to provide base security personnel with proper credentials after arriving at the Franklin Gate entrance, Buczek said.

Base personnel then inspected the van. Military dogs trained to detect bombs were called in.

"The military dogs were alerted to a scent in the cab of the truck," Buczek said. "Guards closed access to the base and notified the Georgia Bureau of Investigation, the Federal Bureau of Investigation and the Naval Criminal Investigative Service."

St. Marys police closed access to an area one-half mile out surrounding the base, and a bomb squad was called in, Buczek said. A briefcase was removed from the vehicle with a remote control robot, but nothing was found in it.

"The dogs were called in again for a second pass of the vehicle, and they didn't pick up anything," he said.

The two men, whose names were not released, were detained and later taken into custody by federal immigration officers in Savannah for possible deportation, Buczek said.

Times-Union correspondent Liz Hampton can be reached at (904) 359-4171.

CPSIA information can be obtained
at www.ICGtesting.com
Printed in the USA
JSHW032343131122
33133JS00002B/7